FOREVER CORNWALL

LYN MCCONCHIE

Night to Dawn Magazine & Books LLC
P. O. Box 643
Abington, PA 19001

www.bloodredshadow.com

Cover Artists: Laduwki @ Dreamstime.com
Editor: Barbara Custer
Published in the United States of America

Dedicated to five real people – one deceased – two of whom live in Cornwall, and the fourth is Canadian. To Mic, Hugh, Maureen, and Diane, who graciously permitted their use as fictional characters.

To Jacqui Smith, who gave me the book title.

And last but never least, to Cornwall, which was once a country in its own right. If an apocalypse ever does occur, may it survive and rise to be one again.

****

I'd like to acknowledge my friends Cheryl and Lynne, whose assistance has enabled me to have the time and energy to continue writing. And Barbara Custer, whose polishing of my work has allowed it to shine. And then there's Sooty. The small black feral cat who strolled through the cat door several months after my house cat died, and announced that this was now their place. Four years later, it seems they were right.

CHAPTER ONE

I woke up to the damned alarm again. A relentless beeping that said there was something wrong in the immediate vicinity of "outside" and I should do something. I did. I slammed my hand down on the alarm, but not in time. Beside me, Maureen rolled over sleepily.

"Hugh? What is it?" I restrained the tart response that she had to know as much as I did and crawled out of bed. I reached the bedroom door and met my grandmother, heading for the alarm's vicinity.

"What is it?"

"The alarm," I said, receiving the sort of look only my grandmother could produce.

"So I gathered... Oh, I see. Well, let's find out why."

The three of us trooped towards the back door of the cottage we shared, and I noticed in the corner of my mind that I'd picked up my shotgun as I passed my bedroom door — it usually lay on a shelf there, right by the door. Maureen had brought her revolver, and Mic — my grandmother but usually called by her name rather than that title — had a machine-pistol on a strap over her shoulder. I blinked, opened my mouth to ask where she'd come by *that*, and shut it again. Now was not the time.

Automatically, we spread out as we exited the cottage. I took the lead, slipped silently around the corner — and something struck me hard in the face. The whatever it was emitted a loud croaking squawk; another something hit me on one side of my head. I felt something warm running down my face and put a hand up.

That might have been the time I panicked, but for two things. After three years of events that were weird or threatening beyond anything I'd known before they began, I'd learned not to panic, plus the stink as I raised my wet hand to my nose, I knew what was going on; to some extent, at least, and that wetness wasn't blood, it was chicken shit. Which meant the things assaulting me out of the dark were loose chickens … which in turn meant something had let them loose, and I'd better find out what.

The "what" was shown in a bright flare of light as Mic triggered the narrow-beam light she wore on her forehead. Maureen followed suit, and the chicken-predator was shown in the cross beams. A large chimpanzee, hairy coat frosted with silver, and an array of heavily worn teeth bared at us. Not a usual sight in Cornwall, even in 2042. In one hand, it held a limp body of a hen, and Mic took a pace forward.

"That's Mrs. Black. Put her down, you hairy brute." Her voice was imperative, and my wife chimed in.

"Mic, be careful, those things can be savage."

The chimpanzee demonstrated that by dropping the chicken — which promptly came to life and fled shrieking — to focus on us. There was a couple of seconds pause, then it emitted a snarling scream and charged. Mic flipped the machine pistol into line and fired. In no more than a heartbeat, a dozen bullets hit the furious beast in the chest, and it went down. Mic caught my wife's eye and nodded. Maureen moved to stand beside her. Her revolver cracked once, and the shuddering hairy body went limp.

I made a slight sound in my throat, and the women turned. Mic touched the light to reduce the intensity as she turned to me. "No choice, love. It would have died anyway; better to give it a quick, clean death. I hope there's no more around as it is. It must have climbed the wall."

"I know." I'd already guessed that. "But where could it have come from?"

Maureen shrugged. "A private zoo, some fancy park. Anyhow, better go tell Thorne that it's all right before he's out here with half the kids."

A very good idea. Thorne was a nice guy, but he could rush into things now and again if he thought a friend was in danger. I headed for the huge old Manor house in time to meet Thorne and two of the older pupils, all armed to the teeth.

"I heard shooting?" The pupils had passed me and were now staring down at the body.

"Sir, sir, come and look at this."

Thorne did so. "A chimpanzee." A couple of hens marched past, muttering something it was just as well we humans couldn't translate. "I see, it let the hens out. I believe chimps can be aggressive?"

Mic snorted. "Not anymore."

"It attacked you?"

"Yes, and it wasn't playing." She sighed. "If it stayed, it would have been a nuisance and a danger to the children. I'm sorry, but these days, we're probably more of an endangered species than it is."

Which, I reflected as we went back to our cottage, was no more than the truth. Three years earlier, there had been some sort of plague—a virus. Where we were, we didn't hear many of the details, but we certainly saw the effects. A staphylococcus A mutation it was claimed. Something ten times deadlier because it had a long incubation period, so pretty much the entire population of the world had it before anyone knew it was around—apart from a few specialists who'd had a suspicion but little proof, so few had listened, including the world's governments. To add to that, it was at least ninety percent lethal. To survive, you had to have had an earlier minor staph A infection *and* been treated for that with the new antibiotic, allodaxin. After that, your chances of survival depended on how recent these events had been.

Thankfully, one of our pupils had returned from seeing his

parents, who were briefly in London, and three days later, he'd given his minor infection to everyone at the small private school where I, my wife Maureen, and my grandmother, Mic, lived. Doctor Di had descended on us, beaming when I phoned her.

"I've just got a consignment of allodaxin. Never used it on a patient before. Supposed to be the new wonder drug. Let's see."

We saw all right. We'd all had the infection, we all got the allodaxin, and we all survived. In fact, we all recovered within four days. Then Doc Di had a phone call at the last from some specialist friend named Mac — what else — in Scotland. It seemed we at the school — and the doc who'd picked up the minor infection from one of her patients — were now immune to the bug, thanks to the combination. He had, however, told her much more; that information had trickled out bit by bit over the past three years. I hoped he'd survived, too; he deserved it.

The first part we heard — probable death rates for the British Isles — had sent Thorne to his suite to drink all night until he passed out. Oddly, the only place in the UK that had been hit badly in this initial phase was on the Welsh/Scottish border. I had no idea why that should bother him, although he'd been tense ever since a letter arrived in the mail a while back. He slept off his binge, emerged from his suite two days later, and was Thorne again. However, as we'd observed since, Doc Di's informant had told the truth so far as he knew, and as Mic had commented acidly when we were hashing it over yet again, it *was* the end of the world as we knew it, and none of us felt *that* damn fine.

****

I corralled the wandering hens, buried the unfortunate chimpanzee the next morning, checked the wall, and discovered where the animal had scaled it. I went back with a saw and removed the branch. I doubted a human could manage the jump from branch to wall, but just in case … Maureen wasn't far away while I worked; blueberries and raspberries were becoming ripe, and she was picking them in the section of the walled garden that had been netted across the top to keep the birds out of them.

In a short while, the berries would be so prolific, we'd have everyone picking. Mic would be overseeing their drying or bottling, and we'd have sufficient for a year again. I stood on my ladder, dropped the sawed-off branch, and before going down, I looked over our shared domain.

It had begun sixty years ago when Thorne's father inherited—and had realized that one more lot of death duties, and his family would lose the estate. He was the next in a long line who'd loved their home but who'd never been nobility or vastly wealthy. He needed an income, and I grinned as I remembered Thorne's comment on the subject.

"Pays be to a trained accountant. Dad wanted a way to get income and give the Government back as little as possible. Something where he could charge just about every single expense back against income."

Gerald Trelen found it quite by accident. He'd gone to a good private boarding school and made friends, several of whom had later employed him as their accountant, conscious that he knew *exactly* how close to the line to take their declarations. That paid well, but not quite well enough. He needed a sideline—and found it when one of his friends was appointed consul in an obscure country where England had financial interests, but where you wouldn't want to raise children.

Gerald had given his friend's children a home during term time. They'd gone to the local primary school, and it had worked so well that another friend in a similar position had made the same request. Both families paid about four times the actual costs—which costs a good accountant could extend to just over eighty percent of expenses, and Gerald had. Nor had the single Inland Revenue inspection spotted anything out of place.

To cut a long tale far shorter, in five years, there were a dozen children staying at the Manor over term times. In ten years, there were almost thirty, and by the time Thorne inherited—Gerald having died from an embolism no one had known about—the school roll had reached eighty-nine and the Manor was their school. If the children started here young enough, they went to the primary school initially. If they stayed longer or were they already older when they came here, they were taught at the Manor where Gerald had added classrooms, teacher accommodation, and other refinements.

From where I stood. I could see the big old Manor house, our cottage, and the second cottage where Annie, the matron/first aid practitioner lived with her dog, cat, and father whom—a year before the plague started—had retired from being a professional gardener officially, but who was now employed here part-time as one unofficially, and paid in food, cash, and other items in kind which suited everyone. Jake was a lean, fit, upright sixty-three-year-old, and happy almost all the time. Annie, his daughter, was moving back to that. She'd lost her partner to a younger woman before the plague and hadn't found anyone else, but as Jack said in a conversation that had started about three weeks before the plague moved into full effect:

"Them as had a happy marriage, goes looking for another, and sooner or later, they find it." He'd grinned then. "And them as didn't have a happy marriage, marries again in hopes that this one will be it."

To which Mic had returned, "If that's so, why haven't you married again?" (Jake's wife had died from cancer fourteen years ago.)

"'Cos you wouldn't have me, sweetheart."

My grandmother snorted. "That's because I'm a smart old lady."

Jake chuckled and left the subject for another. "What do you think about the news from last night, smart old lady?"

Mic sobered fast. "I don't like it. I think the government isn't telling the truth, and things could end far worse than the doomsayers believe."

Jake looked at her and quoted softly from a song they both liked. "*Voices that spoke with persuasive skill, it can't happen here! And it never will!*"

"Exactly — and I think they're wrong."

Thorne looked at her. "If you're right, what can we do?" It was a fair question. Mic would never have claimed to be psychic; she thought all that was rubbish, but she could listen to comments, gossip, current affairs, and learned discussions, and come up with suggestions that almost always turned out to be right.

She thought, then spoke slowly, thinking as she talked. "Stock up for a start. Buy two, three, four times of anything we need, use regularly, and can afford to buy. If I'm wrong, then we'll use it still; it just takes longer to use up. And get a stack of seeds, saplings of fruit we don't already have, nut-tree saplings, a couple more types of berries, arrange our own meat and milk, and…" Her gaze met his, clear-eyed. "Get a new complete set of the eco-electric systems, plus spares, and a barn or three to put everything in."

I didn't know then how seriously Thorne had taken her, nor how glad we'd all be in the coming years that Mic had spoken her mind and Thorne had listened. If I had known what he did, I might have tried to talk him out of it, but I didn't. He'd gone to his bank the next day and borrowed a large amount of money against the Manor; the bank manager, an old acquaintance, accepted what Thorne told him and shifted the money into the Manor account since it wasn't as if Thorne didn't have the collateral.

Thorne had spent a third of it on the power systems and five connect-barns. They arrived, Jake and I put the barns up, and Thorne disappeared again, spent another third of the loan on rainwater tanks, with all the necessary piping and filters. While we were putting tanks and pipes up, he followed those two events three days after that, with the arrival of a convoy of trucks and half the fit, healthy, unemployed locals who would agree to do some work and lived in our immediate area. Since Thorne was paying cash, there was no shortage of volunteers.

The Manor was bedlam, compounded by a second invasion only hours later, this one of a C.B.M. (Computerised Building

Machine) which lumbered, along with feeder trucks containing the necessary materials behind it, onto Manor lands, and with a computer programme activated, it thickened and heightened the Manor's original walls with heavily reinforced concrete. With that complete, it expanded the walled area to double what it had been with a further wall. I'd have asked Thorne what on earth he was doing, but he seemed never to be anywhere around when I looked for him, so I grumbled to Mic.

"I don't know how much money he got to do this, or how he thinks he'll be able to pay it back. The Manor does well enough, but not *that* well; it's crazy. At least it's the holidays; most of the kids are away, and they won't be back for another couple of weeks."

"Why is it crazy?" Mic demanded, and I stared at her.

"Jake's expanding all the food production, more trees, berries, vegetables, Just the potatoes alone, he's put in another three acres. And that new wall, he's closed off ten acres inside part of it and brought in goats and jersey cows." I lowered my voice. "You could feed half the school a vegetarian diet on what we'll be growing next year."

"Maybe that's what he's got in mind," Mic chirped.

I gave her a disgusted glare and left. With school holidays, we'd temporarily lost the majority of our pupils. The number varied, as did who stayed and who didn't, who and how many depending on the safeness of the country where their parents were, the ease of getting to and from that, and so on. This year, we'd retained nine in the senior classes—five boys, four girls—with another six in the junior classes—three of each.

These events took ten days, although it never occurred to most of us in those days that time could be significant. The minor infection had been over just one month, although it was the reason we had fifteen kids here when we usually didn't have more than seven or eight. Some parents had been reluctant to have their children travel far in case they still weren't over the infection.

The berries ripened, and I couldn't recall seeing a better

crop. Maureen organized picking parties, allowing several friends of the Manor to join in, while she started the bottling, too. With the berries mostly picked, we had shelves upon shelves of bright jam and preserved fruit lining the Manor cellars. It was Sunday afternoon, and we had people working, but that was up to them. It could suit them to be here on a weekend if they were over-busy during workdays.

Then Doc Di's motorcycle came thundering in through the Manor gates, pulling up by the front steps, and when I say thundering, I'm not kidding. The Doc has a 1982 Harley-Davidson FLHS, a Shovelhead, and she added fairings herself since this model doesn't normally have them. But it's a real beast, and she rides it in a way that can intimidate even bikers. In two fluid motions, she kicked it up on the stand, dismounted, and fixed eyes like stone on me where I stood. "Hugh, call everyone in, we've got real trouble, and it's going to get worse fast, a *lot* worse."

I looked at her, saw the look in her eyes, and knew this wasn't a joke or even an exaggeration. I jumped for the emergency bell and rang it. Then I counted. Seven of us, including Di, plus the fifteen kids; all present and correct. Then there were the locals—Dave, the electrician who was just finishing up installation and cross-connection for the extra eco-electricity systems; two pensioners picking the final berries; and Paddy, the plumber installing more rainwater tanks and connecting the water-bore Thorne had paid to have drilled. We'd hit good, sweet water only twenty-five foot down. Plus, four kids belonging to the tradesmen, who often brought their children here in the holidays if they were working at the Manor.

Maureen muttered something to Mic and walked over to our people. "Come to the little hall." Mic signalled our pupils and they followed, while I heard Maureen telling the four kids to go to their dads. It didn't take long. We arrived at what was always called *The Little Hall*, and Thorne, who was last in, shut the door; then I heard a click and knew he'd locked it as well. A feeling like a shaft of ice slid down my back.

Doc Di was standing at the front of the hall. She'd taken her helmet off, and her dark brown hair hung in its usual plait almost to her waist, while her green eyes studied us. "Sit down, don't ask questions until I finish, and don't interrupt me. Believe me, you need to hear what I'm saying, and you need to listen and remember every word."

Annie stared at her. "The juniors are only ten or eleven."

Doc Di nodded. "You're right. I can either be graphic, and I think that's needed, or tone it all down, and that may leave some unsure of what I'm saying. Will you take them out, Annie? We'll wait."

It took only a few minutes before Annie was back, the door was shut—and locked again—and Di straightened to look us over. "You've been hearing the news about this virus. The truth is that you haven't been hearing much of the truth. It started in Africa, and by now, almost every single person on that continent is dead. Most of South America has gone, too. It had a long incubation period, and before it went active, practically everyone in the world was a carrier."

She took in a long breath. "Everyone in here, plus your juniors should be safe; you all had the minor infection, *and I treated you all with allodaxin*. The combination, with that having happened within the past two months, means you're immune and you shouldn't even be sick. But out there, it's started in a big way. I've come from the port, the hospital there is overflowing with dying patients, half the staff is dead or dying, too, and the patients' friends and family are rioting, setting fire to nearby buildings, and killing other patients."

"Why?" Annie asked blankly.

"Because without enough staff, they appear to assume if they kill half the patients, there will be some staff available to treat their own people." Annie opened her mouth again, and Doc Di held up a hand. "What we need here, right *now*, are the medical supplies I have at my place. I've been quietly stockpiling for weeks since I had a warning from a friend in Scotland who's an expert. He'd heard from a friend of his in Africa. Also, I know where there's a private library of medical books and another place that has do-it-yourself building diagrams, blueprints, books, and several computers pre-loaded with all that. If we drop everything else and go now, if we move fast enough, we can get everything, bring it back here, and have a better chance of survival."

She saw our stunned disbelief. "We also need weapons, ammunition, gun gear," she grinned savagely. "Common sense and the willingness to fight. It's *bad*, people; it's going to get unbelievably worse, and if you aren't prepared to kill, you'll be the ones who die. I spent half of last night on the phone and internet to overseas—while those still work and those I talked to are still alive. I saw two friends slaughtered right in front of me on Zoom, and please believe me." Her gaze swept over us.

"This is hell, and you're in it. Assume I'm exaggerating, assume all your neighbours are the good kind people you've always known, assume this will all blow over, the Government or the army will come to save you, and assume that it can't possibly be as bad as I say ... assume that, and you won't even be buried because none of your friends here will live long enough to do it."

She clapped her hands together, and we all jumped. "We'll need trucks. Thorne, I know you have two. We need guns; some of you are better with bows; thanks be that you have a tradition of archery here. Some need to stay to hold the walls in case—and thanks be that Thorne built *those*. We need a mix of people to take the trucks, the best shots, the strongest people. Don't waste time; every minute you do, we may lose our supplies and all the other things we need that we can still get if we're fast enough. Okay?"

One of the senior boys stood up. "Are you *serious*? You think we should go out there and shoot people, and steal stuff? You're barking..."

Maureen stood up and spoke quietly. "Geoff, you love cats, don't you?"

"What?"

"Doc Di has two cats."

"Yeah, so what?"

Maureen's voice abruptly cut like a blade. "She came *here*. Her neighbours would know she has medical supplies; any hour now, they could break in and take the supplies — and let her cats out into what's going on out there now or will be very soon. You stay here, Geoff; maybe if the Manor's attacked, you can bring yourself to believe; if not, too bad. But I'm a good driver; I'll take one of the Manor's trucks. Hugh can ride shotgun for me. Mic will take charge of the defence."

Geoff got as far as "B-b-b-b-but..." before she turned her back.

It went quickly after that. Two trucks — ex-army three-tonners Thorne had been offered very cheaply by a friend, a retiring Army supplies officer — if he took both and their extras. And paid cash. Thorne had taken them. With no time wasted, we moved out, Maureen and me in one with four of the seniors in the back as muscle, Thorne driving the second truck with Annie and four seniors. Mic, Jake, Geoff, and the juniors would guard the walls. Doc would ride ahead on her motorbike. We were rolling out of the gates less than an hour after she'd raced through them.

I was thinking as I scanned the countryside. So far, we were ahead of trouble in the deeper rural areas. The port she'd been at had blown up, but it was a large place, and they were a mixed bag: more strangers, a couple of poor areas, and some foreigners that didn't speak a lot of English in town from off the boats docked there. More people in general. Where Doc lived was outside a small town, an old one. And if rioting and looting *did* begin, they'd go for the shops and businesses that held the valuables.

Doc Di's rented house with her surgery was on a narrow side road. The signpost on the corner had fallen down last winter and not yet been replaced, while her house was a faded tan behind a line of trees — out of sight, out of mind with luck. Oh, they'd remember sooner or later, but not until they'd gutted the town centre, drunk all the booze, and recovered from that. Then some would remember her — and that doctors have drugs.

We were the lead truck. I spoke to Maureen, and she signalled; we slowed, and seeing the Doc return, I talked quickly and Doc nodded.

"Follow me. I'll come in from the back. We'll miss town and leave the same way."

Thorne had joined us and he agreed. Doc moved out with us following, and the whole place was so peaceful it was almost unbelievable things could have been as she said. We reached her house and were happily greeted by her cats, Merlin and Spitfire. Doc pointed to where her stockpile of medical supplies was under tarpaulins in the conservatory at the back of the house. We wasted no time; the trucks were parked as close as possible, we formed lines to pass the cartons, and we had all of them loaded in two hours. The cats, muttering indignantly, were in cat carriers, with cartons of cat food stacked nearby. Thorne looked at Doc Di.

"What would you really hate to lose, Di? We still have plenty of space, and if you're right, everything here will be gone in a day or two. When they don't find you, when they don't find drugs or valuables, they'll smash the place up or burn it down." It took another hour as we added bedroom items, stripped the kitchen and bathroom, added books, tools, and clothing. Di called a halt then. "That'll do. The design place and the medical archives are down the road. Let's see what the situation is there." The medical archives had been the passionate hobby and life's work of an elderly woman whose ancestress had been one of Florence Nightingale's nurses. She was dead in bed, very peacefully. Doc Di sniffed the mug by the bed and said some multi-syllable medical terms.

"She was ready when it hit her hard enough to know she was on the way out." She picked up the folded blanket at the foot of the bed, draped that over the small, still figure, and looked down at it. "Don't worry, Miss Madelaine, we'll take good care of your library." She waited until we had everything, shut the bedroom door there, and locked the back door after us. I thought it was futile and yet … it felt right.

The small building containing computers and shelf after shelf of blueprints, magazines, and other paperwork took less time. We boarded the trucks again, and Doc led off, only to halt four miles down the road, walking back to speak.

"I want to check this house here. Old couple. She's been sick; his heart's starting to give out. Cat died the other week, and they were upset about that."

I looked down the narrow drive. "Better you and I go down. Trucks won't do so well with that drive, and we'll do better on the bike if we need to run." Doc nodded.

The house was silent, and I knew as I stood in the hall no one alive here. Doc headed upstairs with me at her heels, and I was right. They were there, two old people, lying together in a big bed. I looked at the doc.

"Food, medical stuff, anything worth taking?"

"They were on the bones of their arse, Hugh. But we'll look in the linen cupboard; her mother quilted, and so did she." We removed two large armfuls of beautiful quilts and headed for the door. I paused to look around.

"Guess that's everything worth…" A small indignant mew interrupted that as a kitten joined us. It was tabby and white with blue eyes and a coat that was fluffy enough to suggest Birman or similar in his bloodline somewhere. I scooped it up. "Nope, looks like there's one more thing worth taking. I guess they got another cat."

Doc smiled at the kitten. "Looks like it. Make sure you don't drop him."

I tucked the kitten into my parka and tightened the hem's drawstrings. We puttered down the drive. I climbed carefully into the truck, showed Maureen the kitten—promptly named (Pussy)Willow—and we were about to drive away, when Doc held up her hand. Everyone froze listening. And distantly, from the small country town about a mile away and borne on the breeze, we heard the first sounds that forecast the end of our

Cornwall and our world as they had been. A massive *boom* and the crackle of gunshots.

Doc lifted her hand, waved it forward in the old sign familiar from countless westerns, and we rolled out, our scout in the lead. We hadn't quite believed before despite everything. Now we did, and our walled home would never look so good.

CHAPTER TWO

I should have known better. You know what they say; assumptions make an ass out of you and me. I was driving, Maureen and I having swapped over, and I thought I'd like a mug of hot chocolate as soon as we got back, when a small figure darted from the side of the road, waving desperately. I saw it was a kid, and automatically braked.

Maureen yelped. "*No,* keep going, it's an ambush." My wife notices things, and I trod on the accelerator. Two men who'd jumped from the bushes to open my door, found it was locked and dived in front of the truck. They were twice late. Maureen had slammed her lock down, and my abrupt acceleration gathered them against the front of the truck, off balance, and already falling as it hit them. There was a bump, and I halted a short distance down the road, seeing the small figure standing frozen by the road still.

Thorne halted his truck and stepped out, flanked by Annie, both with guns ready, and Doc came rolling back. There was a commotion, not so much noise as us scattering to get whatever needed to be done, done. I reached over and hugged Maureen.

"Good thing you saw that; stay and watch. I'll see if I can be useful out there."

I was, as two bodies were removed to the roadside and covered in pulled long grass. Doc Di was holding the white-faced child.

"All right, Bree, men came to your place; your daddy's away, there was just your mum, you, and Billy. Who's Billy?"

"M'friend. He often stays if his dad's away. He's a friend of m'dad."

I gathered that Billy's dad and hers were friends, she and Billy were friends, and both fathers had gone somewhere together. Di elicited more of the story, a deeply unpleasant tale. Bree, her mum, and her friend Billy had expected the men home a week ago. They hadn't arrived. Then two other men had knocked on the door and forced their way in. They'd stayed, taken turns with Bree's mother, used all the food in the house, and decided with everything in chaos they'd be highwaymen, using Bree as decoy.

I relayed that to Maureen, who joined the Doc and made her opinion clear. "We need to get Bree back home. Doc, you should look at the mother. And depending on where the fathers were supposed to be, we could check there if it isn't too far." Bree looked up at us in tear-stained hope, and Doc nodded.

"Yes." And to Bree: "We'll take you home. Tell us where to go; we can maybe get you food as well." I noticed she hadn't missed that mournful bit where there was none left in the house.

We followed Bree's instructions, having to drive around three sides of a square since Bree had used shortcuts to take the marauders where they'd wanted. We turned a bend, and Doc halted us, calling back.

"Listen." Not that you had to do *that* too hard. An entire herd of cows was making it known they hadn't been milked and someone should do something about it. *Right now!* I winced. I hoped Di wasn't going to have us all doing that for the rest of the day. But no. She moved her bike to park it by the farm gate, got off, and walked down the muddy path. She wasn't gone long.

Thorne and I were waiting, and she came to us. "Everyone's dead there. I thought they'd be when the cows weren't milked." She saw my look and grinned briefly. "Don't worry, Hugh, I'm not going to suggest we milk that lot. I'll go and open a few gates. But I looked inside their kitchen. They've got food; we can collect that and take it to Bree's mum. We can come back here and check around afterwards too."

We followed that programme, and the family must have

been believers in being well-supplied because we ended up with cartons of canned, packaged, and frozen food. Bree said they had a fridge and a freezer in the shed. We took everything edible and moved on to where a large white house with green and red trim stood.

Bree was out of the truck and up the path screaming for her mum and Billy, and announcing the bad men were gone, there was food, and we were nice.

Her mother may or may not have believed any of that, but her daughter was there, and ten seconds later, so was she. Doc stepped in. People trust a doctor, and a woman doctor even more so. It worked, and once the initial weeping and hugging had died down, Bree's mum had heard how the two men would come back, and yes, we had food to leave them; she beamed at us. She would be twelve or thirteen years older than Maureen and me, about forty, I estimated. She was a pleasant-faced woman — if you ignored the bruises down one cheek — and thinner than I thought she'd usually be.

"You brought us food? Oh, I'm Mary Leonard, you know Bree, and Billy's here." I'd started carrying cartons inside. "Thank you, thank you so much. You're all so kind."

Annie looked at her. "Bree said your husband and Billy's dad were to be gone a couple of days, but it's been more than a week, and no word. Where were they going?'

"Mark farms next door. He and my husband were going to pick up wheat. Tail end of a big crop, and you know about that."

None of us were farmers, but we'd all grown up in countryside, and most of us did know. The fence-line area of a big wheat crop can be either adulterated by other seeds blown over the fences or harder to mow because of said fences. Either way, the last of the crop can be sold cheaply, more so depending on the wheat farmer's convenience.

"They phoned us; we've bought there the last eight years. It isn't worth their while to do the work, but having the strips of wheat still standing causes problems, so our men started doing it, using a small tractor they still have and doing the bagging and all. Mark and Rick pay for fuel, do the work, and the Harrold's charge them 50p a bag for the wheat. It's a great deal all around. Last time, they came back with over two hundred bags for a hundred quid, plus we took them a couple of hoggets (those are yearling sheep) and swapped those for a weaner piglet." Her smile flickered. "We ate extra well for weeks."

Thorne took charge once all the food was inside, and a pot of soup was heating while Annie sliced potatoes into that. "Can you tell us how to find where your men are, how far it is from here, and there's another thing. Did you have sore throats and a bit of trouble breathing at some time in the last five or six months? When was it? Did you see a doctor about it, and what did he do for you?"

Mary Leonard stared then answered slowly. "Harold's farm is about a hundred miles from here. Can show you on a map. Sore throats, yes, Billy an' Bree got them. Me'n Rick picked them up from her. Mark never had it. We went to Doc Revenson; he gave us some new antibiotic. Only got it in that week. When?" She calculated. "Maybe two months ago now; could be a week or two less. Why, what's that got to do with anything?"

We waited until the three of them had eaten, and the children were starting to fall asleep on stomachs full for the first time in several days. Annie helped put them to bed, and once we were sure they slept soundly, we swept Mary Leonard back to the kitchen and gave her a precis of recent events. Thorne finished. "Your husband and his friend may not be alive. From what you say, Mark Harker isn't likely to have survived, but your husband not coming back suggests some other trouble there. What day did they leave, and when did you expect them back?"

"They went on the Monday; even if things took longer, they'd have been back by Friday." Her face twisted as if she were about to cry, then she forced herself into calm again. "Rick phoned me Tuesday and said it were going well. Wednesday night, we had that storm ... you didn't. Oh, well, we had it here. Not so much rain but bad winds; when I couldn't get a call in or out, I figured the pole at the farm there had gone down. I wasn't expecting them until Friday, so I didn't start worrying until Saturday." She grimaced. "After that, those men came, and I'd got other things to worry about."

Maureen took her hand. "Doc Di will talk to you about that. So, your husband and his friend should have got back Friday, and it's eight days after that now." Mary Leonard nodded. "We must get home. You have enough food for weeks now, but we go to the Harrold's' place in a couple of days. When we know what's going on there, we can come back this way and let you know. Okay?"

"I can't expect you to…"

"No, we're offering. You look after the kids and yours and Billy's dad's farms, and we'll hope, all right?"

"Thanks."

We stayed the night, and once Maureen, Thorne, Annie, Doc Di, and I were alone, we talked quietly. "What do you reckon?" That was Annie.

Di looked at us. "I'd say the boy's father is dead for sure. Mary told me where the phone transmitter is; we'll pass that on the way to the Harold's. If it is down, we'll know one reason there were no phone calls, but that isn't the only possibility. Mary's husband not coming back says a lot. Even if his friend died, Rick should have come back by now. A hundred and some miles. A fit man could *walk* that in seven days."

Her gaze went from one to the other of us. "With the death rate we're starting to see, there's food to be found. And bicycles, vehicles with petrol. No, something happened. But we saved Bree, we killed the men who had them, and we brought enough food for weeks. We owe them nothing, certainly not scouring the countryside to find a man we've never met, the husband of someone we don't know."

There was a long silence before Maureen spoke. "All that's true but for one thing. We *do* know them now. Doesn't have to be all of us. Hugh and I'll go."

Di gave a tiny nod. "If you find him, you're bound to need me."

Two of the seniors had been exchanging looks, and Gary spoke, his sister, Karen nodding. "We're good shots. We can stand watch, pack things, and we can both drive."

I eyed them. "Really, because neither of you has a driver's license?"

"We learned last time we stayed with Dad in Australia. Won't say we're great, but we can manage." He grinned. "Not like the police will be taking us to court."

I reflected that he was probably right about that, and there was another thing there too. It might not yet have occurred to the juniors, all of whom were under twelve. but the seniors were all fifteen or over, and none were stupid. Maybe Geoff's outburst had been triggered by certain thoughts of what might have happened to his family, if he'd see them again, and whether they were even alive still? Gary and Karen had to be thinking the same thing, and it'd be no bad idea if they had something else on which to focus.

I caught Maureen's glance, raised my eyebrows slightly, and collected a tiny nod in return. I looked stern. "Gary, you're the eldest. If we say you can come with us, you're to both be armed, don't make a move without checking, do whatever Maureen and I tell you, and remember common sense."

Karen smiled at us. "Common sense isn't common. We'll be sensible. Honest. So, we can come?" I looked over at Thorne, who nodded.

****

We reached the Manor to find everything peaceful and unloaded our salvage. Di went out to her surgery and bedsit in the container and came back, eyes wide. "Where did you get that addition?"

Thorne grinned. "I heard in the pub a while back that Joe Kindon bought one for his granny. I knew he wouldn't have put it up yet, and you may remember him; he and his family went to Italy for a holiday. I told Jake to drive our tractor and trailer over with a forklift and collect it. Set it up and hook it all into the container and the power. Kindon had a rainwater tank, plus an entire eco-power outfit to go with it. Jake said it was all still in packaging, and it only took him a day to set everything up.

Di hugged him. "Thanks."

"Hey, got to keep our doctor happy. Besides, where would your cats sleep?"

I'd guessed from that what he'd done; I'd heard some of the pub talk myself. Joe had planned to bring his beloved granny to his place once they were back from holiday, and to that end, he'd bought a self-contained granny flat. It was a building with one large bedroom—a good triple-size—another still larger room to be used as dining and sitting room that became a kitchenette along one end and with a bathroom off the bedroom. That contained a bath *and* a shower, both situated and created so either could be uninstalled and a large cupboard—also included—put into their place.

Joe, commenting how muddy a farm could be to grunts of general agreement, had also announced that he'd bought a pair of flat-pak sheds, as the company advertised them, to put on either side of the back door. One for firewood could be filled when the weather was fine, and it would hold, if properly stacked, about ten days to a fortnight's worth, and the other shed as a washhouse/mudroom. He planned to roof over them to give the granny flat a porch. Someone asked about a front porch, and Joe grinned wickedly.

"Remember when Marsh pulled down that glass house a' his?" Many did. "Aye, well, I bought the thing. Got in four by two lengths a' studs an' planking. Once flat's up, I'd put like a glassed-in veranda, right across most a' t' front, same way 's the back door wi' glass roof over it. Gran can grow her veggies there like the conservatory posh folks have. She'll love it."

I opened my mouth to wonder aloud what might have

happened to "gran" and shut it again. I could guess, and so could we all if we thought about it. It wasn't necessary to bring down the mood. Di was so happy, and I gathered her cats were pleased too. That'd do. We split for our various homes. Mic has made a good dinner, although she wasn't happy to hear what Maureen and I planned to do next. Maureen won her over, however, until we found that while Mic agreed we could go, she planned on coming with us, and that was that.

Maureen and I exchanged glances and shut up. When Mic gets that look, it's no use arguing. If we wanted to look for Bree and Billy's dads, we'd have company. I calculated. Okay. Mic, me, Maureen, Gary... Not that bad really; we were all fit, could all shoot, could—if the kids were to be believed—drive well enough, and we'd take two vehicles. Joe Kindon had had something else, a pair of four-wheel-drive Landcruisers. They were three and five years old, in excellent shape, and came with dismountable winches, spare tyres, and assorted extras. Joe took care of his stuff, and it didn't seem to have occurred to either Jake or Thorne that if the Kindons weren't coming home, then one, they were on our boundary, so no one had to see anything we might take, and two, if they weren't coming back, everything was there for the taking.

I shared that with Maureen over breakfast. We'd agreed to leave to look for the men the day after, so we had today to nip over and look around at Kindons. We left Willow, replete with quality cat food, asleep in a patch of sunshine, strolled off across the paddocks, climbed the boundary fence, and Maureen's head came up abruptly.

"Hugh? Look at that?"

There was a caravan parked by the big shed where Joe kept his vehicles. "Can't have been there when Jake got the granny flat," I said. "Joe doesn't have a caravan, and Jake would have said something. Nice-looking thing, one of those Dutch Masters—as that line of fancy caravans is called." I looked at Maureen, and she looked at me. We developed simultaneous smiles and headed for the door. I paused at we reached that. Knocked politely and waited. As Mic always said, better safe than sorry.

And if there *was* someone in there with a gun, I'd prefer not to be shot. It was as well I did. I wouldn't have been shot but having my throat torn out wouldn't have been any better. Judging from the bellowing bark and the thud as the dog hit the door, a canine was in there, ready, willing, and able to do just that. I knocked again, and Maureen moved to the door beside me.

"Is someone in there? Can we help you?"

A weak voice said something, then said "stand down" — to the dog, I presumed, because it went silent. I picked up a plank. Opened the door slowly, and once it was open outward a few inches, I put the plank up to keep it from opening further. A man lay on the nearest bed. He looked to be in his late fifties, and we could see he was dying. The dog went to rise from his side; he said something, and it lay down again, looking at us.

The man reached for a mug, took a drink, and spoke. "Can't talk much, makes me cough. Reckon you can't help me; maybe you can help my dog. You like dogs?"

Maureen nodded. "I do. How is he with cats?"

"Good, likes them. Name's Kaiser." For a moment, I thought he meant his name, and that it was an odd name, but then I realized he meant the dog. "You got cats?" he asked.

Maureen nodded. "A kitten, his name's Willow. We found him in a house where they were dead, and he came home with us."

A smile lit the dying face. "Animal-lovers. Great. Kaiser's Mastiff Rottweiler cross. Almost three. Trained, list of the commands he knows is in the drawer." A finger pointed. "You take him; everything here's yours. What do you know about what happened?"

We told him. It took a couple of hours, and when we were done, he was a lot weaker. Kaiser had come to sniff at us several times, encouraged by his owner. "He's a good dog. Likes kids, cats, okay with other dogs but not living with them." He took a breath. "Don't think I've got much longer. I'm Karl Leethorpe. Come from Somerset, no family left, my parents had me late, and died when I was twenty-one. I'd just joined the army. Mustered out three years back, planned to tour a while then buy a couple a'acres, a milking goat, few hens. Guess I can forget that. Never married, just as well probably. Was camping in Wales, mountains. Kaiser likes rabbits. Didn't hear about any of this. Driving to far side a 'Cornwall, gonna come back zigzagging slow, look for a place for us."

His rasping breathing was painful to hear. "You, Hugh, Maureen, look after Kaiser, an' be kind to him." We nodded. "Kaiser," he said, and the dog came to attention. "Kaiser, friends!" The big dog came to us. "Friends. Kaiser, friends."

He coughed once, and I saw blood in his mouth. He spoke again, his words firm and clear. "Kaiser, go with friends. Good dog, Kaiser. *Very good dog!*"

Maureen stood and took two paces to take Karl's hand. I joined her and clasped his other hand. She sat on the edge of the bed, her voice gentle. "We'll look after Kaiser; he'll be our dog, and we'll love him. Go in peace, Karl."

He gave her a quirk of his lips; that was all the grin he could manage. I saw him gather the last of his strength. "Bury me under an English tree. I saw too many foreign ones." His eyes closed slowly, and Kaiser went to him, whimpering. A small, soft, bereft sound.

We drove home in the caravan. Parked it by our cottage, explained to everyone how come we had it, and we held a sunrise burial back at the other place the next morning before we left. Nothing fancy, just a song and recitation of a poem, and once the grave was filled in, we placed a massive slab of broken concrete over the fresh earth. Karl would lie, now and forever, under the big old Hawthorn on the Kindon farm, just as he'd asked.

We had the Landcruisers. And in an hour, we'd be on our way. Mic would keep Kaiser with her until we came home, and

Willow had gone there, too. Karl had told the truth; the huge black dog instantly adored our kitten, and obeyed Mic. I thought that even if he was officially ours, it was my grandma who'd be his. But right now, we had lost sheep to find a hundred miles away, and while we were at that, we'd get some idea of what things were like out there by this time. And somehow, neither Maureen nor I were optimistic about what we'd find.

CHAPTER THREE

At least we had a clear description of where to find the Harrolds' farm. Mary Leonard had given us a hand-drawn map, we'd related that to official ones, and we were pretty sure we could find the place. As Maureen pointed out,

"The trouble's probably going to come when we get there. Okay, so phones in the area aren't working, but Rick and Mark went with vehicles. They should be okay—it wasn't an EMP that's done this, so where are they?" It was a good point.

After more discussion before we left, Jake was riding shotgun with Maureen, and I had Doc Di ahead of my Land-cruiser. Her cats had gone to stay with Mic as well, and Kaiser was beside himself, having found her cats didn't mind dogs that were properly respectful. I wasn't altogether happy at her coming with us. A qualified experienced doctor wasn't easily replaceable. All I could do was hope like hell nothing happened to her—or to my wife come to that—Maureen wasn't replaceable either; in fact, so far as I was concerned, for me she was even less replaceable.

The countryside was silent. We saw no one, heard nothing, but there were increasing numbers of stray animals on the road. Several times we saw broken gates where some desperate beast had broken through. But that was all, no people waving, no one showed at windows, and I was becoming depressed, wondering if the whole country was dead, were those I knew all who remained? If that was so, we too were likely doomed. There wouldn't be enough of us to rebuild a civilization, or even a non-inbred population.

We turned into the road leading to the Harrolds' place, and Di came back, binoculars now around her neck and more obvious. That wasn't a good sign. She pulled up by my window, signalled Jake and Maureen to join us and pointed. "I didn't go right up to the place, but from what I could see, the main house is burned to the ground. I smelled smoke as soon as I got past the corner; I parked the bike and climbed a tree. It's all flat so I didn't get a clear look, but I'm fairly sure. I'd say we should move slowly from here, maybe just me further ahead."

Jake made a dissenting mutter. "Why you?"

"I can get out of here faster on the bike and I'm a smaller target."

Jake looked at her and said what I was thinking: "Great, and if you aren't fast enough, we lose our one and only doctor, and some of us die because you aren't around any longer. Let me go. I brought my electric moped. She's a good little bike, nippy enough, and silent too. They'd hear you coning; they won't hear me." He chuckled. "Sides, did a bit of poaching in my younger days, I can move quietly, and if I don't come back, you've lost less than losing anyone else."

I disagreed with that and said so. "We won't find another gardener as good or experienced as you, Jake."

"More likely to than another doctor. I won't take stupid chances." He loped back to Maureen's Landcruiser, removed a small bike with fat tires, a carrier at the back, and the thicker frame that said "electric." Before we could continue the discussion, he was astride that, it moved silently away, and the decision was made. We watched as he vanished around the bend and stood listening. We could hear nothing, no shouts or cries, no shots, and after ten minutes or so, we half-relaxed. Time crawled by. I kept one eye on my watch, and after an hour, I straightened.

"That's long enough. We have a choice. We follow Jake, or we go home." I looked from one to the other, inviting their decision.

Di nodded. "If there'd been anything to say he's been ambushed, I could vote to go back. There wasn't any indication of that, and he could have stayed looking around. He could have been trapped somehow."

"By what?"

Di grinned at me. "By a bull, by a farmer asking why he's sneaking around their property, by falling down a hole, I don't know; but with no shouting or shooting, I'm not inclined to walk away. Are you?"

Well, no, I wasn't. I'd known Jake for a few years and liked him. "Drive or walk?"

"Drive a bit further," Di offered, and Maureen nodded. So that was what we did. We didn't hurry; Landcruisers moving slowly don't make that much noise, and we were watching in all directions as far as we could. Nothing moved apart from farm animals, and we pulled up at the gates to the farmhouse drive with nothing to alarm us yet. Something caught my eye.

I spoke sharply, keeping my voice low. "Di, Maureen, over there." I pointed. Something white was being waved. Then, briefly, a figure we recognised stood up and dropped down again. "You two stay here. I want to make sure no one's got a gun to his head. If they haven't, he could have reason to think there's danger if he calls out."

I started moving in, keeping enough cover to dive behind something if anyone popped up with a weapon. No one did. I came to where I could see Jake clearly, and he beckoned. I moved in, watching, but when I reached him, he was … no, not alone. A man was lying there in the doorway of a small shed. He moved, muttered, moved again and the muttering grew louder. Jake dropped to one knee and spoke gently.

"It's all right, he's a friend. The doctor will be here in a minute." Fever-bright eyes opened, but there was no intelligence in them, and I looked at Jake.

"Sick?"

"Injured. I couldn't find anyone else. I'd say this is Rick

Leonard. Call in the others; we need to get Doc Di to treat him, then get him out of here."

I stooped to lay a couple of fingers on the man's forehead and nodded. "He's running a heck of a temperature; I'd say, yes. Hang on a minute."

I moved to where Doc and Maureen could see me in a direct line from where I was and waved them to join me. Doc brought the bike in, but with the scattered debris, Maureen could only drive moderately close. She turned the Landcruiser, parked it, and came walking in.

Doc was already on her knees beside the delirious patient; she looked up at Jake. "Did he say anything useful?"

"No, and I didn't want to leave him and come back. As soon as I went to go, he started talking louder and louder. I didn't know if anyone was around to hear. I knew if I didn't come back, you'd come looking, so I stayed with him. What's wrong with him?"

Doc was running her hands over him lightly. His body jerked, and he made a sound, then another. She reached out slowly, rolling up the legs of his filthy jeans, and my breath hissed out. None of us needed to ask further. Both ankles were broken. In one, the bone was through the skin; both breaks were swollen and inflamed, and the one with the compound fracture also looked infected.

"How in hell did he do that?" I asked, and it was Maureen who answered me.

"He jumped." She pointed. "Look, the house was there. If he jumped from the back upstairs, he'd have landed there. Then if he crawled, here's the first cover he could get to." A heap of rubbish was there, and looking at it, I could see it'd been disturbed. "Then, when they were gone, he crawled to the shed for shelter."

I opened my mouth to repeat her *they.* and saw what she'd seen. It'd been a hot summer and the ground was hard. One of the Harrolds had mowed the grass all around the farmhouse. By my guess, only a day or two before whatever had happened. But if you looked closely, you could see there were wheel marks. They circled the house in a broad, barely visible line that suggested either several motorbikes, or a number of circuits. I jumped to a conclusion.

"Bikers?"

Jake looked up. "I'd say so." He walked over to stand, looking down at the marks. "Can't be sure, but I'd say half a dozen. They'd have guns, though and…"

"And you think they burned the house down?" He nodded. I didn't need to ask why; even out here in the country, we knew bikers. Not the ordinary ones, not those who just got together weekends to ride, and have a meal, a drink, and a pleasant day out. These would have been one of the gangs — or, if Jake was right and there'd been about six or eight of them — what remained of a hardcore bunch. They weren't known for kindness, charity, or a do-right attitude. Now, when much of the population was dead or dying and just about anything they wanted was free for the taking.

However, it had gone, he'd survived, and if the Doc could fix him, clean up the infection, and we got him home again, at least Mary and the kids would have a better chance at living. Not because he was male, but because two adults to two kids would be better than one. I walked to the other Landcruiser, ignoring questions, climbed in, drove it to park beside Maureen's vehicle, and glanced at my friends.

"In case they come back, I'll look around for anything we can use, too."

I circled, then again wider out, but it looked as if either the bikers had taken anything worth having, or there'd been nothing. There had been two large barns, and both had also burned. But in a dip behind bushes, there was a shed. I opened the door expecting nothing of value to find cartons of books, an old canvas and pipe stretcher, an old wooden box filled with the sort of tools you saw a couple of generations ago, and a stack of the old grey blankets the army sold off cheaply years back. Those had been stored in a big tin trunk, which must have annoyed the local moths, none of which had manged to get to them. I picked up the stretcher and took that back along with two blankets.

"Any use?"

Doc Di beamed at me. "Yes, it's exactly what we need. Not rotten?" I shook my head. "Great. Blankets okay?"

"They've been stored in a tin trunk."

"How many?"

"I didn't count, but probably a dozen or more."

"What else?"

"Old hand tools, books."

Jake looked at me. "Sounds as if all of that could be useful. Where?"

The three of us left Di tending to her patient and trooped off to the shed. In very little time, we had it emptied and the contents stowed in one of the Landcruisers. In the other, we'd lowered the rear seat so the stretcher could be laid flat in the back. We came back to report, and Doc nodded. "I've done as much as I can, but he'll need me for a week at least, and that's if all goes well."

I looked at Maureen, and she looked at me and nodded. "Pick up Mary and the children on the way home. If he's okay, they can always go back if they want."

So that was how we did it.

****

Mic took one look at everything when we returned, decided Mary and the children would prefer their own privacy, and asked me. I agreed, so they moved into the Dutch Master caravan, Rick was bedded down in the school's small infirmary, and five days later, we held a discussion. Us seven able-bodied adults from the Manor, with nine more from the village and farms nearest us. By now, Rick Leonard had been awake and coherent briefly, long enough to tell us what had happened. I stood up and relayed this first before Doc Di took over.

"Rick and his friend Mark got there to buy wheat. They both had small mixed farms.

"As the story went, the Harrolds' sons were old school friends of them both, and they'd had a deal on the tail-end wheat for nearly ten years. They got there to find the parents buried, the sons sick, and their wives and children dead. They buried the dead and decided to stay with their friends until they were gone, too. Mark came down with the virus — fast and badly — over the third night. They were all old friends; Rick couldn't get his wife on a phone and didn't want to leave his friends alone. He wasn't due back for days anyhow, so he thought his wife wouldn't worry too much."

I backtracked a little. "He and Mark got there on Monday and weren't due back until Friday. Mark got sick Wednesday night; by then, the Harrold boys had said to take the wheat, the Harrolds wouldn't need it. Rick and Mark had it all mowed and bagged, and the loaded trucks were down in a small gully roofed over as a sort of carport for all the farm machinery. The Harrold boys had gotten sick but more slowly. However, by that time, they couldn't walk, nor could Mark, and all Thursday, Rick was on bedpan duty. The bikers showed up that night around dusk. Mark had a pair of binoculars, and he saw them coming. Eric sneaked out and chained the gate, hoping they just ride off."

"But they didn't?" asked our electrician, then answered himself. "Nah, not that sort."

"No. Rick used a tractor chain, and they couldn't break or cut it, so they took the gates off the hinges. By that time, they'd been almost an hour, and Eric, Mark, and the Harrold men had time to talk."

I remembered how Rick had explained it. The other three knew they couldn't get away. If they couldn't walk to a bathroom, they couldn't make a fighting retreat from the house and escape. Rick hauled in every gun in the house, loaded them, shared out all the ammunition, and silently wrung his friends' hands. He'd look after Billy, he promised. If he got away and could return and there was anything to bury, they'd lie with their parents, and he'd take his friend home again. They'd made only one mistake.

"They expected that lot to smash the door down and come in shooting. They didn't. They had cans of something; Rick doesn't know what, clear, colourless, no petrol smell, but it burned like a torch. They poured it all around the house and the two main barns. They ran out of it just below the attic window and left a gap. No window on the floor above the ground and under the attic, and before Rick could get a rope or something, the whole place was going up. He ran up the attic ladder and jumped. Landed in the gap and crawled for his life. He looked back once he was in cover. He said the Harrold boys waved — they'd been in two back bedrooms — then they started shooting."

As a diversion, it worked perfectly; as a defence, it hadn't been too bad either. All three were good shots; initially, the bikers had been circling close to the house. They'd killed one, hurt one badly, winged another, and the bikers had responded with more Molotov cocktails, not thinking it'd make it impossible for them to access the house. By the time someone tried, the ground floor was an inferno. Rick heard three shots then, one by one, and knew. The bikers stuck around, then rode off, and Rick passed out.

In the heap of rubbish he'd burrowed into, there'd been scraps, a loaf of stale bread, several bottles of soft drink the boys had tossed because only their father had liked it, and the medication for both parents. And while it was just the pain, Rick had eaten everything edible, kept himself hydrated, and used all the pain meds, hoping to heal a bit. The meds ran out; he realised the wound was infected, he was becoming delirious, and he knew he wasn't going to make it home.

"It was Mark, an' Bree, and Billy I was sorry for," he said. "I wasn't going to hurt anymore, wouldn't know anything; but them? How would they manage? Would they be okay? An' what about the kids if anything happened to Mary too?" He looked up at me, his heart in his eyes. "All I can do is thank God you came; even if I go out now, Mary an' the kids are safe."

Maureen took his hand. "They've got friends, walls, guns and they' be fine."

Doc had chased us out then, and we'd gone to pass on what we'd learned. As I pass it on now to others.

Paddy, the plumber, pursed his lips. "Those bikers, nothing to stop them coming back."

Thorne agreed. "No. We have a suggestion. Entirely up to all or any of you how you decide, but the group Rick saw, he says there were eight. His friends killed one, wounded one badly, and one had minor wounds and will probably be okay; that leaves six."

Paddy smacked clenched fists together. "Reckon we can handle that sort."

Thorne shook his head. "Don't count on it. Yes, we could probably deal with six, but what makes you assume the number will stay static?"

"Huh?"

Maureen snorted. "They're like rats, see one and there's ten around. And they gather. Next thing, there's twenty … thirty…"

Paddy scowled. "Yeah, yeah, I guess so. But why'd they live?"

Doc spoke to that. "Many of them are filthy; they catch anything going around. Allodaxin's new; you can take it three ways. Pills for several days, an injection, or a couple of slow-release capsules. Any bikers going to a doctor would get the injection. That's slow release, too. By the time the body's absorbed it all, you're clear of the infection. The government had a project in Cornwall and one in Devon, too. Bikers could go to pharmacies and get a free injection for a list of things; many won't have bothered, but a fair number will have. And as Thorne says, where they run into each other, they'll likely combine. Initially, they'll stick to cities; there's everything they could want there. But remember, nothing's being replenished. Once it runs out, they'll spread out. The group that hit the Harrold farm may have come from Truro, from Plymouth, just riding around to see how bad it is, if there are people still, and the best places to loot."

We all thought about that. I didn't like the possibilities, and the more I considered it, the more I agreed with Thorne's suggestion. It would be a case of "hang together, or hang separately," and I'd prefer not to hang. Mic looked over the silent group.

"Think on this too. Say there are only six. How many people are at your place, Paddy?"

"Four, me 'n' ma, and our kids."

"Against seven adults, all armed, and none of whom will hesitate to shoot. What if you're away, Paddy? What if you've run out of food and gone to look for some?"

"We can go together."

"Then come back and find everything you had burned to the ground."

"Okay, okay, so you tell me, what do we do?"

Mic told him. It took nearly all day, including intense discussion, but most saw the sense in it. Some wouldn't; they'd go home, fort up, and assume things would work out. Some still couldn't believe the government and the army wouldn't cone and fix things. We'd acquired Paddy, though; he wasn't the fool he could act at times. We also got Dave the electrician, two farming families, and a teacher from a primary school.

"Children need education. I'll stay."

We could have asked a lot of questions, but a quick glance between us, and we all left it at that. We could use him; he was a good teacher. He was a sportsman too, strong, good reflexes, only mid-thirties, and pleasant enough. I didn't know if he'd ever been married or divorced. If he had a wife or children somewhere, he didn't seem worried about getting to them. The discussion moved to practicalities.

Not that I joined in. Mic had looked over things from the first and made lists. Maureen and I had added to those, and then when, where, or as we could, together or separately, we'd taken a Landcruiser out and salvaged. The first thing we'd done with Thorne's blessing was to pick up a set of the connectable barns, all with solid lockable doors. We'd filled those. They were in a corner against the heightened wall. Mic and Maureen had painted them in khaki green, and you had to practically stand in front of them to notice they were there. A while later, Mic and Annie had quietly taken one of the three-ton ex-army trucks and brought back more, plus gear, animal feed, and long-lasting supplies to fill them.

Jack had gone out on his moped and circled the nearest township, the one that had collapsed in riots and looting. The bike had a trailer that could be attached, and he'd gone quietly from empty house to empty house. He'd taken seed packets, seedlings, and small saplings, come home and planted them in the most suitable places for them all. Over the time, we'd also brought back the wheat Rick and his friend had bagged. We had the CBM, and with sufficient supplies to keep that working hard for weeks, and we would, just as soon as we knew our parameters. As I said to Maureen and Mic while we had a final cup of hot chocolate together once the outsiders had left: "Tomorrow was going to be a busy day." In which I was even more right than I'd thought to be.

****

It started with Paddy. He arrived with his wife Joy — known to him as "Ma" — and his daughter Ellie, a bright-faced girl of fourteen who planned to be a plumber like her father and already knew much of the work, and Eddie, his twelve-year-old son. Four of us lined up with forklifts salvaged from council yards. We descended on the barns for Lightson and Co., which sold flat-pak buildings. Paddy chose the one they liked, and it was trundled back to the Manor and positioned where it would be convenient for everyone.

Over a week it took time, but everyone pitched in. At the end of seven days, we had two farms extending from the Manor's lands, both walled in a way that might have impressed Norman the Conqueror, while inside a new walled section we'd started a line of houses, each with about half an acre of land, and where Paddy and Dave's families would live. The teacher, Colin Dewenter, had chosen to site his house at the far end of that strip. He had packed all his own items and brought them with a truck, brushing off those who offered help. Paddy admired the walls once his house was positioned.

"Looks like a sort of castle, dun it? You expect another Norman invasion?"

Mic chuckled. "We are likely to get one, even if it isn't the Normans, but that's not all." His eyebrows asked for clarification. "Fewer people, and what increases?"

"Weeds," Dave said dryly, and we all laughed.

"Wild animals and feral ones. We'll have sheep, cows, goats and horses, pigs, and maybe other beasts. Rabbits will be everywhere until foxes catch up. There'll be packs of wild dogs; we'll have rats, mice. Sure, a lot will eat each other, but some will try getting at our livestock. The Computerised Building Machine doesn't just put up a wall; If you use the right combination, another section goes in front, digging a trench about five foot deep and laying a footing."

"So, the walls are to kept predators out?" Dave was interested.

"And our burglar alarms in," Mic waited while his face went from understanding to confusion. "Geese, a breed called Sebastopol. They shriek like demented bicycles at anything or anyone they don't know. We keep them in one place daytimes; nights, they spread out and cover all the land between the walls. Anything climbs over a wall, and every person here gets told about it. They're grazers, good eating, smart, and aggressive towards anyone they don't know — or approve."

Paddy looked at his daughter. "Guess you won't be getting out of any windows after dark, darlin'."

Marnie flapped a hand at him. "Not until they know me any rate." That raised a laugh from us all.

We worked hard, but in ten days, we had everyone in a house, and all the houses where they best fitted. Mic called me in the early morning then. "Maureen wants to do some other things today. I thought it'd be a good time to get the geese." We strolled together to the two Landcruisers. Maureen and I hooked their trailers on, Doc Di joined us, and Mic suggested she leave the bike behind.

"Why? How far is it?"

"Not that far. There's a farm that breeds them."

Di eyed us both. "And...?"

"They have other items too."

"I see." She got in my grandmother's Landcruiser and asked no more questions. The smallholding I had in mind wasn't that far, but it was well hidden, and towards their back boundary was a lake. It wasn't huge, maybe ten acres or so, and it was semi-man-made. There'd been a large shallow saucer just a part of the way the land lay; over time rain had worn a narrow ditch leading off to a stream some distance from it. Until the Bremmers bought the place, spent a day with a bulldozer widening and deepening the dip, and rain the following winter had filled the saucer.

They'd used old concrete posts to create a dam and spill-way into the original ditch. The lake was no more than six feet at the deepest part, but they'd added small fish, some sort of cat-fish, I believe, and it worked. I took the Landcruiser ahead, drove up the winding drive, and called out as I stopped.

"Otto, Eva? Anyone home?" If there was, they weren't answering, so I stepped out of the vehicle and wandered around the yard and sheds. Thorne purchased chickens for school dinners from the Bremmers, and I'd usually been the one to collect them. They were pleasant people, getting on a bit now. Their children had all left home; the two girls had gone to stay with relatives in Germany and work there; the boy, oldest of the three, had married and moved to his wife's home in Glasgow. I reached the back of the house and felt a small pang of sorrow.

Di spoke from behind me. "Do they usually leave the back door open?"

"No."

"I'll take a look, if they're okay, well, I'm a doctor; I was worried."

She checked the house, opening doors, looking into the utility room, and then she made a quiet sound, a "ah, yes," sort of noise, and I joined her and Mic who'd followed, catching up behind me. Di swung the door wider, and we all saw the bodies. They lay neatly disposed on the bed; beside them lay an elderly dog and cat, and a dead canary at the bottom of a cage on the windowsill. Mic had walked around the bed to pick up a sealed envelope.

She opened it, read quickly, and looked up. "They ask whoever comes to take only whatever they honestly need. If we can, they ask to be buried with their pets. They say if we kill any of their creatures, to please do so quickly and cleanly, for food not for amusement." She turned a page, and read on, condensing what had been asked. "Their valuables are in a cupboard; we should hold them a year, and if none of their children come, they're ours. Any clothing, furniture, or other household items we can take."

Mic put the letter down. "Take a look around. What animals *did* they have, Hugh?"

"They always had a sow and a litter," I said. "Other than that, just the geese, the hens, quail, pheasants, and some guinea fowl."

"They're good watchdogs, too," Maureen said, and Mic and I nodded. That was no more than the truth, and like geese, they were edible.

"All right, we take some of everything. Younger stock, mainly female, we take the pig and any piglets, get them into a trailer, and the birds in the other. If there's anything smaller we can use, we'll come straight back as soon as we drop the animals off. Take a quick look now and see if there's anything we really want."

We scattered in three directions. Mic returned with an old-fashioned but beautiful ankle-length fur coat and a slightly shorter leather one. She handed one to each of us, and we tried them on. They fitted, so they went into the vehicles. I checked the shed, a few smaller useful bits and pieces, along with a four-wheeled pony cart, the type with a spare dismountable shaft and sets of matching harnesses. That way, it could be drawn either by one pony or two. I made a note of it. Mic returned with a sack of footwear in each hand.

"All good quality. Better to take it and find we can use it than not and find we needed it." That's my gran, very sensible. It was easy enough to decide too; there was enough still here we'd like, so we'd come back.

Maureen was looking thoughtful, as if some thought was nagging at her; she didn't know what, but it wouldn't shut up. We got back, unpacked the creatures, settled them into safe places, and took off again. I was driving into the Bremmer yard when Maureen yelled triumphantly in my ear. I almost put the car off the drive, then the word registered.

"Cellars?" I pulled the car up, half-turned to stare at the big old farmhouse, and saw the edge of a narrow ventilation slot. The others had dried weeds, rubbish, and several old cans piled in front of them. I vaulted out of the vehicle, strode over, and kicked some of them aside, and yes. There had to be cellars—so why were they hidden and what was in them? Then I knew. I remembered quite a long conversation on wars with Eva Bremmer about seven years ago. Their grandparents had lived through the Second World War as children, and I remembered what she said they'd told her.

We hadn't locked the back door. I shoved it open and headed for the rear of the kitchen. There was a large ancient cupboard in one corner. I grabbed it and swung it to one side. Nope. The other? Yes. It rolled away, and beneath it was a trapdoor. It opened in silence, and Mic grunted.

"That's been used recently; the hinges and the bolt have been oiled or greased." Doc slipped by us and dropped down the ladder. I heard her breath catch.

"Come on down to Aladdin's cave, people." There was a minor traffic jam until we all reached the floor and could look around. Di had found a light switch and turned that on as she stepped off the final step, and none of us, looking about, could say her comment was inaccurate.

Mic blinked. "Dear grieving gargoyles, what were they *expecting*, an apocalypse?"

I couldn't help it; I laughed until it set the others off, and we stood in that cellar howling like idiots for a good five minutes. Maureen walked to a pot stand once she caught her breath again and picked up a small leather-bound book. "It's a diary; it's in German, but there's another one under it that looks like the translation." She'd have started reading, but for Mic, who caught our attention.

"Hugh, you and Doc get back home. Get the army trucks. Get hold of Thorne and tell him about this *quietly*! No one's to know but us seven. Not the kids, not the outsiders. We'll put it all down in the caverns. There's only us know how to get into those; then if anything goes wrong, we'll have this as backup. It could save our lives."

Our gazes met, and we all nodded silently. We were starting to learn that when life gets terrible, the people you trust all the way are those you know — all the way.

****

We worked quietly, long hours after dark, circling the outer walls where a light wouldn't show until we had everything down in the large dry caves under the Manor. And once that was done, we announced we were taking a road trip to check on a few things — just in case. We went to a place we knew; it was a small hotel. As we'd guessed, the owners were dead, the staff fled, and there was sufficient food for us to eat well for the weekend. We did and took turns reading the translation of

Anders Bremmers' grandmother's diary to the others.

It was a generation older than I'd thought. Anders had been Otto Bremmer's father, and it was his grandmother Monika's diary. She'd been thirteen when the war started, and her father had given her the diary. He'd told her to write down what happened without fear or favour. That one day, the war would be over, and people should know the truth, but no war was ever the last, that when another came, her diary could save those who knew what to expect, fear, avoid, or plan for.

She read, and we listened. The end was sickening; if it became that bad, I didn't think I'd want to live. It was a miracle Monika had survived, and I wondered how many had known of the events she'd written down. It took most of the weekend, and once I recited the final page, I looked up.

"What do we do with these?'

Mic took them from me. "We put the German diary back where it came from. The English one goes with an explanation into the caverns. Somewhere in there where only us here will know where it is. I'll go through the translation and make notes that may be useful. I'll also start a diary, and that will be hidden, too. If we get through this, a record might be useful, and if we don't, well, if a historian finds it sometime in the far future, it'll be a genuine historical record and — enlightening." I nodded; oddly, I'd started a diary myself right after Doc had taken us on the first salvage run. Maureen knew where to find that, but only she and I knew I was writing it.

I said nothing, but as I drove home, it occurred to me that if Mic's or my diary were as brutally truthful as Monika's was, then any historian who found it, and if their time had gone back to what ours was before the plague, they'd be at least as horrified as we had been. I made a mental note to suggest to Mic that some names were changed, as they say in books, "to protect the innocent." Although there were few of those in Monika's dairy, and I suspected it could be so in ours, depending on how life went from then on.

CHAPTER FOUR

Life went on quite pleasantly for months after that. Everyone settled in; those who'd declined to join us had no problems. We had a school set up, and with Maureen and I working part-time there, Thorne taking classes, Annie back as matron and school nurse, (and after Doc Di's approval, Annie, whose hobby had been herbs, had taken that up again, and one of the juniors had become interested as well). Colin Dewenter from a local primary school was teaching full-time, and with Jake on gardening classes, we had a day run to a schedule, kept the children educated, and out from underfoot.

Rick Leonard was improving. Billy Harker missed his father, but with Mary Leonard mothering him, and Bree, who'd been his best friend for much of his life, and all the interesting new events, he forgot to mourn for as much an hour at a time. Usefully, too, Rick could hand milk, we found him an electric wheelchair that was basic, light, and strong, could be lowered so someone using it could pick up anything they dropped, and every morning, Bree and Billy got the cows and goats in. All three milked them, the children carrying the buckets of still warm milk around to each household.

Mic raised another subject four months in. "How are we managing for eco-electrical systems?"

Dave and Paddy were there, and Paddy answered. "We've got everyone on power and plumbing, but we could do with more. The spares we have mean we could replace about half at need. But no system lasts forever." He glanced over at Dave who took that up.

"A basic household system was intended to last about

twenty years before it broke down completely and needed replacement. Top quality systems they'd started selling in Cornwall over the past couple of years do thirty and are more easily replaced as parts. Parts are better quality too. Forget generators. They'll probably stop working about the time any fuel goes."

"How long for those then?" Mic asked.

"Depends," Dave said thoughtfully. "Petrol, diesel, you can get water in them. If that happens, they won't work. We could look for the new tankers. They were made to keep water out, including condensation. Fuel in those could last thirty-forty years, but not much longer is my estimate. Lots of electric vehicles about; if we collected the tankers and electric machinery, we might, if nothing goes too wrong, live our lives as they were before this happened — maybe for fifty years. After that we'd likely need to start back-engineering."

Paddy nodded. "I'd go with that. Unless we get a good mechanic here."

Mic looked around us: me, Maureen, Jake, Thorne, Dave, and Paddy. "In other words, we can't sit around; we need to start from the ground up. Barns first, a lot of them. Get those up, bring in all the packaged, canned, bottled food we can find, animal feed too, then collect the most expensive eco-electricity systems, electric gadgets, white-ware, cars, and other vehicles. And while we're gathering that lot, pick up hand items, stuff like cast iron frying pans and cooking pots, beaters, anything that works by hand."

Maureen grinned. "We won't need to go far." We all looked at her, and Mic grunted.

"Of course. The museum." It was quite a decent-sized place about thirty miles from the Manor. A depiction of life at the start of the eighteen-hundreds. "We could use everything they have, just one thing. We'd better drop everything and go there fast before anyone else gets the same idea. There's electrical stuff in every house and half the businesses, but that sort of collection won't be in many places. Another thing I was thinking about is weapons."

That had occurred to me while she was talking. Bullets would run out; they weren't casually made by some amateur, unless you were a black powder re-enactor. And even then, your guns wouldn't last forever. I said that, and Mic took it up again.

"They have guns like that in the museum, too, but better to collect bows and arrows. Both can be more easily made." She grinned at Thorne. "Thanks to you."

It was true. Many private schools have a specialised interest — riding, a team sport, an art or craft of some kind. Ours was archery. Thorne's father, Gerald, had been an Olympic competitor and a British champion. Thorne had grown up using a longbow and had diverged in his later teens into crossbow and pistol crossbow as well — mostly I think to differentiate himself from his father without doing something substantially different and losing what they had in common.

Thorne considered that. "Better we get as many crossbows as possible and pistol ones," he said slowly. "They're more difficult to make. But there's something I know most others won't. I was at the competition they held at Looe a few months before this happened. I was talking to Tommy Berenson; I've known him a while, and we always got on well. He makes crossbows and good ones. He was telling me he could be moving up our way. His uncle died last year; the man had no wife, no kids, so he'd left everything to Tommy. Tommy's place is on the edge of Looe, and some developer came right after that offering a real packet for Tommy's home and the land he has there."

Mic straightened in her chair. "Okay, where's the place he was left, and did he give any indications of when he might move?"

Thorne took a slow drink from his mug of tea as he thought. "Last two-three years, he said it's spread out more, so there's trouble. His workshop's been broken into twice in the past three years. He's got three kids, twins — a boy and a girl — they'd be going on ten by now. Yes, that'd be right. At the competition, he said they'd be starting year five and be at Intermediate at the beginning of the new year."

He took another drink and was silent as he recalled old conversations. "Third kid's another girl; she'd be about seven. This developer wanted to start the project asap and offered extra if Tommy got out fast. Tommy said it was enough to make it worth their while, and his wife wanted to get away anyhow. She said it was better to start fresh, new school for the twins, and the school the younger one attends is rough, and getting rougher. The Looe competitions would have been five months before the plague got started. I'd say there's a pretty good chance they'd moved by then."

"Where?" Mic was insistent.

"Don't know, he never said the village name. I don't think it's in a village anyway, just a house and some land, somewhere between Padstow and Bude."

"Did he say anything at all about the place, how far it could be to either? Where they'd shop? If merchants would drop things off there? Anything that could give us a place to start looking?"

Thorne nodded. "I remember I asked if getting stuff to it would be a problem. I said places on the coast were often down a path or stairs to a beach, and it could be a real problem. He said they wouldn't have that one even if there were others. The loop road to it was third class and sometimes went out in the middle of winter for a few days, but the ground was in the lee of a sort of hummock of ground, kept the worst of the wind off, natural drainage, and the hummock hid the house." He paused. "Yes, and he said if you looked over from Bude, you could see the hummock; it had a whole line of yews along the top Some legend they used to be used for longbows by soldiers out of Bude."

Mic dug a while longer with questions, then sat back. "I'd say I can make a darn good guess where their place is."

"When should we go then?" That was Jake.

"We need to discuss this with some of the others. No sense in taking a Landcruiser or two. Better we do it in bulk. The two army trucks, the Landcruisers, and farm utes with trailers, anything that takes a good load. It's a fair way, and it'll use up fuel.

We go straight to the Berensons. If they're dead, we salvage; if they aren't, we offer to barter for any of the gear they'll sell; Jake would have pointed out the uselessness of money these days. We offer to take them to Padstow if they want to go there; we can check there out as we pass; we'll say we'll go there, haul back all the salvage we can carry, and leave it with them as payment. That may suit them."

I added a comment. "We can look up sports shops at Padstow too, Bude, maybe. They could have bows and arrows, other weapons and ammo we could use. Clothing as well, lot of sports clothes aren't only comfortable; they're hard-wearing."

"Plus, tennis balls, cricket gear, other stuff for the kids for fun," Maureen added. And so, after discussion with everyone over the next two evenings, it was decided.

****

It was a bright morning, about 6:00 a.m., and Mic and Jake were singing as we fell into line, some ancient song their parents had liked about a convey. Something about "It was the dark of the moon on the sixth of June." Annie pointed out that it was a sunny morning on the eighteenth of July and was told it was the thought that counted. We were a convoy, which was enough.

That we certainly were; a discussion had decided each vehicle would have two adults, and two more in it who could drive — not necessarily adults since most of the senior kids could, even if they didn't have a license. That way, if we found suitable vehicles and salvage, we wouldn't have to leave them behind. That had allowed us nine vehicles. It was agreed, too, that if anyone came across a better vehicle than theirs and with no apparent owner, they could take the better one.

Mic had ensured everyone was up and breakfasting by six by making sure everything was waiting ready before dark the previous evening. We'd left Rick Leonard behind; he still wasn't in any physical condition for a trip as long as this one was likely to be. The Merrison mother and grandfather, and Tilliker uncle were all slower and weaker physically, but they could shoot. With them were all the small children, besides which the geese were out, so if anyone tried climbing in, there would be a very prompt warning.

The day stayed clear and sunny, we knew where we were going, and we were with friends, so the songs kept coming, a lot of them Cornish folk songs or traditional—I think we must have sung "Trelawny" half a dozen times. Once we got near to Padstow, however, Thorne silenced everyone.

"The doc goes ahead." We'd found her a lighter—and silent—electric motorbike for some occasions. "She scouts, comes back. You all take the chance now to, ah, use the facilities, have something to eat and drink, and stretch your legs. Once she's back and we hear what she's seen, we'll be rolling, and I'll want everyone alert."

We had a pleasant break that lasted an hour and a half before our lookout on the rise signalled Di was coming in. She pulled up and looked around at us. I noticed her face was a shade paler than usual, and I tightened up. Maureen took my hand, and Mic took my other one. Di took in a breath.

"Depends on how you look at it, whether good or bad. Half the town's burned. Not so bad for salvage, it's the suburbs that've gone. I didn't see many people; that's why I was a while. I found a vantage place and watched." She paused, and I could hear the indrawn breaths. "There were kids, a scattering of them; all looked to be around maybe seven or eight up to around eleven or twelve. I didn't see more than about twenty. One of the older lots chased some younger ones and took anything they carried. I'd say we can salvage anything. They didn't look to have any real weapons, but whatever we do, we'll have at least one major choice to make."

Thorne took that up in a quiet voice. "Whether we take any of the children along with us. If what Doc says is so, most, if not all of the adults caught the virus and weren't treated in time or not with allodaxin. Two other questions are, do we look for Berenson's place now and come back here afterwards, or do we find Berenson's and go from there to Bude and circle home?" The talking got into gear as soon as he stopped.

I won't say who was for or against; some of their reasons weren't that far wrong, but those who come after may not understand. To some, it was a balance. We had twenty-five adults, counting the senior pupils, and eighteen smaller children. Right now, we were moving slowly to where we could manage food, shelter, power, and schooling for everyone; it was taking all the adults to do that. If we doubled the number of children, we'd lose one or more of what civilized things we had. We couldn't afford to go backwards; too many things needed stockpiling before they were gone.

I won't list the votes or the names. I'll just say that it came down on the side of walking away from Padstow. We did, and the Berenson home wasn't hard to find in the end. It had four inhabitants, three of whom were human. The younger girl had caught the infection about nine weeks earlier and given it to the twins. Her mother had kept her away from her and Tommy, and when the main plague got there, both parents caught it. My Landcruiser was in their yard right behind Di's motorbike—after all, the family knew me—and all three kids came out screaming my name. I was wrapped in weeping kids, thin arms, and small, desperate faces turned up to me.

"Mr. Rogers, Dad said you might come; he left you a letter. Please, take us away from here; they're dead. There's just us and Rasti. Please, can we go? Can we go *now*?"

Rasti was their cat, a beautiful Seal Point Tonkinese. The letter was, in many ways, a wildly optimistic prayer. Tommy had assumed—on no foundation whatsoever—I'd survive, and once I'd had time to recover from the initial trauma, I'd remember him and his family and come looking. He wanted me to take the children, to save everything at the property for them, and he assumed that nothing had been as bad as it appeared. The government would be running again shortly, all would go back to normal, and this letter gave me official guardianship when the Social Welfare got going again.

It added information about bank accounts — no longer existing — other relatives who'd take in the children and their goods if we didn't want to or couldn't — if they'd survived, which I thought unlikely, and in any case, even if they had they were in north England. I could guess what that city was like by now, let alone the impossibility of us travelling there or them making it here. And I must also see the children went to church every Sunday, made decent friends only, they should keep up–their archery — and that was just about the only practical item in my opinion.

I questioned the children. No, they hadn't read the letter; it had been sealed, an' Daddy wouldn't have approved, with a hint that his disapproval would have been painful. No, he hadn't told them what was in it. Why? I said he'd asked us to take them with us, to be their guardians; yes, Rasti could come. Yes, their two goats as well. I'd noticed them as we drove up, both nannies, Nubians by the look of it, an excellent breed for milk and meat. And we'd be taking everything in the place, no, not their possessions, but we needed the other things. They seemed quite happy with that. I passed this on to Thorne, Mic, and Maureen, crumpled the letter into my pocket, and started salvaging in Tommy's workshop while Mic and Maureen gathered goats, the cat and his food and belongings, and the children's possessions.

I don't like lying to children, but we couldn't afford to hold everything here waiting for them to be old enough to inherit, not when the weaponry might at some stage be the difference between life and death. As for most of the other demands, that I must see the children go to church every Sunday, there wasn't one nearby, and there was a ninety percent chance no minister had survived. As for decent friends only, that depended on your definition. I'd always known Tommy was a bit narrowminded. Oh, well, he could rest in peace; we'd care for his kids, but our way.

Driving them and everything he'd left them the length of

England, even trying that would be madness, particularly with no guarantee any relatives had survived or would be prepared to take them in. And telling the children any of this would be dangerous. They'd then expect us to live up to what "Daddy" had said, and we couldn't and wouldn't deliver most of Tommy's list, so they'd come to resent that—and us. And it would be a source of contention so long as they remained. And if they didn't, where would they go?

I looked at Mic, who'd read the missive; she held out her hand and I passed over the foolish letter. When later, just before we left, having quietly brought out the shrouded bodies and laid them on a pyre, those sheets of paper served to light it. As I said to the children:

"The house is here; if, when you're old enough, you ever want to come back, you can. It belongs to you." I thought it unlikely. By that time, they'd be probably ten years older at least, and they'd have long since learned what happened to only two or three people who lived in an isolated house. Mic, Maureen, and I had talked about this, and where things would likely go. At the Manor, we were reverting to a walled village, where a lot of buying and selling would be barter-based, and where it was us against them, and everyone outside our walls was classed as allies or enemies. It hadn't got to that last yet, not quite, but it would, and probably within those ten years.

It took the remainder of the day before we had everything packed up. We were only taking the contents of Tommy's workshop and a gleaning of rarer things from the house—any house would have ordinary ones. The children, fully fed on pleasant-tasting food for the first time in a couple of weeks, had gone to sleep in sleeping bags in the back of our Landcruiser. We headed for a place one of them had mentioned. A house belonging to a family their dad knew, people called Holly. The children knew only the name and general direction; however, they'd never met them. That I thought would be better; we'd be halfway to Bude, and with the kids sleeping like logs, we could do any required house cleaning and get them into a bed before they woke.

As it was, no cleaning as required. The house was locked—I jimmied a window and let everyone in. The owners had probably gone on holiday and been caught by the plague wherever that holiday spot was. But whether that was why they were gone or for some other reason, they weren't here, and we were. We slept in their beds, ate a hearty breakfast from full cupboards, and, pausing only to add all that food, and a gleaning of rarer items as was becoming our practise when further from home, we drove on.

Bude was empty. In many houses, bodies lay and rats swarmed. Some of the bodies were fresh; it hadn't been the plague that got *them*. Dogs ran in small packs and fought the rats. I saw no cats, and wondered, but there was no time to look for answers that wouldn't be of any use to us. We took books, paper and exercise books, pens, and pencils, any food at all that had been secure from vermin, new clothing and footwear, skeins of wool, bolts of fabric, pins, needles, thread, buttons, and anything else that would become scarce quickly and be difficult to replace, or irreplaceable, in the longer run.

We circled on the Launceston Road after a night in Bude, camping on the forecourt of a small B&B. Mic looked that over when we arrived.

"Attic, look." We did. "You find interesting things in attics," my grandmother added. "Sometimes they come from a long time ago."

Maureen and I checked, and she was right. I don't know the story, except that from the look of the place, it had originally been a large house and was probably at least two hundred years old or even three hundred. Some of the attic contents appeared that old. Half a kitchen's worth of cast iron cookware, assorted hand tools, room and fire screens and fire tongs, three hammocks, four birdcages, two cages for a cat or small dog, bed frames— one baroque iron curlicues, and the spaces between larger items stuffed with everything from eiderdowns and feather pillows, to nine, count them, nine, fur coats, of various sizes, species, and lengths.

There was a large attic window, too. I'd brought a portable hoist, and with diligent use, we got out everything of use to the window, dropped most of that in front of Thorne's three-tonner, and helped him load it. He looked at the curlicued bed frame, two feather mattresses, all of the feather eiderdowns, and six pillows.

"You taking those?"

"Yes."

He nodded, and that was that. Mic grinned. She'd been the one to tell us. Back some forty years ago, a friend of hers from New Zealand had come over. She'd stayed with friends and having been in Belfast before Cornwall, she'd raved to Mic about the fantastic warmth and comfort of a feather bed, eiderdowns, and pillows. At the time she came, it had been winter and far cheaper, and winter in Belfast that year had been *freezing*. She'd stayed very warm and comfortable however in her feather cocoon at her friends' place, and she'd told Mic about it—several times. Mic's got a memory like an elephant, and as soon as we were in the attic and she saw those items, she'd pounced.

I'd grabbed the bed. It was a Victorian fantasy, like something a princess would have slept in; it was high off the floor, the iron painted in a cream picked out in gold, and my memory isn't bad either. I remembered on our honeymoon that we'd slept in a similar bed, and Maureen had looked wistfully at it when we were leaving. Her look met mine, and I saw she remembered, too, and loved me for thinking of it. I recall thinking later as I set it up again, complete with feather mattress, feather eiderdown, and pillows, that it was a bed fit for a princess, and that was who'd be sleeping in it with me. *My* princess.

It all took time. We stayed an extra night in Launceston proper since Di, doing a scout alongside roads, had found a place that made connect-barns, and it was filled with them, of various shapes and sizes, but too many even for our convoy…

"There's trucks, too, though, forklifts and hoists."

We understood; this was where we used the additional drivers. It was another fine, clear day when we left, heading home. We had an extra seven trucks, all with full fuel tanks, and at the rear of the procession, there was a fuel tanker, also full. That had some lifts and hoists attached to it by ropes. Mic started singing "Trelawny" again as we rolled along. In many ways, it wasn't quite appropriate for our trip, but it was Cornish, a song of triumph, and right now, that how we all felt—triumphant.

A good sword and a trusty hand!
A merry heart and true!
King James's men shall understand
What Cornish lads can do!

And have they fixed the where and when?
And shall Trelawny die?
Here's twenty thousand Cornish men
Will know the reason why!

Chorus:
And shall Trelawny live?
And shall Trelawny die?
Here's twenty thousand Cornish men
Will know the reason why!

Out spake their Captain brave and bold:
A merry wight was he:
"If London Tower were Michal's hold,
We'd set Trelawny free!

"We'll cross the Tamar, land to land:
The Severn is no stay:
With 'one and all,' and hand in hand;
And who shall bid us nay?

"And when we come to London Wall,
A pleasant sight to view,

Come forth! come forth! ye cowards all:
Here's men as good as you'

"Trelawny he's in keep and hold;
Trelawny he may die:
But twenty thousand Cornish bold
Will know the reason why!"

Chorus:
And shall Trelawny live?
And shall Trelawny die?
Here's twenty thousand Cornish men
Will know the reason why!

We bellowed that out, and the song picked up and ran from vehicle to vehicle. We were coming home, not with Trelawny—who in my opinion had been something of a twerp, but what we had now were items still more valuable to us in the here and now. They meant life and hope, and—please all the fates—the survival of the Manor and our people. Our convoy rolled on steadily as the song rang out across the countryside.

CHAPTER FIVE

After that, I assumed things would be quiet for a while. When I said that to my grandmother, she retorted that I should have known better. "Life doesn't work that way, Hugh. It's rarely what you expect, what you hope, or what you want. Old saying, my lad. 'Life is what happens while you're making other plans.' And while you're about it, maybe you should talk to Thorne about an official cemetery." I thought about that for much of the next day.

It wasn't a bad idea; thus far, we'd lost no one, well, we had, but Karl lay buried where he'd wished to be, and as for that other ... my mind went back to the time two days after we'd returned with the Berenson children.

They'd settled in with the Merrisons. As Maggie Merrison said comfortably, "We only ever had one child; those are good kids and Dad and me and my dad, we wouldn't mind. Tad likes them. We've got room, and they can call us aunt and uncle. We asked, but they never knew either granddad, so they won't mind calling my dad that." So, it was settled. The Ikea flat-pak we'd moved to the Manor had been a three-bedroom house. We'd moved in one of the self-contained "tiny homes" for her father, and by coincidence, we'd left sufficient space between those buildings to insert more bedrooms opening into the main house.

Hayden Merrison had surveyed the result with pride. "We're leaving Tad, an' us in our bedrooms; Dad keeps his tiny house. But with those rooms, we've got one for each of the Berenson kids and a spare for visitors. Should do us nicely."

Thorne, who was looking over the result with us, agreed. "And with the passive heating system, it's all good." We'd added piping room to room. Where the pipe entered a room, there was a cover that could be rolled around down to shut off any heat — or undue noise — not that noise travelled well through them. But it meant rooms didn't need individual heating in winter, which we'd found to be a blessing for all concerned.

Thorne, Mic, Maureen, and I had discussed some of this. As Mic pointed out, "For the next while, we've got things, but they won't last forever. Get flat-paks in while they're still in good condition. Get seeds, seedlings, and saplings — food ones first. Get books, the DIY sort, information, herbals, and we'll stockpile medicines, particularly the long-life items. All the food that's used the new preservatives."

Thorne nodded. "You know Dewenter dug a cellar before we put his house down? For storage, he said. Seemed like a good idea to me."

Maureen looked up. "Would it be possible to lift our place and do that?"

****

The discussion on that and other possibilities went on and started again the next day. We'd just stopped for morning tea when the commotion began.

Ollie Tilliker came running in. "Sir, Mr. Trelen, there's a lady, me 'n' Pete found her. I think she's sick."

Thorne sent one boy for Doc Di, the other to show us, and the four of us followed the lad to where, outside Trelenwold Manor walls, there was a small, huddled figure. It raised a face in which the eyes were unfocused. Mic took the woman by the shoulder in a grip that, while gentle enough, also demanded attention.

"What's your name?"

"Lana. I'm Lana."

"Are you with anyone, or is someone with you?"

"Daisy, m' little Daisy, she's gone; he took her; that's why I come. Lives here with some rich guy he does. School didn't get rid of him fast enough. Kept it all quiet." Doc had arrived, but she stayed back a little. I moved to her.

"What do you think?"

"She'll be all right if she's properly treated; she'll be okay if I wait a few minutes more to do that. Let Mic see what else she can get out of her." Her gaze met mine. "I don't like the sounds of any of what she's saying. If it's what it sounds like, best we keep all the others away. Hang on a minute." She called the Tilliker boys over.

"I want you both to go home. Straight home. Stay there. It's important. Tell your mum, dad, and grandpa I'll be coming to talk when I can, and—listen to me, this is really important. You don't stop to talk to anyone or tell anyone anything about this lady. Go home, and you can tell your family, but say it's an order not to talk to anyone else. It's Manor business. You all stay home; if anyone asks, you're busy, you don't know anything. Now go."

They ran, and I looked at her. "Think they'll all do that?"

"If I'm right, I hope to hell they do. If so, we may get through this without too much trouble. If someone talks, we could be in—a deep mess." She turned back to listen as I did to my grandmother's quiet questioning.

"Lana, Lana! Someone took Daisy. What about the rest of your family?"

"Just me 'n Daisy, others all gone. Weren't losing my Daisy. Never learned to drive so I walked, I walked n' I walked n' I walked. Found his place, no one there, met a man, said Colin'd gone to posh place, walls all around."

"Trelenwold Manor?"

"Yeah, rich folks, some fancy place kids board, heard people talk about it at Daisy's school. Sort of knew where it was, an' I come here. Get my Daisy back. He'll have her hidden somewhere. I know about him; his school knew too; gonna fire him all quiet." Her head lolled to one side as she became unconscious, and Doc moved up.

"That'll do," She looked at the four of us. "We don't talk about this; we don't let anyone know Lana's here. If anyone asks, the boys found a woman; she was just overtired. I gave her something, and she went on her way."

"And we get Lana to our place," Maureen said quietly. "If we circle and come in the back way, use the Manor to screen us." She glanced at her watch. "It's close to mealtime. Thorne, you get everyone in there to come to lunch. When they're in the dining room, go and pull the curtains; it's a sunny day. If anyone asks, say you have a bit of a headache and the sun's making it worse. We'll watch for that. Okay?" Thorne nodded.

Maureen turned to Doc. "We need to move her without making much noise. What would be best?"

I grinned. "What about the pony stretcher?"

Mic looked at Doc who nodded approval. "Mic, if you circle and watch the dining room windows. We'll get there as soon as we can, be watching. Hugh, you get the pony stretcher."

I was gone, not making a show of my hurry but wasting no time. The pony stretcher had been a creation of Jake's, not meant as the genuine article, but as part of a door-to-door, one hundred and twenty years since an "end of the First World War" commemoration evening at the end of 2038. All he'd done had been screw in a method of attaching the four stretcher arms to sit securely in four old leather cup stirrups. Someone led the front pony, the other followed, a "wounded" patient, surrounded by "medical" staff, lay on the stretcher, and because that was affixed to stirrups there was sufficient give and take in the stirrup leathers to prevent problems any time the ponies got a bit out of step.

As a system, it was quite smooth. It was soundless, and I remembered exactly where the items had been left. The two ponies belonged to the Manor; normally they either pulled a four-wheeled cart or were ridden by juniors. They were Welsh cobs, fourteen hands, quiet, sensible, and matched grays, each with a characteristic dished face. I whistled them in softly, tacked them up, and was back where my wife and Doc were waiting, in about ten minutes.

Getting Lana onto the stretcher wasn't easy. I guessed

that was why Di had sent Mic to watch. She'd have wanted to help with the lifting, and while, at sixty-one, my gran was fit and healthy still, she was less capable of moving a heavy weight, and we did need someone watching the Manor curtains. I took Lana's shoulders, Maureen, and Di a leg each, and we moved her as smoothly as possible. Then we started walking.

She'd made no sound, and I asked Doc, "Is she injured anywhere you could see?"

"No. I'd say it's exhaustion. Her feet are in bad shape; she may have been eating unsuitable food or had gastroenteritis from bad water. If I get her treated, she could be back with us as soon as day after tomorrow."

"Gives us time to…" I broke off.

Doc Di nodded, a look on her face I wouldn't like to have turned on me. "She gave us something to start with. If the school knew, they may have the information there. I want you three to go there first thing in the morning. Maureen's very good with computers. If there's no power at the school, bring computers from the headmaster's office, or any other you think could be worth it, back with you. Come to that, go over the place if you have time. If there's salvage, we may need to return for that."

Maureen agreed, adding. "We can take a battery pack, even a couple. That way if there's no power, I can fire up any computers we think could tell us something. We'll have to hope they aren't password coded."

We arrived at the back of the Manor. Mic came towards us silently and kept her voice down. "He pulled the curtains just now. Leave it a minute in case."

We did so, and it was just as well. One of the juniors, Noni Carter, came to the window that would have shown us and stuck her head through the curtains.

I heard Thorne's voice. "Noni, what are you doing?"

"I thought I heard something, sir."

"And is it likely to be an attack on us?"

"Um, no, sir?"

"Good, then we don't have to worry about it, do we? Sit down, eat your lunch. And *don't* get up without asking permission." Dimly, I could hear other juniors making smart remarks at Noni, while one of the seniors cut in to point out the geese were around, and no invader would be strolling past them. Which, I thought, as Doc silently led the ponies to our back door, was true.

We left Lana on the stretcher. I took the ponies back where they'd come from while Maureen returned their gear, and Mic vanished upstairs. We had agreed to take Lana up to one of the storage rooms. Our cottage was two stories; there was the ground floor which had all the common rooms, plus our bedroom. And when my grandmother joined us a year later, she'd claimed the next floor up. That'd been the attic, which totalled about three-quarters the size of the floor below.

Mic had considered those, marked out an area from them that gave her a bedroom, a sitting-room, a kitchenette, and bathroom, which was about half the area, and the other half was designated as storage again. The bedroom and sitting-room were merely separated by a curtain, and if that was opened for a party or to a larger group for some reason, the bed in the corner was shielded from view by a large, folding, beautifully painted — once it was carefully cleaned — bamboo screen Mic had found at the garage sale of an old man's possessions, and bought for a pound.

Mic had the door open that let into her rooms, she'd moved fast, there was a clear space in the storage room nearest that. There'd been spare mattresses and bedding in storage, and she had a stack of two mattresses out; they were made up with sheets, pillows, an eiderdown, and a light bedspread over that and tucked in. And, anticipating, she'd placed a water-proof sheet over the mattresses. Doc, Maureen, and I placed the stretcher on that, and carefully raised Lana while sliding the stretcher from under her. She settled into the bed, with a tiny, contented sigh.

Mic looked down. "She's filthy; her clothes are worse. She'll have to be washed."

Doc considered that. "Let her sleep until tomorrow. I'll come in and wake her enough to get soup into her about the time you're going to bed. Then around 6:00 a.m., I'll come in and feed her again. We'll have breakfast; you can take off for the school, and I'll stay here with her. Depending on how Lana does, I'll get her stripped and washed, into a clean nightie, and outside another couple of meals. By that time, she should be improving. You'll be back, maybe with something to prove or disprove what she said, and we can then call the others in. Okay?"

"Should we say we're going to the school if anyone asks?"

Doc smiled. "Why not? Even if they want to come, what would they see? And there may be useful items while you're there anyhow."

We followed her programme, and when we left, it was in our two Landcruisers with trailers attached. Kaiser came with us; the sight of his massive head poked out of the window, ears flying, mouth open in an enormous doggy grin, amusing us all. His friend Willow had stayed home. There was a nice warm bed, inhabited by a nice warm person who seemed to be staying put, and Willow wasn't going to miss out on that.

I kept my speed cautious. It was over a hundred miles to the school, but it was now almost a year since the plague started; some roads were partially blocked these days, and there was wandering stock. I sped up where I could see the way was clear, but it still took a few minutes short of three hours before I pulled into the gravelled circle by the main entrance. It looked quiet; no sounds, no movements. I let Kaiser out, and he vanished. We sat waiting. Kaiser came back, effectively reporting no people, and nothing he could identify as dangerous either. I stepped out of the vehicle and headed straight to the front offices with Maureen at my heels. Mic disappeared with Kaiser, and I left her to it. We found the headmaster's office. To my sour amusement, there was a note on the desk—behind his locked door, which I'd opened with a screwdriver.

To Whom It May Concern:

Considering the development of this pandemic, I have made the decision to shut the school until further notice. Should the authorities enter and access the computer for any legal reason, I draw their attention to the file labelled as C.M. Dw. I looked at my wife, she looked back, and we fell about. I couldn't *believe* this guy; did he think he was being subtle or what? We kept reading, me over Maureen's shoulder. *Alicia Oakley was removed from the school after the first accusation. Her parents do not intend her to return.*

The file contains all testimony given by anyone involved, including a psychiatrist's evaluation of Alicia. It also contains a statement by the teacher, whom, I may say, vehemently denies the child's accusation, claiming it a misinterpretation of events.

However, it is my personal opinion that the evidence is sufficient to order his dismissal. Any further action will be decided by the National Education Board of Cornwall, who have been sent both an e-file and print copies of all documents.

It is my closing statement that the teacher in question has been formally dismissed from the school, given a written statement to this effect, and that he has been paid up to the end of the month for all monies owing.

John Radcliffe

Maureen put the letter down. "Let's take a look at this file on the computer."

We did. I read the file aloud, already seeing the problems. Alicia's testimony was clear. She'd been upset over an argument with a friend. She sneaked off into her classroom to cry and sulk, Mr. Dewenter had found her. He'd put her on his knee, cuddled her, said not to cry, and then he'd "done things." The psychiatrist described said "things," having gotten them from Alicia by degrees over three interviews. She was adamant she believed the child. Alicia, she said, was only five. In play with the dolls she's been given, she was very clear what the teacher had done.

One of the more damning items was Alicia's six-year-old friend, who'd come to find her and make up. She'd seen Alicia on the teacher's lap, seen her struggle. Heard her say "Let me go" or "let me down;" she couldn't be certain which, but it was one or the other, and Maureen made a small sickened sound in her throat.

"The headmaster says he isn't certain," Maureen said. "I am."

I nodded. "Print it out if you can, twice at least. More if possible."

"Thorne?"

"To us three here, to Thorne, to Doc Di—she may be able to speak to this better than us anyhow—and I want every adult to read it. I'll call a vote to be cast once they have. Do we search his house?"

"And if there's nothing there?"

"I'll put it to Thorne that Dewenter goes anyhow, based on the file and that the Education Board found that sufficient for the headmaster to annul his contract, pay him to date, and dismiss him."

Maureen looked thoughtful. "Yes, what they really meant is 'we believe the child; it's a low-end offence without much concrete evidence, but he has to go.'"

"Yes." Maureen turned to the computer again, and I went in search of Mic.

As I went, I was considering how Thorne would decide. I was pretty sure he'd agree that at the least, Dewenter packed up and left Trelen Manor. It wasn't known to anyone but Thorne, the two of us, and Mic, but Maureen and I were able to ask for that.

****

It had started six years earlier, not long after we'd married. I've always been something of a twiddler, I liked making minor items, inventing things to make doing something easier, and I'd read about a problem an American firm was having with one of their systems. I found it interesting. I twiddled and fiddled and came up with a gadget that'd work for them. I'd have just sent it to the firm, but for Maureen. I told her about it when she came home from lunch with a friend. She was looking excited as it was and still more when I told her.

"No," she said firmly. "Patent it, then send it."

"We can't afford that."

"Oh, yes, we can. I bought a lotto ticket last week, and it's done nicely. We patent your idea in as many countries as we can. It's a windfall, and we use it that way."

We did, then I sent the gadget to the firm in America. It took them a year, but after they'd looked over my gadget, they couldn't come up with a cheaper variation that'd still be as good and wouldn't infringe my patents; they made me an offer. A lock, stock, and barrel one, and I accepted. I sold them all rights, and in return, I got a lump sum that just about laid me in the aisles. Maureen, Mic, and I had another talk, and from Mic, I learned something I hadn't known, that Thorne was in financial trouble. Even private schools have building standards—enforced by an agency, and they said the Manor had fallen below code.

The entire Manor roof needed replacing; so did much of the electrical wiring. Ideally the buildings—all of them—should be painted, and in another three years, when next things were checked, he'd have to replace a few other things. Thorne had obtained estimates, a minimum—which would leave things to be done in three years—and a maximum, do every item, and even better. That way, it'd be as much as twenty years before further upgrading could even be mentioned.

Mic looked over the table at us. "He told me how much for the maximum; it's about half what you and Maureen got from Tilzley and Co. I didn't say anything to Thorne, but if you paid for all that, you could take the big cottage over the back to live in, and maybe I could come, too? You'd get a share of the profits, you could teach part-time if you wanted, put the rest in the bank on deposit, and sit back. Thorne does well with the place; it's just that what he gets isn't enough to pay out that sort of money on a lump sum over only a year or so. And that's the time he's got."

We knew Thorne's finances. Mic's dad had been an old school friend of Thorne's father. Mic had babysat Thorne, and I'd grown up knowing him as a trusted older cousin or something similar. I had a fair idea of his finances, and Mic would have a better one. Apart from anything, I'd run free at the Manor all my life. I loved the old place, and I knew it was swings and roundabouts on this. If Thorne sold, some outfit would turn it into a hotel, pull everything down, and put in a development, or something equally horrible. Thorne would go to live in Portugal or someplace where expats went, and we'd never see him. And every time I ever saw the Manor — whatever was left of it — I'd know I could have saved it.

I looked at Maureen; she looked at me, and we nodded to each other. "Mic, we'll leave it to you to talk to Thorne. If you think he wouldn't want to do that, it's okay."

Thorne *did* agree. And if we insisted he had to get rid of Dewenter, I was sure he'd agree there, too. A Trelen still held Trelenwold Manor because we'd stepped up to save it — and because he knew we loved the place almost as much as he did.

****

Now, I swung the Landcruiser through the gates and stopped by the main steps. None of us had wasted our time at the school. Maureen had ten copies of the computer file, and she'd made ten of the headmaster's letter, too. No, there'd been no power, but the portable batteries we'd taken had worked. Mic and I, with Kaiser's assistance, had gone through the whole place while Maureen dealt with the paperwork.

We'd stripped the staffroom and canteen. The school had closed officially, and it seemed no one had returned afterwards. We found food — large amounts — and all I could say on that was someone had been slow on the uptake. We'd stripped the infirmary next, and again it was the same thing. No one had been there. Mic had gone to take a quick look over the craft rooms, metalwork, sewing, art, woodwork — and been struck almost speechless to find that applied in those as well.

When we met up, I was almost as flabbergasted. I'd been to the caretaker's home—and his storerooms. "You won't believe it," we said simultaneously. We'd taken everything we could load, and we'd go back for the rest just as soon as things were resolved here. As to that, we left the loaded vehicles and trailers, and went to find the doc. I wanted to show her copies of the file and letter and see what she said, and find out if Lana had said anything useful either.

Di read the letter and file, listened to me, and shook her head. "What she said was very simple. She was out with Daisy. The child went off on her own without Lana realising. Lana went looking for her, and was in time to see Daisy climbing into a car. She got a good look at the driver, who didn't see her, and she's positive she knew him. One of the teachers from the school where Daisy had started a couple of months earlier. A guy called Dewenter, and she'd heard some very odd talk about him, and that he'd been fired."

"And she's been looking for him and Daisy ever since?" Mic said in a quietly lethal voice. Doc nodded. "Okay. Hugh and Maureen, start unloading. If anyone offers to help, let them. And before you ask, I'm taking this lot around to Thorne, Jake, and Annie first. I want to hear what Thorne says. If he agrees, we'll call in the other adults as well, let them read these, and take a vote on your question, Hugh."

"Do we know where Dewenter is?" asked Hugh.

Doc did. "One of the seniors mentioned it when I was outside. Dewenter said he needed clothes and he was going look around. That was about an hour ago, she said. I got the impression he intended to be gone several hours—only the best for Mr. Dewenter."

It was time enough. In half an hour, the three I'd named had read the letter and file, and Thorne had agreed. We called in the other adults, including our seniors. Twenty-seven of us, two hours after we'd returned from the school, had read the letter and file, had talked, and listened; we were agreed. The vote was twenty-seven to nothing that we search Dewenter's home for anything incriminating.

Jake spoke thoughtfully. "I always wondered why he wanted to live so far from anyone else. Thought maybe he just liked being private."

"Do we wait 'til he gets back or search now?" Annie questioned.

"On his return," Thorne said. "Two of you senior boys, watch the gate, play with a ball or something; once he's through and can't see, shut the gate and put on a chain and padlock" He pointed to the wall corner where he'd placed those. "Mic, take Kaiser. If Dewenter tries to run for it, have the dog stop him. *Whatever* we do," his gaze swept over us. "He'll be present, it'll be fair, and we'll have an honest record."

I looked at the man I'd known all my life, and for the first time in all those years, I saw his ancestors, those who'd dispensed justice within their lands, and I was glad I lived at Trelen Manor. Thorne was their true son, and his justice *would* be fair and honest.

CHAPTER SIX

In my experience, if anything can go wrong, it will — and does. For once, however, it didn't. Colin Dewenter returned in his car at five o'clock. He zoomed through the gates, paying no attention to the boys playing soccer, but as soon as he was around the corner of the road leading down to his solitary house, the gates were shut, chained, and padlocked. We had been waiting; once Colin got out of his vehicle, I appeared with Mic.

"We need a word, Colin."

"Okay, give me a hand with this salvage, and we can have a drink and talk."

Something possessed me then; I picked up the large cotton bag that clearly contained some of the clothes he'd gone for, and without his seeing what I did, worked the top open — noticing it had been looped securely shut to prevent that. I tripped — accidentally on purpose — dropped the bag and shook it so the contents landed strewn on the ground.

Mic had quietly taken a smaller package and gone ahead, so she paused in the doorway with the door half-open.

"Hugh! You are *clumsy* ... hold on, those are children's clothes. Dresses for a little girl. Why would you have those?" With her attracting his notice I'd stepped back by the car. Dewenter, either from guilt or intuition, saw the game was up. He dived for his vehicle, not realizing I'd quietly removed the keys. He was in the seat and grabbing for them before he saw they were gone, and he wasted no time there either. He vaulted out, and ran for it just as Thorne and half a dozen others closed in. He was fast, but Mic whistled sharply, and Kaiser, who'd been at her side, was gone. He brought Colin down flat on his face in the grass in less than fifty yards, and Colin rolled desperately, trying to get the dog off him, get up, and run.

Thorne and the others joined the confused tangle before Colin could do more than thrash and yell. Dog and man were separated, Kaiser more gently than Colin. Jake and Paddy took a firm grip on the human portion of the duo and held him securely. Kaiser loped back to us, tongue hanging out as he was patted and praised. Colin Dewenter straightened up, glaring at us defiantly.

"What's going on? Why'd you set the dog on me? What's all this, Thorne? Am I supposed to have done something?" Mic picked up a girl's dress in each hand and displayed them. Colin sneered. "So, I picked up some kid's clothes for someone I know. That's a crime now?"

Thorne shook his head. "No, but Lana Blake says she saw you abduct her five-year-old daughter, Daisy, and that is. The headmaster at your previous school says you were dismissed from there for sexual activities with a pupil named Alicia. We took a vote: we'll search your home, and depending on what is, or is not, found, we'll make further decisions then." He waved to us. "You know what's to be done. Do it."

Mic had dropped the dresses and was already inside walking through the house to the back. She called sharply, and Thorne, Annie, Maureen, and I joined her. "I got a glimpse of the cellar he dug before the house went on top. I'd say there's a trapdoor into it, and it'll be in this vicinity," her hand indicated the parameters. "It's probably disguised. Move furniture, rugs, carpet, anything that could be between it and being opened."

Thorne was the one who called us shortly after that. "This set of bookshelves. There's a couple of brackets that hold it to the wall, except that they don't." He moved those, and they turned upward, not attached as they'd appeared to be. Thorne took one side of the bookcase and pulled outwards. It moved fluidly, and he said a word we rarely heard from him. "There's a trap door right here."

We joined him. The trapdoor was quite light and came up easily. I laid it back against the wall, and Thorne paused. "Annie, you and Maureen—and Mic, you too—go down. If there's a little girl in his cellar, he's had her there for a couple of weeks; better she sees women first."

To sum up: There was a little girl, and it was indeed Daisy Blake. She flew to Annie, holding on to her and screaming wordlessly. Kaiser had gone with Mic, and Daisy hugged him next. Thorne was getting a quiet running commentary from Mic, and he moved everyone else back, giving orders.

"He had a little girl locked in his cellar. We know who she is; she was a pupil at his school." Doc Di went down the steps. "The doc will sedate the child and examine her. But there's little doubt in my mind. Colin Dewenter, at the very least, leaves Trelenwold Manor." There was a snarl from the assembled adults. Doc came up the steps, Daisy in her arms, and carried her through a now silent group to her car, where she placed her in the front seat and fastened her in.

She turned to face everyone. "I have her heavily sedated now. I'll run a line with fluids, and I'll examine her. I'll be out front of my surgery in an hour and a half to tell you what I find. Maureen, can you and Annie come with me, please, in case I need extra hands."

****

We ended up in a straggling group outside her surgery an hour and a bit later. Some of us were sitting, some with a book, reading, and Mic and I were whispering. "What do you think?" I asked my grandmother.

Mic looked at me. "Do you have any real doubts?" I shook my head. "No. And think about this, Hugh, what would he have done with the body of a child of that age? She'd have died after a while. No sunlight, no exercise, no proper diet. And if she got sick, he didn't dare call a doctor. Would he risk hauling a body out with the chance of someone seeing what he was doing?"

I felt sick, icy horror. "Mic? He's been here for months. We only know about Daisy because Lana saw him, recognised him, and had already heard talk of where he'd gone, so she headed for here. What if there was another little girl before Daisy, or maybe more?"

Mic stood and wended her way through the gathering. She reached Thorne and talked, her back to the crowd. I saw his face change as he spoke to Mic, and she came back while he walked into the surgery.

Mic reached me. "Thorne says he'll have Doc Di hold things up a bit. We're to go back to the house and take a quick look around the cellar. He says don't take too long, but don't miss anything that's there." I snorted but followed her to where our electric bikes leaned against a wall. We were at the Dewenter doorstep in minutes, and down in the cellar. We started at opposite ends of that, Mic going counter-clockwise and me going clockwise. I scrutinized walls; we met. Each was now checking the floor.

Mic looked at a set of shelving, sat on the floor, and studied its base, then stood and looked at where it met the ceiling. "Ah." Her hands went up; she made a motion as of turning a lever, then, "Hugh, here, love. Pull this forward."

I took a grip on the shelves and pulled. There was no movement. I took a better grip and *hauled*. And they moved, inch by inch, swivelling outwards—and behind them, there was a patch of fresher concrete. Beside it, there was a hole with a board over that. Neither were large, both, I judged the size to be one a five or six-year-old girl would fill if she were curled into a ball and rammed into it.

I looked at my grandmother and felt something inside me. All the little girls I'd known and liked, who'd trusted me, the daughters of friends, with whom I'd played, showed the things I could do with electricity like flashing Morse with a batteries and bulb fixed to a small board. I'd read fantasy books to them; I'd taken surplus fruit from the Manor to those who were sick. Maureen had cuddled Manor juniors who were homesick, taken them for countryside walks, taken them riding on ponies or pushbikes. All I could see now was a redness that blotted out everything.

Mic said something I didn't understand. There was a pick in my hands. I smashed it repeatedly into the concrete until it gave way and pieces fell, then a larger one, and I could smell what it had hidden. *When there's no laws left, outlaws come into their own.* I ripped barehanded, and the pieces remaining that hid the tiny, helpless form tore away until it tumbled free. I had a blanket in my hands. I wrapped her in that.

We were walking back to the Manor-house. I carried her carefully; she was a child. She should not be jostled or frightened. I saw faces turn as we approached. Mic spoke, and they moved aside. Thorne was there before me, and I talked to him.

"She was behind the shelving in the wall. There was an empty hole waiting beside her. I had to bring her out; she shouldn't be left in the dark."

Thorne's hand came out to grip my shoulder in one hand, holding me with all his strength. "There will be justice, Hugh; I swear it. But it must be *justice*. Lay her on the grass in the sunshine and let those who will judge see the truth." They saw; they filed past, some retching, some weeping, some hard-faced and grim. Some ran away to return with flowers until all but her face was covered.

It seemed only seconds before Doctor Diane came to give her testimony after that. "I have examined the child found in Colin Dewenter's cellar. She is malnourished. She has bruising that has been caused over days, and, I can only say this brutally: There is no kind way to describe it that might not be mistaken for less. She has been regularly raped. In my medical experience, most recently sometime within the past twenty-four hours—during the hours of last night," She stopped speaking and stepped back.

Thorne took her place. "Bring out Colin Dewenter." He was brought out by Jake and Paddy, a whining mess, far from the arrogant sportsman and teacher he'd appeared previously. Thorne looked at him. "A child was found captive in your cellar; Doctor Diane has testified she was most recently raped last night. That house was yours, the cellar you dug. No one lives with you. And Hugh has found another child. Hugh?"

I moved to where I could look at his face. I don't know what mine showed, but he cringed back. "I went to your cellar and moved the shelving. Behind that, there was a fresh patch in the concrete. I broke that open and brought out the body of the child I found there, for everyone to see. Beside it there was another hole, empty, waiting." My voice broke in rage and horror. "How many patches would there have been in the concrete if Lana Blake hadn't known you? How many, you..." Two men caught me back, and Maureen was there, saying my name.

Thorne spoke. "A question without any certain answer, but the number ends here and now. Bring him behind me." He paced to the ancient oak that shaded the oldest part of the stables. They'd been built from stone, and there was a massive, stepped mounting block, never used these days, in one corner beneath a bough. Thorne entered a door and emerged with a coil of braided nylon. He looked at Colin's captors. "Lift him to stand on the mounting block." They tried, but Colin fought in a crazed desperation. "Hold him."

He walked to stand face-to-face with Colin. "Understand this, Dewenter. You hang today. Step onto that mounting block, and have the option of jumping off; if so, you may die quickly of a broken neck. Or stand on the ground, the noose will go around your neck, and I doubt I'll lack volunteers to haul you up, so you strangle slowly. But whichever choice you make, you die today. You'll lie naked in an unmarked grave, and any mercy that comes to you will be by God's choice. You'll get none from any of us."

There was a cacophony of agreement and threats while Dewenter blubbered, mucus trickling from his nose, tears running down his cheeks. "It isn't fair; it wasn't me. I won't be hung; it isn't legal. I'll have the police on you. *You can't hang me!*"

Thorne had been weaving a noose, and now he placed it over Colin Dewenter's head, tightened it about his neck, tossed the other end of the rope over the branch, caught the end as it came down, and took a grip on it some feet up, leaving near thirty feet lying behind him.

"I can. Colin Dewenter. You have been found guilty of the rape of two underage girls, their imprisonment, ill-treatment, and abduction being done to facilitate the greater crime. One you murdered, or else she died from your lack of care. The people of Trelenwold Manor have found you guilty. Judgement has been given. Sentence shall now be carried out."

He held the rope, and I saw his hands whiten with the power of that grip. He walked backwards so the rope tightened, I was there in half-a-dozen strides, my own hands adding to the pull. Mic was behind me, Maureen, Doc Di, Paddy, Jake… Colin Dewenter shrieked, ran to and fro; then he did under duress what he'd refused to do under offer. He scrambled up the mounting block. We saw he would try to escape all of his sentence and we accelerated. Before he could jump and utilize the slack the block provided, we moved faster, and as he jumped, it was already too late.

He rose slowly into the air. Fighting, eyes bulging, mouth open as he tried desperately to get a final breath—and failed. Jake had let go of the rope and gone to the loose end. He took that, snubbed it around a stable post, and tied it off. It took minutes more as one by one we let go, and found the rope held. Colin Dewenter danced. Twisting, turning, hands flailing, until slowly, all movement ceased. I'll say nothing further; we've all read of what happens after death, and his was no different then.

Thorne moved to stand by the dangling figure before facing us all again. "Go home. Keep your children inside until the morning; we'll take the body to be buried at first light tomorrow. You were all given a piece of paper and on it you wrote L or R. or S. Give them to me now before you leave." He collected the squares of paper and looked at Jake and me. "We'll take him to the stables in a few minutes, strip, and wash him then lay him in the back of my station wagon. We'll leave with him at first light. I'll drive."

****

I'd wondered later that evening what the paper squares were for and found out once we were driving away in the station wagon. Jake had brought two spades, and I was handed a cloth bag containing the paper squares. "Take one out when we come to any corner or crossroad and tell me the letter," Thorne instructed, and I understood.

We moved past the gates. I dipped out a square and spoke. "L." The vehicle went left. and over the next hour again and again, I dipped, called a letter, and the driver followed. A long and winding road, and at the last, I think none of us knew exactly where we were, just that ahead there was a clump of trees and a track meandering through them to who knows where. We parked the station wagon, moved Colin's naked body onto the trolley Jake had loaded with the spades, and followed the track. It came out in a long, muddy stretch of grass along a slight slope. There was a tumble of small boulders, but nothing else that was memorable, including the boulders.

Jake picked up a spade. "Reckon here's as good as any for an unmarked grave."

We buried Colin Dewenter as Thorne had said. Naked in bare earth, without a gravestone or acknowledgement. Jake took one final action before we dumped the dug earth back until the hole was filled and mounded the original sods above it. They'd sink over a few months, and once level, nothing at all would go to say anything was beneath them or that they'd ever been displaced. Once we were done, we stepped back and looked.

Jake heaved a sigh. "No one's going to look at *that* and think 'grave,'" he said. "Nothing in it to identify him and if someone digs him up by accident, they won't recognise him." That, I thought, was true. Jake had smashed the body in the face half a dozen times with all his strength, using the flat of his heavy spade before we started filling in the grave.

And with all the ducking and weaving we'd done on the roads, I'd been on the trip, and *I* couldn't have told you where Colin was buried. I thought it probable Thorne and Jake couldn't have either, and without road maintenance, with road signs all over Cornwall rotting and falling, even if one of us had known, in another few years, we couldn't have found the spot, or not in my opinion. So that was it. Done and dusted. We went home, a quiet journey, but after I'd spent the rest of that day doing hard physical work and eaten a great dinner Mic had cooked, before sleeping peacefully all night, I got up the next morning feeling comfortable with myself again—and stayed that way.

****

A month after that, Thorne announced that we should have an official cemetery. That sheep would graze it, no sacrilege; it'd keep the grass down which was common sense. He had the CBM hauled out and supplies set up, and it busily enclosed a section of land that had once belonged to neighbours of the Manor. They'd had a smallholding of twenty poor-quality acres and hadn't survived. We'd salvaged most of their stuff, taken the sheds and smaller moveable buildings, and now their tidy two-bedroom bungalow would be the cemetery's records and administration building.

After several gatherings to discuss it, it was agreed that the dead would be laid in the earth. They could be clothed; a quilt, blanket, or some similar item could be laid over them, but when whoever officiated said earth to earth, they would be allegorical and factual. The alternative would be ashes to ashes, again literally. The whole of the cemetery wall was a double layer; the inner one had niches from about three feet up to two feet from the top. That wall was ten feet, while the wall that backed it was nine inches thicker and two feet higher.

As for the "ashes," if that was what you wanted, you saw to it the cemetery records had that information plus the money to pay for the pyre. Either that, or your family were willing to pay, or your friends to supply the dry wood. I listened over the next year and realised that most preferred the idea of ashes. A tidy, polished coffin was one thing. A body that still looked like someone and allowed you to think of decay, worms, and … no.

Maureen saw an opportunity when I reported that, and we made a trip to a place Mic knew on the edge of Dartmoor. We drove the two army trucks and returned to everyone's pleasure, with a third. The first truck crowded with Nubian goats, hens, and Sebastopol geese, while the second had six ponies and an entire stack of horse-drawn vehicles with harnesses.

Thorne arrived at the door of the third truck I'd found in a yard and driven back. "What else did you bring home, Hughie?" I lifted a corner of the tarpaulin lashed over the truck's contents and showed him. He gaped. "How *many*?"

"About a thousand, maybe twelve hundred; I picked all the medium-sized ones and a few small ones. Pretty well all of them are coated brass, but they're engraved and nice-looking. They all have a shield on the front, and the place where we got them had manual engraving pens and electric ones. We cleared out all their unused record ledgers, pens, and stuff like that; they're in here too, and," I grinned like an idiot. "We've got rabbits."

"Rabbits." Thorne's voice was flat.

"A breed from New Zealand. They're a huge, docile, breed like, well, rabbits, and Mic says they're fantastic eating. Years back, her New Zealand friend told her about them. She's the one with Sebastopol geese; that's where Mic got the idea for them as watch-geese. Her friend had them for that over forty years and was never once burgled."

****

Our salvage was shared out item by item. The hundreds of urns went to the cemetery's Administration House, and a selection were displayed there in the foyer. Some of our people bought one if they really liked it, then carved their name and details, leaving only the second date blank. The horse-drawn carts, traps, and so on we'd brought back went into the Manor stables along with the harnesses and ponies. We'd found a farm that seemed to have bred them, a Dartmoor Arab mix, they averaged around fourteen hands, were sturdy, sensible beasts, their hooves didn't easily wear down, and the six we'd taken were all mares broken to saddle and harness.

The geese joined the Manor flock. The hens were shared, given to those that didn't have a flock, or added in lower numbers for genetic diversity where there was a flock already, and the eighteen Nubian goats — sixteen nannies and kids, two billies — went to Lana and Daisy as a business.

"Milk and meat," Thorne said. "Opposite season from the cows, breed them in early autumn. Spare males are meat. Nannies that get too old and any badly injured are pet food. One or two as your pets are okay, but be realistic."

Daisy, who seemed to have come out of her traumatic captivity well so far as anyone could tell, promptly claimed a charming little female Nubian. "Her name's Mic." We looked from one to the other and even my grandmother was flummoxed. And Mic, the little goat became and Mic she stayed until she died at a ripe old age, allowed to die naturally because no one would have felt it right to slaughter "Mic."

After that, life settled into a peaceful routine. Now and again, we took a convoy out. We had lines of the connected barns, all full. Another trip the following year, and we bought back more urns, goats, ponies, their vehicles, hens, and bunnies. I pointed out that would be the final time for bunnies; we'd come home this time with practically every youngish, healthy New Zealand rabbit we could find. Still, that was fifty spread in small pens and hutches throughout the households.

We'd also taken every suitable urn, and after Mic, nosing about, had read some of the files, we'd gone twenty miles on and raided there. More urns, more unused ledgers, and a trailer full of incidentals. All sorts of items like hand tools, cast iron cookware, bedding and mattresses, linen, and books. At a crossroads, there'd been a village library. And behind that, the large, rambling home of the rich old lady—The Honourable Emily Smythe-Harris—who'd endowed it, and whose home held even more volumes.

We returned to her place once Thorne had heard some of what remained them. She'd had a large greenhouse—amateur hobby, professional quality. It was filled with English heritage food plants, seeds, the records of and books about them. We emptied the place, brought that all home, and added everything edible to our gardens and orchards. She also had a heritage orchard, and we got as much of that as we could salvage in saplings, seeds, and ripe fruit—with a note to return.

I wasn't to know for another year or more that Mic, happily vanishing into rooms, corners, and cupboards, had also found the unobtrusive cottage sited behind a tall hedge and painted a neutral colour. The occupant was decomposing in his bedroom, had been, according to letters Mic found, a pensioned-off soldier wounded in the line of duty, and a relative of the lady who'd provided the cottage as "grace and favour." However, as I've said before, not much gets past my grandmother, and she rarely lets a chance go by.

Winter came, we sat back, and took life easier. It was almost three years since the plague began. Maureen and I had enjoyed our thirtieth birthdays, and Mic her sixty-fourth. Thorne's estimation was that as many as three-quarters of the entire population of our Isles had died from the plague; more would have died from secondary reasons—a little old lady who lives alone on her pension without family or friends, and who at ninety can't walk far, isn't likely to survive long.

Those who were bedridden or had chronic diseases or conditions requiring daily medication would have died even faster. Death would also have gathered in the too-stupid, too-reckless, or those who later developed a need for medication that was no longer available.

Then the night came when I heard our chicken house alarm, tore out expecting a fox, got a chimpanzee in a lousy mood, and Mic produced a machine pistol and calmly shot it dead at my feet as it charged. That was when I heard about the Honourable Emily Smythe-Harris's ex-army relative and where Mic had found the gun. I went back inside once the excitement had died down, with a distinct impression that our quiet times were over again. Something I discovered quickly was all too true.

We coped. Life went quiet again for a while, and then it wasn't. That started with a massive explosion we heard from a man fleeing it, caused by a gas leak in the town. We moved out as a convoy and were halfway there when another explosion occurred. There was a quick consultation, and we camped up for twenty-four hours to see if this would continue. There was a third one, then silence, so we advanced again.

CHAPTER SEVEN

The man, a Barry Griffith, found no reason to stay in a town that seemed to be blowing up in stages and had fled on an electric bike with a small trailer.

"I've been pretty much living out of my suitcase anyhow. I was offered a job at the start of 2139." He smiled bitterly. "Paid very well, so I took it. The firm put me up in a tiny house, furnished, power supplied as part of my job. Not fancy, but it was comfortable, and I transferred my bank account."

"What were you doing?" Mic asked.

"Financial officer. The Company was Melling and Co. Good people. Town's okay, too. I'd been working over the border before, in Exeter. Thing I really regret is not having my library. I rented an insulated container and paid them five years upfront when I left for here. I'd planned to move the container once I'd been in town a year and knew if I wanted to stay on. I've got over five thousand books in that, and once things went to hell, there was no way I could get it—or even get to it."

"What sort of books?" That was Maureen, and only a heartbeat before I could ask.

"Mix. I enjoy a good mystery, animal books, and true-life humor, but about two-thirds of them would be Science Fiction, fantasy, a sprinkling of horror and ghost, and some series that crossover with that and mystery or something." A hint of red showed on his cheekbones, and I bit back a grin. So maybe the "something" was risqué SF. There's always been a few of those published.

Thorne looked at the man. "If you'd care to join us, you'd be welcome." Ah, he'd summed Barry up as I had. Worth a trial.

I took a longer, harder look while our potential recruit considered. About five foot ten, lean, and, fit, I thought, light brown hair, blue eyes, and aquiline features, and any visible skin was moderately weathered and tanned. His electric bike was cared for, trailer neatly packed, and the man wore clean, tidy clothes, although they weren't new.

"Yes, okay. On a proviso." Barry's voice broke into my train of thought.

Thorne nodded. "If it's to take the tiny house you've been living in back with us, that's fine. I'll go further. We've been talking about going to a city to look over what may be available as salvage. Exeter is within our reach. I'm not making any guarantees, but if we do go there, we'll bring your books back."

Barry shook hands, parked his bike, and became the fourth in our Landcruiser when we moved out the next morning, his bike and trailer loaded into one of the ex-army trucks. Maureen drove, and with only the Doc ahead, we rolled down the road towards where smoke rose lazily into the sky.

Mic glanced at Barry. "What do you know about the explosions?"

"Not a lot. There's a sort of gas tank farm. It's in the middle of the industrial area, and there's a suburb starting to circle it. Old chap where I worked was the night caretaker, lived near the place, and used to grump about it. He said the tanks weren't maintained as they should be, that when the wind was right, he could smell gas, and if he could have afforded to, he'd have long since moved out. He couldn't; he was in some boarding place for pensioners where the rent was fixed; anywhere else, and it'd be double."

He broke off. "Wonder what happened to him. Anyway, I've ridden by the place several times—I got my electric bike when things started going bad. I know where the tank place is— was. My company was a couple of miles away, and the house is parked on a piece of land they bought to expand into. Poor old George. Nice old boy. Since I'm coming back, I guess I'll take a look and see if he made it."

Ahead of us, Di had parked on top of a small rise, produced binoculars, and studied the road ahead. She put them away, turned the bike, and came back to us. Thorne left the truck he was driving and joined us to listen.

"The town's pretty much a write-off. The explosions flattened half of it, and those started fires. The unflattened half is mostly burning. There don't look to be that many people in the streets; probably grabbed anything they could carry and already got out. I'd like to look for drugs."

Barry eyed her in disgust and opened his mouth. I nudged him hard in the ribs and hissed. "She's a doctor." He shut up, and Di was continuing.

"I know the hospital, a couple of surgeries, and the dentist. I'm going to those first."

Thorne nodded. "I'll come with you. We'll take Jack and Annie and the Tillikers. You can collect anything from those places you want. Hugh, what do you, Mic, and Maureen have in mind?"

"You told Barry we'll get the tiny house for him. Plus, there's someone from the place where he worked he wants to check on. After that, we'll salvage; anything in particular we should look for?"

Doc Di nodded. "Medicines, first aid supplies, any relevant DIY books, or books of that sort. Then the usual items, food, and arms, footwear, heavier clothing, eco-electrical systems. You know the sort of stuff. Do you want to take anyone else?"

"Ask the Leonards if they'd like to come with us?"

The Leonards joined us in their Landcruiser in minutes, the children, Bree and Billy, with a bow and a quiver each. Rick and Mary had belted guns. They all carried the ubiquitous large, folded cloth bags we used for salvaging and trundled a small, sturdy wheeled trolley that could take three bags filled and stacked.

Barry gave us directions, and a block or so before that, we saw a small clump of four shops. Their backs had been to the blast and their frontages were intact, so we could see they appeared largely unlooted. Mic halted, and waved the Leonards up, pointing at the shops. "Salvage there; if there's room, go there afterwards," she pointed at what looked like a small factory just past it, "then join us."

They halted by the shops, waved, and we headed for old George's boarding house. It was partially destroyed, but he was there, lying on his bed, still looking dazed, but he stared up at Barry as he entered and dropped to his knees by the bed. "You come back, son. Good to see you, but you don't wanna stay long."

Mic looked at me, and I understood. She was taking that as a genuine warning from a man who could know something. I stepped up to look at the old man, and he was old. If he was a day less than eighty, I'd be surprised.

"Why shouldn't we stay long? Is it the gas tanks?" His eyes turned to me, and he nodded slightly, his eyes clearing.

"Aye, never told Barry here no details, but back aways, I worked there. Once I turned sixty-five, they said I could stay on four hours a day an' they'd pay me part-wages. Didn't need much, so I kept on another ten years. Retired completely then, started doing night caretaker for Welling. I've allus been fit enough, and Welling didn't know I were that old. But I had friends at gas place still; that were bought by some American outfit years back. As time went by, company skimped more n' more on maintenance where inspectors wouldn't notice; some of the lads wondered when they going to have sommat happen an' if it were to claim insurance. Glad I was I got out when I did. I'd a' liked to move further away, but I couldn't afford it. I knew what I heard when first tank went. But only three on 'em blew. S' five more, and son," his eyes turned to Barry. "The five's all connected."

Mic moved forward, sat on the bed, and took his hand in hers. "We can get you out of here, George. You can come with us. We've a nice place, Trelenwold Manor."

He squeezed her hand. "I take that kindly missus, but it's too late for me; last few years I've just been waiting to see my Jenny again. Now, you listen. Them tanks, they'll have lost the connection they had to the others, and when the connection went, they'll have lost some pressure, but it'll build up again. I knew t' system well, and it ain't changed since I were there. Can't give you an exact time, but I can give you a fair guess."

Kaiser padded forward and stuck his nose under the wrinkled hand, and the old man stroked the dog's ears gently. "Nice beast." He paused to breathe deeply. "Listen now. How long ago were the third blast?"

I glanced at my watch and told him — that'd been at 6:00 a.m. four hours ago. Old George nodded. "Right. It won't take less than twelve hours from now, could take as much as twenty; they got bleed-off valves, but one could stick; the further past another twelve hours from now, though, the more you'll need to get away. Understand?" Everyone nodded.

His gaze fixed on Mic where she sat holding his hand. "Remind me of my Jenny you do, lass. Nay, I won't come wi' you. I'm too old, got nothing more to give, and Jenny's less'n a mile from me here." He was old. In my estimation and from what he and Barry had said, he'd be well into his eighties, and he was right. If we hauled him home, he'd need someone to look after him, someone to cook and clean, someone to provide food, medicine — if not now, then soon, someone to do his washing, and… Mic stiffened, and in a single careful movement, swept the blanket over him to one side.

"You were hurt in the blast."

George smiled up at her gently. "Aye, my Jenny allus noticed things too. I were standing when it hit; window were wide open, so blast came straight at me. Felt sommat go in my back, an' I fell on t' bed. Been here ever since. Reckon it broke m' back. So you see, ain't no use taking me anywhere, less it were to lie by my Jenny. Don't fret, Barry, nor none of you. I lived long, had good friends, and I had my Jenny. She's been gone four 'n a half years now, an' I've grieved less, knowing she missed all this plague fandangery. It don't hurt. I'll be joining her next few hours anyways, I reckon. Just wish I could be laying beside her when that happens." He fell silent, and my grandmother was on her feet, her eyes determined.

"You will be, George, you will be." Her gaze swept over the four of us. "Find something light to carry him. A mattress, an eiderdown, a couple of good pillows. Now!" We scattered. When we returned, George was in a clean nightshirt, his face and hands washed, and he was sipping his way down a very large glass of what I thought to be whisky. Mic had a bag at her feet and was nodding at something he'd said.

He looked at us wonderingly. "Allus knew folks could be kind; I'll go the happier for what you do for me. But before you move me and in case that don't go well, I kin do sommat for you. The young lads at the tanks, I told them we should get away, but we shouldn't go empty-handed. So last couple 's years, we been salvaging." He grinned. A cheerful wicked grin that lit his face so you could see why he and his Jenny had stayed together and loved so long.

"Go to the gas tanks," he gave explicit instructions. "Back behind t'longest building, around between that and t' high fence. Looks like that end o' that's blocked wi' rubbish. It ain't, and ever'thing should still be there, building's solid brick, should still be standing mostly. You take whatever's still a'tween building and fence. It were mine and t' lads, and they're gone. Time first tank went, they'd have been cooking breakfast in shed in front." He sighed. "They were good lads; mebbe I'll see them too where I'm going."

Mic spoke very gently. "I'm sure you will." And to us, "Barry, Hugh, pick George up carefully. Take him down to the Landcruiser in the back."

We obeyed. In the Landcruiser, propped up so George could see out and tell her which way and with Kaiser lying at his side, Mic drove to the cemetery, and there we dug down where he showed us. We found the coffin, the brass plaque making clear we had found Jenny Carrington. Then we expanded the hole until we could place George in it, lying on his impromptu bed, mattress under him, eiderdown keeping him warm, and two pillows allowing him to half-recline. His half of the cavity was a fraction shallower so he could lay his arm over the coffin without strain, and he smiled contentedly up at us.

"You couldn't a' done more for me if I'd been family.' I noticed his voice was blurring, and his eyes seemed to be becoming unfocused. "You can go now; Jenny'll be along in a minute." His eyes went to Mic and seemed to clear briefly as he gave that wicked grin. "Live long an' prosper, you an' all a' yours. An' mebbe you kin sing me a song now so's I leave t' music, Allus loved a good song."

His eyes closed. Mic stood straight and sang, with Maureen and I joining in. The first song matching his comment, a humorous SF anthem known as "Star-Trekking (Across the Universe,)" and a smile lit his face. The second was also an anthem, one every Cornishman would know. The last words rang out, Mic dropped to stand by George and nodded at us.

"He's with his Jenny now," and very softly she sang the last lines of the song again. *"For this is'my Eden, and I'm not alone, for this is my Cornwall, and this is my home."*

She drew the eiderdown over his face, and without needing instruction, I covered him. Once that was done, Barry and I—he'd gone looking—carried the unmarked stone over, filled in the grave, and placed the stone flat over the body where it lay now, with his Jenny forever.

I laid a bunch of flowering branches I'd found nearby on the stone, and we followed Mic to the Landcruiser. She climbed into the driver's seat, Kaiser beside her, dropped the bag she'd found somewhere back under her seat, and started the engine. I saw we were heading for the blast site, and I admit to feeling nervous. If George was right, we had at least ten hours. If he was wrong …

Mic circled to come to the blast site at the rear, and advancing at a crawl and dodging flung debris, we got close to what I thought was George's fence. Nearer the blast, a small, prefabricated building was a heap of red-strained splinters, under which nothing moved. That had been George's lads' kitchen, I thought. The fence was solid in a big way; it looked like poles of some description, possible old telephone ones that'd been dumped there when they became redundant. And then set upright and sunk half their length into the earth. Mic exited the Landcruiser, walked to the end of the fence, and reached underneath the piled rubbish.

There was a creak. She hauled, and the whole rubbish pile moved outwards. It looked to me now as if it had been a light slanting square of metal and the rubbish, probably all light, had been fixed to that.

With it clear, I could see a long line of empty space between the building's back and the fence. The gap would have been around twelve to fourteen-feet wide, and as it stretched the entire back of the brick building, as much as two hundred feet or more long. But it was a gap no longer; instead, it was full. I stared at half a dozen self-contained caravans crammed with boxes, bags, and small items where they could be tucked between. Metal containers, all of the eight by eight, by ten-foot type. Also crammed, and from some of the marked items, much of it, long-lasting food.

I started walking down the line. One container was filled with books, more with footwear and clothing, one had labeled wrapped first aid supplies. Many of those with heavier items were filled with those only two-thirds of the way, with lighter things like sealed bedding on top. At the far end, there were six containers filled with eco electricity spares, while the final two behind them had complete units of solar and wind power.

I turned to look at my grandmother. "Jeez, Mic, what was he going to do with all this, start another town?"

"Yes. He told me he never told his 'lads' that he wasn't leaving. But he wanted them to have a chance, a hope of making a decent life again. He said they almost made it. They'd have been leaving in another two weeks once they'd finished salvaging a few more places. They had bigger trucks they could put the containers on parked elsewhere in two different places so they wouldn't draw attention here. There are forklifts with those and a lot more fuel."

"These 'lads?'"

"Yes. He worked here most of his life. The company started hiring teenagers. He taught them on the quiet, so the bosses were pleased. I think he was a father-figure. Their families mostly died of the plague; some of the boys, too. And he took the rest under his wing." Her smile was kind. "He told them the old stories. They were going to build a new Camelot up on the heights near Bodmin Moor. They'd pasture horses and livestock on the moor. Take over several of the big old places there. Once they had that safe, they'd start finding people to join them."

I thought of how all that would probably have gone and sighed. Mic nodded. "I know, but it could have worked. He hoped it would. He didn't want it for himself; he never intended to go. It was for them, for a future, a chance for lads he'd known and liked, to maybe survive. When he knew they'd never have a Camelot now, he gave it to me, to us. He said someone should have their salvage rather than it sit here and rot."

It hit me. "Yes, and we only have a few hours to get it all out of here before those gas tanks all go off. What do we do first?"

Mic concentrated. "Maureen, go and find the Leonards, send them here, then go and find Thorne. Tell him we have a bonanza waiting packed and ready. Hugh, George told me where to find the haulage trucks. Go and bring the biggest one we can load with containers. George said there were forklifts; bring four."

I was gone in one direction, seeing Maureen from the corner of my eye, diving for the Landcruiser. The first place where there were trucks wasn't that far away as the crow flies, and I did my best. Half an hour later, I was getting the first forklift onto a massive thing like a car transporter. The biggest, Mic said, and that was what I was bringing. After, it was organized chaos. I won't describe events; it was a madhouse of people, vehicles, gear, and goods going in all directions.

To add to that, Lana and Daisy had found a pet shop. I have no idea why the owner had kept it open or how he'd managed. I suppose he kept finding canned pet food. He'd died in the blast, transfixed by a long sliver of wood. But his stock had survived. No fish or reptiles. But puppies, all adults now, of course, and birds. Thorne had given orders, and two of the senior girls, driving a large station wagon, had packed up the lot, plus pet food, medication, and equipment, and headed straight home.

For any who read this and wonder, that's where the budgies, canaries—and the funny-looking parrots that live free around the Manor—came from. The puppies were mostly terriers; they're larger now; a few of the puppies had been Dobermans, and while we mostly kept them as separate breeds, now and again, someone slipped up.

We made it out of the town in time, but some not by much. Thorne had told us the timeline and said he wasn't our father; if we wanted to take risks, it was up to us once we'd got our George-given windfall cleared. We had that heading back well within time, a good two hours clear. But after old George's salvage, there was the rest of the town, some shops still part-full, some of the big old houses that had belonged to the wealthy, still standing—and with contents. We salvaged the closest to the tanks at the start, moving out in hopes some places still worth salvaging would survive the blast.

The Leonards, Lana, and Daisy left. Paddy and his family, Dave the electrician, and his daughters stayed a while, the Merrisons and the Tillikers a bit longer. The Manor seniors and juniors had been ordered home by Thorne, and we'd backed that. They went under protest—but they went. Jake, Annie, and Barry stayed—almost too long—while Doc Di moved out of town to where she thought even if everything went up at once she'd be okay. She parked there and waited.

As she said, "I'm a doctor; if any of them get caught, they'll need one."

As it was, they didn't; they left in time to reach her. She moved out smartly ahead of them, and they'd gone another mile when there was one of the loudest noises anyone had ever heard. (Yes, the three of us stayed with Doc Di in case. And for some reason, Mic had transferred everything we'd salvaged to one of the trucks) The sound was shattering. It roared, bellowed, rolled over the land and returned, and the earth heaved under our vehicles. Kaiser threw back his head and howled. Maureen made comforting noises, while Mic sat there until everything was quiet again.

"Now," she said as the last echoes died away. "Do we go back and see if there's anything worth finding?" Everyone but us stared at her incredulously, and she smiled. "Just checking. Get going." They did with Di out ahead again; we stayed.

Mic looked at us. "If you don't want to do this, stay here, I'll be back in a few hours. Well?" We went back with her. Back where I'd expected, to the small quiet graveyard where George lay with his Jenny. That was flat, broken trees with grass and headstones. Some of the graves had broken open, but not the one we'd made. We stood there briefly.

Mic smiled down. "Sleep peacefully, the two of you. I think it'll be a long time before you may ever be disturbed again."

She turned and walked to the Landcruiser. We followed, wondering what she had in mind and found out when she drove off, partially skirted the town and stopped outside a massive old house that was intact apart from the windows. "Come with me." We followed again, through the ground floor, up a flight of stairs, another, and across a corridor into a huge room filled with books.

"George told me he and his lads had planned to come here in a day or so," my grandmother told us. "He said, for a start, it's got some interesting plants, and that isn't all either."

It certainly wasn't. Downstairs in a conservatory, there were marijuana plants, opium poppies, high-yield digitalis foxgloves, and several other plants that could be used as medicines.

Upstairs there was a collection of herbals—handwritten—from the seventeen and eighteen hundreds, kept under lock and key. And in the garage, there were vehicles. I gaped until Mic suggested I shut my mouth against the flies and that the old lady who'd owned the place had loaned some of the contents to staff for convenience—it made sure they got to work on time.

I daresay it did. On hooks along the walls, there were *twenty-five* electric bikes—under those where were crates of spares, batteries, tires, and the sort of small tools used on bikes— there were a dozen bike trailers, and then there were four vehicles. One was a majestic ancient Rolls. One was a small electric town car. But two would be handy. They were a sort of utility, with heavy electric engines, four-wheel drive, and long covered decks, each with a trailer, and both utes and trailers were *big*... We stayed the night, Mic assuring us Thorne knew. Kaiser was in seventh heaven exploring. We were busy all the following day. With drugs, books, and herbals all loaded onto the utes but with some room still, we parked the Landcruiser by the front door and started on the house.

Some of the furniture was old and beautiful. Where it would also be useful, we took it. The bedding was all feathers: feather mattresses, feather eiderdowns, feather pillows, we took everything. There was an enormous pantry and a walk-in freezer—contents still frozen—that had probably only stopped at the final blast. We gutted the pantry, freezers, and what seemed like half a mile of cupboard shelves. Managing to get it all—but only just—into the Landcruiser and trailer. Kaiser ran about from one to the other of us, convinced he was helping. He was; so long as he wasn't alarmed, we knew we didn't have to be.

At last, we had everything in the vehicles, Mic led off, I followed, and Maureen was third—until I glanced back, and she wasn't there. I leaned on the brakes and horn, slowed, and spun the car in its tracks. The second ute was halted in the drive; Maureen was running towards the house, and I could dimly see something moving through the glass of the front door, which, being some sort of smash-proof, was the only piece of glass that remained. I got out of my vehicle, swearing under my breath, and started walking back.

Maureen had the door open. I could see the mover now. A very fluffy, very large, silver-striped cat. One of the most beautiful animals I'd ever seen, a Maine Coon, I suspected, some of the boys of that breed I'd heard, could be huge. I reached Maureen, who was hugging and talking to him. He was meowing back. I'd been scared when she vanished from sight, and I was still feeling the adrenaline. Dratted cat, why hadn't he come out earlier, oh, right, probably not sure about Kaiser. But really, we didn't need more animals.

I looked at the pair and said so — a bit tersely. "We have a cat and a dog, and more dogs just went home with the others; we don't need another cat, particularly a male."

Maureen met my glare head-on. "He's neutered. We took all his cat food. This was his home; now there's no one. His name's Jason. He'll be company for Willow, Kaiser will like him, and I'm not leaving him to starve. *He's coming with us.*" He did.

CHAPTER EIGHT

After that, all we did for most of the next year was integrate everything we'd salvaged. Not Jason; he managed any integration on his own. In two days, Willow was cuddling up to him; Kaiser *did* like him. Barry, who'd parked his tiny house next to ours, was a willing slave. Jason could go anywhere on Manor lands and be sure of a welcome, and even I fell for him, *and* he knew it. He was a people cat,

If Maureen or I, or both of us went off salvaging, Jason would often come, too. After a few weeks, I accepted that he could look after himself quite competently if it became necessary. From assorted evidence, I guessed his owner had died several months before we'd arrived, and he'd managed perfectly well. But he *was* a people cat, and he liked us. Life was better if a fellow had people — more so if they were his own. And we were.

****

Winter had been close on that last trip, so it was months before the weather improved to where we could make another one. This next trip intended to be really long and a fair distance away. Not that life had been static. We'd twice gone back to Old George's town, and yes, places on the outskirts had either survived or still been salvageable. We'd found, too, that word of the Manor had spread. And just as Jason was a people cat, so are most humans, "people" persons. A solid sprinkling of families or solos had survived the virus, and while at first, they'd stayed in their homes, some found a plush house and moved there to enjoy the luxury.

But living alone meant there were no other voices, no one laughing, or no one to joke with; sounds in a strange house are threatening. Families had the familiar sounds, but the plague wasn't the only sickness. One family caught colds; they were the standard, usual symptoms, typical colds, but it started them thinking. What if they'd been bad flu, or even something worse? What if the adults — mum, dad, and granny — had been too sick to look after the children? They appeared at the Manor gates, begging admittance.

On their heels were the family they'd met salvaging and who'd given them the cold. The outcome was that in three days, we acquired fourteen new members. We sent vehicles to their homes and brought back everything they wanted; several of their sheds were removable, and we put up a pair of flat-pak houses for them. Those came ready insulated, and the families were content. They planted vegetable gardens, fruit and nut trees, berry bushes, and fenced sufficient land to have a house cow, two goats, several ponies, and a sow each. By spring, they were a part of the Manor community.

They weren't the only ones, just the only families. Towards the heart of the winter when all the days were short, cold, and grayly bleak, we got the first solo. He was in his late twenties and came riding in on a powerful squat electric tricycle, a heaped trailer behind with a cat sprawled on top in what was clearly a cat-designed travel hollow. By now, we had a guard at the gates, and they were usually shut.

He hailed the guard, Mic today. "Lady, is this the Manor?"

"It is."

"Can I come in and talk?"

"Are you armed?" Mic was always armed, but unobtrusively and Kaiser was with her.

He laughed. "Isn't everyone these days? Yeah, but you can check and hold them while I'm here, okay?"

She let him through and petted the cat who yawned, stretched, and purred. "Nice boy. What's his name?"

"Mally, for Marshmallow. Look, I like living on my own, but just in a house. I found I'm not so keen on being alone in a whole area."

"You and Mally don't look to have been deprived of much."

He laughed again. "Nope. I won't say I'm a survivalist, because most of them follow a philosophy and I don't. I just like being self-sufficient. Fact is, that was what I was planning, going to work on one of the islands. I only had a final exam to go when this damn disease hit, and that was that. I was staying in my uncle's caravan; he died a bit earlier, and left everything to me. I was a useful place to stay. He had half an acre, the Dutch Master caravan — thing is huge — two sheds, a jeep, and personal stuff like books and so on."

Mic's very good at summing someone up. By now, she considered him a good Manor candidate; she turned, rang the bell by her small gatehouse, and one of the seniors came running. "Take over a while. I'll be escorting this applicant to Thorne." She left Sue to guard the gates and waved him to follow her, resuming the conversation as he did so.

"What's your name?"

"Merrion, usually Merr, short for merman because I'm a good swimmer..."

"Sussex?"

"Mum was. How'd you know?"

"Merrion's a Sussex name; don't hear it much these days."

"My great-grandfather, a fisherman, drowned in a storm when mum was seven. She loved him and wanted him remembered. She and Dad moved to Somerset for Dad's work, cabinet maker, real expert. Plague got them. I knew where my uncle — great-uncle really — was, so I went there with Mally and the cycle. He died a year back, not from the virus, just old age. Said I got everything; he was just so glad he wasn't dying alone, and anyhow, I was family. Said I should get out once he was gone and look for a community. He said that was it with people; any disaster was bad, but sooner or later they'd regroup."

His mouth drooped. "If you take me, could I go back and get everything?"

Mic nodded. "I can tell you this: if you're in, there'll be any help you need. Besides, a Dutch Master would make a good home for you, and you could swap it for a house if or when a time comes, you need more room. So, Merr...?

"Godden. Merrion Godden."

"All right, follow me. I'm taking you to Thorne Trelen, Lord of Trelenwold Manor." She saw him frown. "No, you don't have to bow; it's just that all this land was his, and we're polite about living on it. If you settle here, you'll call him Thorne, if you become friends and he asks, or Mr. Trelen."

"Oh, okay."

She walked him into Thorne's study, shut the door behind them, and introduced the boy he'd brought, Mally, with him, and Thorne spent the first few minutes scratching the cat until he purred and asked his details. They could see his owner relaxing with a fellow cat lover. Thorne waved Merr to a seat. Mic made hot chocolate with the small hot-water jug, offered that, and once he'd taken a few mouthfuls — looking ecstatic — Thorne asked questions. Nothing was different to what he'd told Mic or what she'd observed so far, and she answered a tiny quirk of Thorne's eyebrows in question with a confirming nod. He went to the heart of it then.

"You told Mic that you'd missed your final exam by weeks? What sort of exam?"

"Practical. I'll give you the short version, but I guess you'll want to know. My best mate at school's dad was a dentist, and I know people think it's funny or weird, but I always wanted to be one too. He taught me some basics and recommended me for a scholarship when I was eighteen, and I got it. My parents could afford for me to board; you can't do that sort of stuff in the country, so I started at a place in London that taught classes. Once I'd done all those, Mr. Carren let me come and do practical work at his clinic in Somerset."

He sniffed once. "They all died when the plague hit. That was early. I went home, and they died too. Anyhow, while Mr.

Carren was alive—he died last—he talked to me. Said I should go where there wasn't anyone much, wait until things settled down a bit, then start asking around for someplace that needed a dentist and where they were decent people. Not some thieves' den. He said when things go bad, you get outlaws, and if you're in with them, even if you're not doing anything bad, people lump you in, and if a time comes, then you die with the other thieves."

Thorne nodded. "Your Mr. Carren was a smart, sensible man."

"Yeah. Once he was gone and Mum and Dad, I made for this area, and my great-uncle. I lived with him for two years, and then he died. But before that, he told me now was time to start talking and listening. Find my place and see if they'd take me." His head lifted, and he met Thorne's look squarely. "So, will you?"

"Mic, take him to the dining room; he can have a meal. Get Hugh, Maureen, Annie, and Jake."

My grandmother conducted Merr to the dining room where he'd not only be fed, Mally would too, and walked briskly away to find me and the others. We assembled in Thorne's study and listened as he and Mic shared their opinions and our candidate's story and decided. Merr was called in to sit, cradling his cat and looking apprehensive while Thorne spoke. Not a man to waste words if it wasn't necessary, he was brief.

"Probation, but you're in. A year and a day from now, you'll be confirmed as a Manor resident if you haven't done anything anyone can protest."

I was interested to see Merr checked that. "How protest? What if they don't like my cat or my caravan, some silly thing that annoys them?"

Mic answered that. "Then we might start looking harder at *them*. No, if they protest you becoming permanent, they have to have something fairly bad and genuine."

"Fair enough. What do I do now?"

What he did "now" kept him busy enough to be occupied for a week. Our threesome plus Kaiser drove to where Merr had been staying, hooked up the huge caravan, and trundled it the eighty miles to the Manor, positioning it near Doc Di's home and surgery. With the location settled, we added a flat-pak: waiting room, supplies room, study, and a generous surgery room. Merr was overcome, his voice a squeak.

"That's fantastic. I never expected anything this good."

Jake grinned. "Man does his best work if he's got room, the right gear, and comfort. Look around you, too. You'll want someone as a dental nurse if there gets to be a lot of work. I'd say there won't be yet, but that could come."

Merr squared his shoulders. "I'll be ready." He was, and while he might have been the first solo at the gates, over the rest of that winter, he certainly wasn't the last as occasionally, another small group or family arrived in hope. We didn't accept them all; some were obvious freeloaders, but fifty-seven people found a new home with us by late spring. And that was good.

Merr and Mally settled in well. People liked him; he was a polite, sensible, and good-looking young man, with fair hair, bright blue eyes, and a lean figure with strong shoulders. He was also an efficient dentist, and he shared some of the drugs he'd gathered on his journeying with Doc. It turned out that he was twenty-eight, a year older than Maureen, and I had been, when this all started. Of course, we were thirty-two now, and life was anything but what it had been when we were coming up to *his* age. I said that, and Mic roared.

"I bet people said that when the Romans came, and the teenagers of the time said a few smart things back. Things rarely stay the same for any real length of time, my love. Now and again, you get a few generations where not much changes, but that's not the usual; that's the anomaly."

I opened my mouth, then reconsidered. I knew a fair bit of history, and she was right. Just in the last few generations, there'd been two world wars, others in Korea and Vietnam, that virus that'd hit the world around the early twenties, the Russian business … each time things changed—and sometimes, they didn't go back as they had been.

I nodded. "Mic, maybe we should start teaching history here. This is in some of our post-holocaust books, that people forget, confuse fiction with real events, become fixated on an idea, and follow that until it kills them. We're lucky Thorne isn't religious; we aren't. None of the ones who've joined us have been. I read not long before the virus, that every census saw fewer saying they belonged to a specific religion."

My wife was tart. "No, most these days watched ninety-nine percent of everyone die, and decided it was nothing to thank God for."

Mic chuckled. "True. Thorne talked about this to me one evening. He won't accept in any who are what he called overly devout or fanatic. Apart from anything else, he says it invariably causes trouble. If you have the not particularly devout in any religion, they don't like to be told to thank God for a death, a major injury, the loss of a baby. The 'it's all in God's hands,' isn't great either when it's a case of 'we need to do these things' and you get told 'God will provide.' They won't help, and you end up watching someone die when it wasn't necessary. No, I'm with him there."

****

Summer arrived in a way that said it was going to be long, hot, and with sufficient on-going showers to make the land fertile and the atmosphere muggy at least half the time.

That was when Thorne announced *the* convoy. We'd go to Exeter, on to Somerlees in Somerset, and home via the coast, Torquay, and Plymouth.

"This will be what I might call a breakaway convoy," he said to all the interested faces. "Some of you have been making lists of what you genuinely need, with backup lists of what you'd like but that aren't essential. We'll start out with about three-quarters of us who can drive. Where we fill five or six vehicles, they form a minor convoy and head back home. They unload, take a two-day break, and head back to rejoin us. If you see a vehicle like a tanker that's already loaded, you take that home. Some of those who can drive will be reserved for that, and we have a number of cars or electric bikes here that can be used to rejoin us wherever we are by then."

"How long?"

"All summer," Thorne said flatly. "This is the fifth summer, people. Side roads aren't what they were; some older buildings are rotting or crumbling. Livestock is dead or gone wild. Apart from anything else, to stay mobile another couple of generations, we need fuel, and the eco-electric systems. I'm hoping in Exeter, apart from anything else, we find publishing machines. The kind you fill with ink, covers, and paper, set parameters, and they copy any book."

There were murmurs of agreement. Thorn continued. "We'll have to start gearing-down at some stage. When or if a time comes we can't run really heavy farm machinery, we'll need to have learned how to use horse-drawn and have some of that waiting. Right now, we have a ton of sugar and other sweeteners, but most don't come from here. We'll need apiarists for honey, someone growing sugar-beet, maybe sugar cane, and there's all the small things we never thought about before this happened. Have any of you gone to the shops and bought pins, needles, hair clips, rubber bands, paint, a new watch, or a headache pill lately?"

This time the murmurs were wry understanding and agreement.

Maureen and I exchanged looks. We hadn't wasted our time this past couple of years. Maureen had raised this then, when she had a headache and no pills, and again when she found she needed rubber bands. Mic had nodded.

"If you don't have it, you can't buy it, and how long before any place that had them had fallen down on top of what was there. We salvage now and stockpile, or we go without for the rest of our lives." Mic grinned at us. "For me, that could be ten to twenty years, and that's bad enough. You'll be a lot unhappier a lot longer."

Which was why the start of that winter over a particularly foul weather week, two and a half years ago, we'd had a quiet word with Thorne. We'd gone off and come back with a flat-pak building, but before we'd put that up, we'd dug, in the pouring rain and the mud, using a mini CBM, and produced a large cellar. It stretched under about half what we had always called our cottage, but which was two storeys, and then under almost all of the new building we put up on top of the extended cellar.

The cellar itself was ten feet deep. It had drains, shelving, very strong pillar foundations, and it was, once we'd done everything, bone dry. It was an experience, but Maureen and I were motivated, strong, fit, healthy, and determined. Mic was just motivated, healthy, and determined, but that was sufficient. And once we had a cellar, we started filling the shelves. In the rooms above ground, we filled shelves too, mostly with bulky, more easily found and numerous items, like bedding and linen, but below-ground we had sealed water containers, food, medical supplies, weapons and ammunition, but we also had shelf after shelf of the items like needles, thread, fabrics (stretch ones in particular), socks, underwear, and leather gloves. Hair clips, brushes and combs, tampons, and half a ton of paint and varnishes in cans that ranged from a couple of ounces to buckets — which would remain useful even when emptied.

We'd spent months carrying a notebook and pen everywhere. Writing down all the small conveniences, the tiny vital items, the little things we'd miss incredibly if we were without them. Currently the cellar was about a third full while the above ground rooms were about half of that. Now, with this massive convoy that would last months as we came and went, we could add to our supplies. We wouldn't be taking items others could find and bring back, we weren't going to be depriving anyone. But we weren't going to go unnecessarily without useful things for years either, because others had been lazy or thoughtless and hadn't thought or bothered to salvage where they could be found.

****

The convoy set out for Somerset at 6:00 a.m. one fine morning in 2044. We had brought Kaiser, but firmly removed Jason, to his indignation. On a trek such as this would be, there were too many dangers for a cat. Instead, he and Merr's Mally went to stay with the Merrison grandmother, who was seventy, loved cats, and was going to be spending her time bottling fruit and vegetables as they were brought back — the bottles she already had since she'd been, as was explained to me once by her son, "bottler from way back, her do like bottling." And considering the vast number of preserving jars, pans, and rubbers rings she brought with her, that was no exaggeration.

The drive was peaceful, but all three of us noticed as we discussed over dinner when we halted for the night, the growing deterioration that Thorne had given as a reason for this excursion. We mostly kept to the main roads, but now and then, a vehicle saw something down a side road they thought worth investigating, and they'd done so in twos. One duo returned with most of the stock in a saddler, everything from harnesses, saddles, halters, and bridles to hoof oil, leather softener, and two wagons they found in the big barn behind.

The other duo had found a small timberyard. Two large trucks peeled off to join them and loaded everything, not just timber planks and plywood sheets, but insulation, a huge stack of bags of cement, several mixers, and other items like nails and screws. It took a third truck to take it all and, and, according to Thorne's earlier decision, the five vehicles left us the next morning to return home, unload that lot, and then rejoin us. It was accepted that major supplies of that sort were for general use, but you could fill a bag or two or take a fancied item for yourself without protest.

We wound our way along roads where the grass and weeds encroached on the edges; where panicked feral livestock fled as we came towards them, and where, an earlier flood had left mud or minor debris as a high-tide mark on the road's surface. Some buildings were burned, rotting, or crumbling, and the towns we passed, the smaller ones anyhow, seemed deserted. Here and there, someone came out to stare; however, they made no approaches, and this had been discussed already. On the final journey where we were going home, we'd stop and talk, take anyone who looked suitable but not until then; that way if later, we found we'd made a mistake, all of us would be there to deal with it, which would be safer.

"If you pick up someone, they could be a Trojan Horse," Thorne had said. "We have walls and gates and a guard. But if half of our adults are away, what if someone we think we've '*saved*,' hits our guard over the head, opens the gates at two in the morning, and maybe thirty armed people come in and start killing people, taking whatever they want. It's quite possible, and I'd rather not see people I know lying dead, girls raped, babies with their skulls smashed in, and everything someone valued gone."

There was complete agreement on *that*, along with the addendum as Thorne agreed, that we'd stretch a point for a baby or toddler.

We passed the Somerset border. Merr directed us, riding pillion on Doc Di's motorbike, and we halted late that afternoon outside what had been his mentor's dental surgery. It hadn't been a one-man practice by any means. Mr. Carren had been senior partner, but he'd had two juniors, and the sprawling building had also provided rooms for a physiotherapist, an optometrist, an optician, and an elderly woman who read auras—and made a very good living at it.

Merr told me later that she gave advice claimed to be based on auras seen through crystal readings, and even those who didn't believe in any of that valued her advice which was invariably accurate, useful, and sensible.

Kaiser was out of Mic's Landcruiser, peeing in the gutter then racing around the building and those on either side. Across the road, up and down, and he returned to indicate there was no one about. Mic beat Thorne after that and was opening the door to the rooms a step ahead. Maureen and I were on his heels, Kaiser by me, and we poured together into the building and spread out.

We knew what to do, Merr was into the dental surgeries, indicating apparatus, along with smaller items and dental supplies, and it was all being packed and loaded into vehicles outside. Di was doing the same in the physiotherapists, optometrists, and opticians. Maureen and I headed for the aura reader rooms. I'd brought in soft cloth bags and into those we placed all the beautiful crystals, and the many glittering crystal ornaments and jewelry.

Mic had listened to Merr talk about those and thought that somewhere along the line, they'd be useful. We added a set of beautifully embroidered velvet hangings with gold cords, a pair of curtains ditto in silver, matching sets of cushions on light but strong and comfortable bamboo chairs and other miscellanea. After that, we found a fabric shop. It was large, heavily stocked, and while Mic whipped through, taking pins, needles, measuring tapes, a multitude of different sizes, shapes, and colors of buttons, and the most useful and best fabrics in untouched bolts, we helped before calling in someone else to finish the salvage there.

We had all three of our Landcruisers and trailers full; we gathered up a couple of other vehicles in that happy state and headed for home. Three days later, we were back on the road. Our convoy had left Somerset, and we met them on the way, turned and followed them into Exeter, wondering what remained of that once proud city.

CHAPTER NINE

What Exeter looked like was something out of a war movie. There'd been fires, but that was the least of it. We heard vague talk of a war between two sides. No one seemed to know who or why, and those who'd survived didn't care. Not that there were many *left* to care. In our time there, we saw maybe fifty or sixty, most of whom chose to leave with us.

Barry joined us and led the way to the storage place. It was what they meant when someone says, "no mean city." It was no mean storage area. It gave the impression of stretching for miles, and as the storerooms were metal containers, nothing had burned, not outwardly anyhow; inside could be a different matter. Barry dived for his container, got that open, and heaved an audible sigh.

"Everything's okay." I considered the number of books in there and groaned silently. My back was *not* going to enjoy this.

"Have you got cartons?" I demanded. Barry nodded. "Right, let's get started."

It turned out that while he had cartons, he didn't have any kind of writing implement. Fortunately, I did, so we spent hour after hour, filling a carton, listing contents on one side filling the next, listing contents, ad infinitum. Towards the end of the day — breaks for lunch and stretching — we were done. I estimated that any one carton had an average of fifty books, and there were a hundred and forty cartons. Seven thousand books.

"Barry, I thought you said you had under six thousand books?"

"Yeah?"

"I calculate there's over seven thousand."

"Oh, yeah, well, that's my grandfather's as well."

"And you didn't bother to count those," I said flatly, with an edge to my voice.

"Uh, I guess not."

"Because you thought if you told the truth, we might not bother?" My edge was sharper. No response, just the sort of guilty look a dog gives you if he's done something he knew he shouldn't have. "Barry, not saying something is the same as a lie. How can we trust you if you get us into something we don't know?"

"Huh?"

I decided to make the situation clear.

"You didn't tell us the truth. There were a lot more books here; you knew that. Then you say, 'Oh they weren't all mine; some were someone else's.' But they still meant extra work and time. So next time, we ask you how many enemies we face, you say seven. We attack and find there were ten, and you say, 'Oh, but the extra three weren't with the others, they were just there.' If you don't lay out everything, you could get people killed."

Barry looked bewildered, "But it's books."

"And next time, it may be enemies. How can we trust you?"

"It's *books*."

"No, it's the difference between telling the truth, and hiding it." I couldn't tell if he genuinely didn't understand, or if he was playing me. I'd talk this over with the others later, but if he was playing me, we couldn't risk it, and if he was genuinely that dumb, he could end up as a risk to us anyhow. "Never mind. Get in the vehicle."

It was about time for dinner. I drove to where the others were camped up in a park, joined the line for food, and went off to find my wife and grandmother. They and Kaiser were eating at a park bench and table. Mic took one look at my expression and asked.

"What happened?"

I told her.

"I see, do you get any sense of which it is, dumb or player?"

109

I shook my head.

Mic nodded slowly. "Okay, wait until we're home again and we can talk to Thorne, Jake, and one or two others. We may have to keep an eye on Barry; we can always put him in a similar situation in a while where it's to his benefit to lie and see what he does. If he does it again, we dump him. As you say, we can't risk it."

Maureen nodded agreement. I started on my dinner, reassured that Mic and Maureen saw my complaint as sense, and that we could sort out something that was right and fair.

Maureen switched subjects. "There are people here. Thorne's had a dozen asking what our place is like, and they all sounded as if they'd join us if we were okay with it." I focused on her, and she expanded on that. "There's trouble here, feral dogs, a *lot* of them. And I guess you could say feral people, too. Two lots are families. Parents and kids. One of three, one of five."

"You saw them?"

"And heard, yes. I liked both, and there aren't any medical personnel left here."

Ah, I got that. They'd realized we had a doctor, and there weren't even nurses left here if Maureen was right. "Why a doctor in particular? Rather than just, 'a doctor is a good thing?'"

"The family of three were here at the hospital. They lived in Holsworthy. Their second son was premature; the mother was in hospital here a month while they tried to delay her having him. He was still weeks early; then he was sick. He'd improved to where the hospital was about to discharge him when everything went — you know. One of the nurses came from Holsworthy, too, and talked to them privately. She said to take the baby out of the hospital, stick around in case they needed to come back, but best to be away."

Maureen looked at me. "I think she guessed how bad it was going to be, Hugh. She gave them a key to her place, said to go there. Joanna said she came back once, six days after, said it was bad beyond belief. By that time, the premature son was sick.

She looked at him, and said she could only tell them the truth: he wouldn't make it. The other boy — he was about two years old then — had the infection a couple of months earlier, and they'd caught it off him. She told them they'd probably all be okay, but the baby wouldn't be."

"And?"

"He died. She kept saying, after all that, after everything, and he died. Now all they want to do is either come back with us or go home."

I considered that. "Holsworthy? Mic?" She tended to know things.

"Market town, population was probably around three and half thousand when the plague hit it, big caravan park and storage place there." Mic sat back, and Maureen and I looked at each other. *That* sounded interesting. We'd talk to Thorne.

A day later, our three vehicles, plus three more, including the large truck Barry was currently driving, were on the way to Holsworthy along with the Jensons, Mara, Jonas, and their now six-year-old son Max. Jonas had worked on a farm there, and they'd had a tied cottage — that is, one they had as a part of his payment for the job. At the farm, we paused to check the main farmhouse. There was no one there, however Jonas had a key, and on opening the door, we found a note addressed to him from Whitestead, the farmer.

Jonas,

Me and Meg are sick, kids look as if they're coming down with whatever we have. Meg's bad off so we're going to the doctor. I've opened all the gates, and as the cow's dry, there shouldn't be anything that needs to be done, even if we're away a couple of days. You said you'd be back for the weekend. Come find me if we aren't back by then. If it takes longer or things get worse, you know where everything is,

Evan Whitestead.

I reflected that from what I'd already heard from the Jensons, the letter was almost four years old, and it was unlikely anything much in the letter was relevant. Jonas looked up from reading the letter aloud to his wife and the rest of us.

"I never got back that weekend. Looks as if they never got back at all." He looked at me. "What do we do now?" Fortunately, we'd talked about this with Thorne.

"You suggested to Thorne you'd like to join us. Do you still feel that way?" I asked.

Both adults nodded.

"I talked to Thorne, and he's agreed. Since it appears as if the whole Whitestead family are almost certainly dead..." Well, the farm was only a mile from the village, anyone who'd survived could have walked home from the tiny cottage hospital there, and from what Jonas had said, the Whitestead children were fifteen, seventeen, and almost nineteen, so even if their parents had died, they would have returned, and they hadn't. I took in a breath.

"I'd say the family are gone, Jonas. And with the death rate, there's a very strong chance so are any heirs, and even if they survived, they can't get here, or haven't bothered. Under Manor custom, anything portable here is yours. Are there farm trucks?"

"Coupl'a good 'uns."

"Then go through your place first and load everything you honestly want to take. Then go through the Whitestead house. After that look at the livestock, any farm equipment; you drive one vehicle, and your wife drives the other. We'll be coming and going around Holsworthy; we'll check in on you regularly and meet back here for dinner. Okay?"

Mara looked at Mic. "You think so?"

Mic nodded. "I do, if there's things you can use, why leave them to rot? If you join the Manor, who knows when you'll come back here again, if ever? Take anything you honestly want, Mara, goods, gear, animals, even clothes, footwear, jewellery, toys, or books."

"Okay." She swept up her son and husband, heading for the back of the house, probably to the bedrooms. "Let's go gathering."

I grinned as my mind added the next line, "Nut's in May, nuts in May…"

Mic moved towards the door. "And as Mara says, let's us go gathering too. A good place to start would be the caravan and storage place mentioned."

In which my grandmother was right. That was a bonanza. I suspected any place like this would be. We opened the gates, did a quick walk-around of the caravans, looked at the storage containers, almost every single one with a chain and padlock — locked. And called in Thorne. He arrived on the back of Doc Di's motorbike and nodded.

"Yes. Take only useful items from storage. But we can use about half of the caravans; they're self-contained and a decent size. Every vehicle that leaves here for home is to tow one if they have a towbar and no trailer. Put them in rows in field seven. We can shift them to permanent places from there; it's fairly central. If anyone coming to us needs a permanent or temporary residence, I'll give them a note to say they can choose one and move in."

Di grinned at us. "And I hear there's a fairly big health centre. I'll be stopping off there, never know what may be sitting about."

What was there, were a whole long list of vaccines, medicines, equipment, and a car park filled with vehicles, as we heard later. Di took Thorne back to the city, returned with two cars filled with people, and gutted the place, along with taking many of the heavier vehicles. They emptied fuel tanks, added plants from the landscaping outside, and collected other useful items.

The Jensons stripped their own home and the Whitesteads'. Then, having checked we would not object, they disappeared to five nearby farms and added from them. Mara's livestock truck ended up carrying away three sows and a boar, three Jersey cows, one with a gorgeous little bull-calf still at foot, plus half a dozen goats, along with chickens and ducks. The remainder of the vehicle had been crammed with — to Di's later delight — a powered wheelchair, two large cartons filled with first aid supplies, a light mobility-scooter, six pairs of crutches, and several large cartons of other lower-level medical supplies. It seemed the furthest farm had housed a qualified midwife, who was also a disaster first aid volunteer.

We also found two filthy half-feral children — twins. So far as they could tell us, they'd turned ten a few weeks before their mummy drove Daddy to the doctor and never came home. Nor did anyone else ever call. But Mummy came from one of the outer Scottish Isles; she'd believed in having full cupboards just in case. In this case, it was as well. Between the orchard, the berry bushes, and the vegetable garden, the pair had survived quite well. They had rabbit snares, too, and as, with the absence of humans, rabbits and hares had proliferated, they'd had meat, not only for themselves, but for their two cats and three dogs.

The cats were ordinary moggies and neutered. But the three dogs were Border Collies from, as I saw when shown the papers, good lines. The youngest, at four, was worth breeding. The children alternated between hanging onto us and skittering away, but one of the Exeter couples, grandparent age, were related to them, second cousins I think, and as they'd lost everyone else, were delighted to have a family again. We settled them in a flat-pak two-bedroom house, with a caravan at a right angle to the back door. It acted as a windbreaker, a bedroom for the twins, and left a house bedroom available for the single woman, Jasmine, who had no one, but wanted to join us. Mic judged her as useful, and she convinced Thorne, so Jasmine came along.

After that, it was load, drive, catch up on energy and sleep for two days, then drive, load, drive, repeat. Others of the Manor diverted to small villages, and they went to and fro, seeking salvage and people. Both were found, the former in far greater quantities than the latter. Before this effort, we'd had about a hundred and fifty on Manor lands. By the time summer was gone and autumn was progressing, we were up to two hundred and thirty. And I hoped, as I knew Mic did, that we hadn't made too many mistakes. We needed unity, not dissent.

The first trouble we had, however, was a death. We'd emphasized to everyone to be cautious entering anything. Floors could be rotten, someone living there could panic, there could be animals that considered it their territory, and other dangers. We hadn't considered the one there was, but if the man entering had been cautious, he'd have probably survived. As it was, he barged in; there was a massive *boom*, and he fell backwards, rolled out down the steps, and sprawled dead before his family.

The family, consisting of a sister, a mother, a grandmother, and a dog—also female—stood there contemplating for all of a second, before taking off screaming. As it happened, Mic, Maureen, and I were nearby talking to Thorne at the time, providing an update on events at the Manor we'd just returned from. We intercepted those fleeing and asked question, heard the answers, and I saw Thorne and Mic visibly *not* say what they wanted to. We followed the family back to the house, assured them that yes, their relative would be decently buried, and please stand back.

All four of us spread out and circled the house. Mic called. "Found a window I can force." We gathered, watched as she inserted a knife-blade. moved the catch, then slowly raised the window. Nothing. Okay, it was at the back, well away from where the gun had fired. I entered. No sound, no movement. I drifted to the inner door, hooked a loop of string around the handle, went back out the window, and we all moved to an angle before Thorne pulled the string in slowly. The door swung open and there was no reaction.

I went back in the window, advanced to the door, and peered. "Looks clear. I'll check the door." I picked up a chair, pushed that past the doorway, and swung it, covering the whole of that space. No boom, good.

I crept through the house. It had belonged to someone wealthy; the furniture was old and beautiful, the drapes and carpets were lush and expensive, and the ornaments lovely antiques. I could see why the dead man had chosen this place to salvage. I would have, too, if I'd seen it first. I glanced back at a small sound, to find Thorne some ten feet behind and to one side of me, Mic and Maureen behind him. I found a smile twitching the corners of my mouth. Talk about all for one.

We made it nearly to the front of the house, and then I could see. I motioned everyone forward and we stood there, looking at what had killed an incautious man.

"If he'd have done what he was told," Mic stated. "He'd have seen that."

The "that" was an old form of trap. A shotgun tied to a heavy chair with string leading to the door and back to the triggers. Open the door, and once the string tightened to a certain point, the gun fired — both barrels. It had worked perfectly. Not that the trap-setter would have known. We found him, long dead, lying in his plush bedroom, with his door half-open. Something warned me, and I checked that, to find of all things, three hand grenades behind the door, another trap that would have exploded as soon as the door was opened wider.

Thorne dismantled that, and we considered the house. Mic turned, shut the front door, and spoke quietly. "Tell that idiot's family they can find another house; the one on the corner down there looks bigger, just not as fancy. Tell them if it has vehicles, they can take them too. Say, once they get to the Manor and unload, they can come back for another house, as a death benefit."

I did that. The family turned and headed for the bigger house, looking torn between gratification and sorrow, and I returned. "I think they're happy with that. But why, Mic?"

"Because I think the Manor will find this useful."

I don't know what made her think that, but she was right. She told me later it was the hand grenades. No one has just three. The house itself was a boon; the furniture, drapes, and all the other usual items we loaded, took to the Manor, stored in a line of containers at the Manor intended to take that sort of item, and went back. Mic had stayed and hunted to some purpose. She'd found the cellar and led us down.

"I don't know who this guy was; I haven't looked for papers. But he had authority of some sort; either that, or some generous friends in high places. And over the next twenty or thirty years, we should find his cellar contents *very* useful."

I contemplated the stacked floor and shelving and agreed wholeheartedly. There were weapons of a dozen types. There were lanterns and primuses, plus the fuel for those. After that were shelves of knives and swords, a host of various other items from whetstones to oil, and, through a steel door and in a second section of the cellar, there was food.

I walked down the lines of that, almost chanting. "Salt, sugar, powdered milk, tea, powdered eggs, dehydrated fruit, flour, coffee ... what didn't the guy have?"

"Very little," Mic said dryly. "The other thing that occurs to me is that we should read his papers. If there's another lot like this where we can reach it, I'd like to know."

Thorne gave a grunt of agreement. "Me too. If there *is* a place near us, we could leave it be, just keep on eye on it. That way we'd have backup."

We split up and scoured the house. This time it was Maureen who found the papers, squirreled away in a not very secret abditory—a place to hide valuables. It held valuables this time too. Jewellery, gold coins, silver ingots, and the papers we wanted. There were letters, emails that had been printed out (and probably then comprehensively wiped from any computer), and maps. Some were of larger areas, and others that showed those areas in greater detail.

Thorne grabbed the letters, Mic the emails, while Maureen and I pored over the maps. After half an hour, we looked at each other simultaneously.

"There's a place..."

"Outside and inland from Falmouth..."

"It sounds even bigger so far as storage...'

"And it's close enough to us to be almost perfect."

Thorne summed up. "It's hidden, you need half a dozen passwords to get in, and if those there didn't survive, there's enough to see we do for fifty years."

Mic glanced up from the emails. "Intelligence outfit; this man was a boss. I suggest we finish doing what we're doing here. If everyone's dead over there, there no hurry, if they aren't, there still isn't. Get this done and take it easy for the winter. We can go there in late spring, drift in, look around, but for now, find everything useful in this place, take it with us, and get back to salvaging."

It made sense, and we did. Autumn went slowly, but with winter establishing itself firmly, and with our salvage stacked to the proverbial rafters at the Manor, we made one final run, and returned home for the winter, almost twice the number of the people we'd been with more homes, animals, storage containers, and our lives considerably improved as to comfort. The first major winter storm hit, and we hunkered down.

****

However, even a winter isn't only storms. In preparation of the last salvage convoy, we'd spent the tail end of last winter plus early spring, in gathering up storage containers. We'd also done something else. It had been the outcome of an evening the three of us had spent with Kaiser, Willow, and Jason. It had started with a discussion on what the installation between here and Falmouth might be. After that, it rambled all over the conversational map, culminating in the conclusion it'd be underground.

There's been a pause, then Mic had commented, "We need a hill."

I'd said, "We could build one."

And Maureen had concluded, "Dig it partway down, then build over that?"

That was it, the whole basic plan. We did have a hill, about two hundred feet high and from where it rose to where it flattened again was about a hundred acres. But any digging would be under cover, and we had the automatic machinery and fuel to run it. We had a consultation with Thorne, Jake, Annie, and our two tradesmen, all of whom agreed it could be done. And over winter, we did it.

By the end of spring, we had a massive cave under our hill. We'd dug the floor to about ten feet below the surface, then about ten feet up into the hill. Effectively, that gave us around eighty acres. We'd put in reinforced pillars and a roof, and ninety percent of our storage containers were in there and out of sight. They only took up around thirty percent of the area. Unless the secret installation was bigger than we thought, our hill would take most of what was likely in there too.

After that, we gathered up more storage containers. Exeter was a city, and you don't get many livestock in one, but we'd been all over the surrounding countryside, and we'd collected them there. We'd been selective. Cows, horses, goats, self-shedding sheep where we could find them—and two of the forests within reach now held small herds of pigs. The animals we'd moved here were young, fertile, good quality, and healthy. Most we simply let go free. They'd be on hand if wanted.

We'd also collected horse-drawn machinery and vehicles. They were in a series of camouflage-painted barns in a gully a mile away. No harnesses, all that and riding gear we had under cover elsewhere. Both sites had a flock of the non-flying Sebastopol geese pasturing around them too. The odd fox arrived— and left again smartly. People, if they arrived, could either leave the same way or stick around. If they did the latter, sooner or later, we'd hear the geese.

Over winter, too, several more solos had come in. One, usefully, had been in the SAS. "Yeah, I was a sergeant, I know where another couple of us live if that's any interest." It was, and we ended up with the three of them plus the families of the other two. They came, looked us over, liked what they saw, and stayed.

"How'd you do so well?"

Thorne looked at Mic, and we all grinned. "I've got about four shelves of post-holocaust SF," Thorne told him.

"I've got a couple more," Mic chimed in. "I had a friend on the other side of the world, knew her for years. She wrote a number and sent me copies. Plus, that last time she was over here and we had a day together, she'd brought half a suitcase for me, ones by Australian and some American writers. Never heard of most, but they were good too. Different countries, different writers, and they have different ideas. If you read a stack of books on the same basic theme, you pick up a lot of ideas…"

"And generate some more of your own." Maureen added.

It's not bad when you can impress the SAS. Our cavern under the hill did, they came up with an extra suggestion or two as well, and finally when it came late spring, the land was drying out, our family and a sprinkling of others from the Manor, had drifted down towards where the secret installation was and camped, ridden around, talked innocently, about plans that were non-threatening. We generally looked like a bunch of harmless gormless survivors—and we'd drawn no discernible reaction, so at that point, we took a deep breath and gambled.

The papers we'd found in that house were moderately clear as to where the main entrance was. We went there, and in effect, knocked. There was no response. Mic, as probably the least likely to look dangerous to anyone watching from inside, stepped up, punched in the code, and the first door swung open. Nothing moved. She ambled to the speaker and spoke to no presence, or none that replied, the next door was coded, opened obediently, and again, there was no reaction.

We knew there were a total of six. She opened the fifth, talked to the speaker and was ignored, so before anyone could prevent her—she said later that there was no sense in risking someone else—she coded the last door. It opened into darkness and silence, and we were in. I was only a couple of paces behind her by then, and I had a staff and a very large lantern. I flicked the switch; light shone all over the place, and in its glow, we could see some of what the installation held. I went to move my staff ahead as a precaution.

Barry had come with us, and now he burst past. "Oh, wow, look at that motorbike, look at the…" A searing pinpoint laser line flashed across the doorway; it met Barry, left him lying open to the backbone on the concrete, and shut off. He looked up. "What was *that*? I feel … I feel … I…" the last of his blood drained onto the concrete, and he was gone.

Thorne spoke softly from behind us. "The willing sacrifice."

Maybe he was; maybe he wasn't. But we knew what to watch for now. We found other traps and disabled them. After that, the installation was ours. We found the living quarters full of long-dead bodies. Some had left letters. There were no pets or service animals. Pets had probably been prohibited, and when the last few people were still alive, if there *had* been any service animals, they'd probably either put them down mercifully or let them go free. Maybe one of the letters? Maureen saw my gaze, gathered them up, and began reading. I looked over the treasure trove of what we had and felt a deep gratitude to the shotgun man. We might survive beyond a generation or two after all.

CHAPTER TEN

I looked at Maureen, and we exchanged smiles. That had been my grandmother's favourite poem for half a lifetime; this little episode could move it into that category for others. As it was the last verse was ringing out when we swung into line, slashed — as we'd done before — between sea and the enemy rampaging through the city and brought those of them who saw, to a sudden, staring, standstill.

Thorne yelled an order as soon as we had them completely cut off from the sea and their boats. We turned in our tracks at that, and charged towards the city and those who had been setting fires, looting, and where, here and there, a man held a small child or a screaming fighting woman. Those were dropped smartly, men grabbed for guns laid to one side, and on one occasion I saw, his would-be victim grabbed it first and shot him dead.

It was a scrambling confused mess of a fight, but those in the city came out and joined us. The Polwithin boats sailed in and targeted the two enemy vessels which, again, seemed to have left no one onboard one and only one person on the other. He was shot before, I think, he even realised he was under threat, and Polwithin put sailors aboard both enemy vessels and started for home. That panicked many of the enemy who headed for the beach, screaming demands that the boats return — which were ignored. That had been our agreement, so, undistracted, we hit the stranded with even greater enthusiasm.

It was dirty work while it lasted, but after several hours, having put in place above the city a guard to watch for that, we were certain no one had escaped. The boats, as Jake had pointed out, were no larger than the one that had sailed into Polwithin, so they probably carried no greater numbers, or not much anyway. That one had had forty; at the highest, this pair were unlikely to have carried more than a hundred together. We collected bodies and their weapons. It looked as if he wasn't far wrong; there were ninety, although weapons were far fewer; probably local citizens had gotten to those first.

A few of the said citizens came cautiously to greet us. Thorne and Mic met them, talked, shared a meal, and we found we had applicants for the Manor. One was the woman who'd shot her would-be captor.

"I'm Gayle; that bastard shot my mum, my dad, *an'* he was crippled, and my little brother. Grady was only fourteen. What kind of pig shoots a fourteen-year-old kid?" I guessed she was about sixteen or seventeen herself. "That man says you got a place inland, and you got a democracy." From the way she said the word, I thought she had no clear idea of what that was; after all it was nearly ten years since the plague. But I nodded.

"Maureen?" I called; she came over. "Maureen, this is Gayle; she'd like to apply for the Manor. Gayle, this is my wife, Maureen; talk to her, and there's no hurry to decide."

No hurry translated to two days. By that time, everyone interested had considered and been considered, and we left with fifty-four new residents. Gayle, we discovered, was bright, had managed a fair education via her father, and was a natural at basic math. She ended up as a senior clerk for Thorne, and he found her invaluable. This year, however, she joined convoys, guns belted on, a long-gun over a shoulder, and an entire willingness to shoot anyone she thought to be like the raider who'd slaughtered her family—we'd helped her burn those on a pyre on the beach, and that was the last time anyone would ever see her cry.

We went over the bodies of the raiders. Some had keepsakes from their original lives, everything from photos to driver's licenses. Two had small bibles, which sourly amused me. What they'd been doing hardly fitted "love thy neighbour as thyself."

But then, maybe it had happened to these men, and they'd chosen, "do unto others" instead. We returned to Polwithin, considered the two boats, agreed they belonged there—fat lot of use they'd be at the Manor as Thorne commented quietly to us—and went home.

Not that we'd be there long. We'd been planning to go on a long convoy, as they'd become known, and this had occurred early and fast enough to keep our schedule on track—or would be if we left in another fortnight. Roads off the main highways were getting worse, and we didn't want to risk getting stuck somewhere, so we'd leave only when they should have dried out to a fair extent.

We departed on time. Gayle had asked to ride with Maureen, who'd agreed; Mic had Kaiser, and I had decided Bree Leonard and Billy Harker could come with me. Both were in their teens now, sensible, and good shots. Both preferred bows, and while Bree used a pistol crossbow, Billy was deadly with a longbow. They'd lived near each other, been best friends forever, and now I was interested to note that the friendship could be developing into something more. I'd have a word with Billy on that subject. I sighed. His was probably the last generation for a long time to come that could do something effective about that.

That thought segued into a mental note. I should mention this to Thorne and Doc Di. We would be salvaging through a lot of places, and it'd be a good idea to collect the items like condoms that I had in mind from pharmacies—or any of the chain stores. Come to that, houses with adult males could have a few, the chains sold them in boxes of fifty for not much, and a few only part-used boxes would up our supplies as would acquiring any feminine supplies.

I glanced back as the head of our convoy rounded the bend at the top of the hills. The convoy seemed to wind behind me forever. Most of the vehicles were large ones. Everything from ex-army trucks to car transporters and stock-feed carriers. We didn't know if we'd ever make another run as long and far away again, and Thorne was determined to bring back every possible thing we could find that was useful. Three things in particular: people, electric ecosystems, and materials for the two CBMs we had.

We were close to self-supporting. So was Polwithin, and we had it in mind to start a new village to complete a triangle with the two places. An oak forest had been planted on government land a few years before the plague hit. It was a perfect spot for a new village, as beside the forest was a slightly elevated plateau. Not large as plateaus went, a little under three hundred acres, but that was a comfortable size, a CBM with the materials required could wall that nicely, and with the plateaus' own elevation added, it would make it a difficult place to take from the occupiers.

Those there would have the standard fruit and nut trees, berries, vegetables, and animals for milk, butter and cheese. They'd specialise in pigs and alpacas. I grinned. One of the Plymouth families had relatives who owned an alpaca farm. We'd gone to check, found them alive, but happy to join their relatives and come to the Manor. They informed us, when we hesitated about taking thirty alpacas, that sheep were good — alpacas were better. They were shorn only once a year, the wool was stronger, finer, and the fibres are warmer since they're' hollow, whereas *sheep's* wool only contains pockets of air. In addition, alpaca wool was hypo-allergenic and almost waterproof.

That, they added, wasn't all either. Alpacas could sometimes be a bit delicate, yes. However, alpacas are light on their feet and don't compact the soil or encourage erosion; they are easy to work with because they are quite bright, and they're lower maintenance than most farm animals too. Plus, their cria — the babies — are far more sensible than lambs. We left Plymouth with thirty alpacas, all their equipment, and the two families plus their two dogs, three cats, two ponies and a pony cart, and as Thorne said:

"Let get going, before they decide to talk us into something else."

The families, all Amcots — the husbands were brothers — had already moved to what would be the third site.

The Plymouth family's mother had grown up on a pig farm, took one look at the Oak Forest, and announced they would run a few small convoys of their own to stock up on pigs. They decided on a Duroc/Long White cross, already had a few of both, and sties and sheds were going up. Since we'd had this site in mind for several years, we'd already had food trees and berry bushes planted, but three Amcots each driving a vehicle, had come on the long convoy to find better animals if they were to be found, plus a list of equipment, and other items they might like if they saw them — including books on either pigs or alpacas, written by experts. Any they didn't have already, that was.

We rolled out of the Manor at 6:00 a.m., and we — as the song said — had us a mighty big convoy. It was ten years now since the start of the plague. We'd begun at the Manor with 15 schoolchildren staying over the holidays. No parents had ever come demanding them back, and the assumption was that either they'd been stranded too far away when everything collapsed, or they'd died from the plague. Then there's been us six adults. Doc Di had joined us within days, and from there, we'd initially picked up locals who considered joining us as safety in numbers, with our walls a bonus.

More convoys, applications made, applicants accepted, and today the Manor counted almost seven hundred inhabitants. Polwithin, too, had grown, and counted themselves as our staunch allies, numbering a handful over two hundred. They had five boats now, and they traded fish, seaweed as fertiliser, other seafood like crabs and lobster, and they had started salt pans. In years to come when we ran out of salvaged salt, this could be incredibly valuable. The new village where the Amcots had settled had already come under discussion as to a name. We'd left the families thinking about that.

We rolled on, past Plymouth, along the coast, and into Brighton where we stopped. We could come and go from London there — and several other towns if we had to run. We could have gone in one of several ways, but Mic had a friend right there. A doctor who'd inherited money from a patient and retired, but who would still only be fifty this year — if she'd lived. The bus depot and nearby train station were empty of vehicles, so we parked there, in long line after long line, spilling out down neighbouring streets. Two hundred vehicles and three-plus hundred people. A mighty big convoy indeed.

****

Liz, Mic's friend, was there — along with three cats, a dying neighbour, and his dog, a young Doberman. Mic fell on her shoulder, hugging, while Liz hugged back, and they wept together. I watched and mourned for all those friends I'd had too far away for me to ever go there, and who'd I'd never see again — never know for certain what happened to them, how they died, or if they lived on still. No wonder Mic was so happy; she'd had friends who were further flung than I did, including the woman in New Zealand. A writer, cat-lover, farmer, and who'd come to stay four times over the years, bringing copies of her books, and some hilarious stories about her animals — and her neighbours. But Mic knew where she was; she'd died three years before the virus came.

Using Liz's knowledge and suggestions, we trawled Brighton. Her neighbour died, his dog chose Bree Leonard as his new human — Liz not dissenting — and he and Kaiser got on well, so that was fine. We salvaged through shops, chain stores, factories, and offices. Several times, I saw Doc Di and Liz in discussion, and I hoped like crazy that'd lead where I wanted it to. Liz sent us to the railway yards.

"They had a lot of storage there; some of the freight will never have been unloaded. Check *Lost Property* in the bus depot too. Then the Police *Lost and Stolen Property*. You'd be amazed at what can turn up in places like that."

The three of us went there the next day and *were* amazed — Police Lost Property had an entire crate of wind-up watches, confiscated as illegal. We added timber yards to the list, too, then a wholesale plumber and an electrical supplies storage. By now and with some of the vehicles filled, they were returning in groups of five or six to unload at the Manor and come back. Taking into account the worsening roads and watching as you drove, what had originally been a twelve-hour journey now took two days if you didn't go crazy. It mostly depended on the smaller group's joint decision.

Twice, a five or six-vehicle convoy left before first light and made it to the Manor by about ten o'clock that night. They could then afford to sleep for twelve hours, have a meal, and lounge for the remainder of that day and the next. Those who'd stayed home did the unloading, and as we'd spent part of our winter putting up a *lot* more storage, which wasn't a problem. It took most of a month before we'd salvaged Brighton of everything portable, useful, and that we might not find closer to home. After that, there was a discussion.

Thorne was talking to Liz. "How many people still living here would you say, if you had to guess?"

She considered. "No more than a couple of hundred now. The plague hit us hard. Many older people used to retire here; they didn't get the original minor infection, and they died in droves. Then there's Brighton Marina, yes there's all sorts of places like shops, and so on. But the thing when you factor the plague in, is that it has thirteen *hundred* berths. And, about ninety-nine percent of them had a boat tied up there."

"Wow!" I said, while Mic and the others gasped.

"So," Liz continued. "When the plague got really bad, many people grabbed a boat and left. And some weren't the owners. I know one case where three families, all related, disappeared on a large yacht. Some knew boats, and the owner was living in the hotel where one worked. He died. She took his keys, collected everyone, they marched down to the marina, and took over the boat. I don't know where they were heading, or if they made it. For all I know, there's a yacht floating about loaded with corpses.

But that accounted for around thirty living Brighton residents alone."

"I suppose other families left if they survived too?"

"Oh, yes. A lot of people who were checkout operators, basic clerks, counter staff, those on minimum wage and renting. They didn't have anything to stay for. There weren't going to be jobs for the foreseeable future, and while there wasn't rent to pay anymore, they didn't like their options here. My neighbours a few doors along packed up and went home. Their family were farmers in Wiltshire, and they thought they'd have a better chance of eating regularly on a farm. They said goodbye and told me quite a number of people who came from farming families were doing the same thing."

"How far into the plague?"

Liz nodded. "That's the point. It was quite early on. I know most were latent. It's my guess that the majority of those who left died in days anyhow. Many people seemed to think that if they didn't die in the first few days, they didn't have it." She glanced over at Di who was listening, "They were wrong, but I never argued. Take someone's hope away, they can get very unpleasant about it, and it does no good." Di nodded agreement.

"Anyway," Liz continued. "You're leaving tomorrow. Will you come back this way, or do you plan to head home in a different direction?"

"London outskirts, then Reading, Swindon, Bristol," Thorne recited. "This is about the furthest that's reasonable for us, and I doubt we'll come so far again. One more place I'd like to get to."

"Where?"

"Cardiff, Newport, and around that area in Wales. Some of our people at the Manor and Polwithin village are sailors. They think there'd be cargo boats in Cardiff we could use to return via Land's End." He took a deep breath. "Some of the people here have decided to come back with us. You've never said if you'd be interested; if you aren't, your choice. If you are, you'd be most welcome, but we can't wait longer than tomorrow. We're leaving the morning after."

Liz eyed him sternly; then her face broke into a wide, wicked grin. "Wait for what, Thorne? I've been packed since the start of this week."

CHAPTER ELEVEN

We moved towards London a day later. The entire convoy, we weren't going deep into London — or that was an initial decision. Ten years after the plague, the place could still be dangerous. There would probably be rats, feral dog packs, and some people who'd survived may have chosen to stay too.

Thorne led out in one of his ex-army trucks, with Di on the motorbike a few hundred yards ahead. We'd decided to head for Staines. It had a lot of government archives and storage facilities, and a considerable number of storage depots and warehouses. The archives could give us information, too, on where to look for specific supplies. Thorne had fuel, bulk ammunition, and weaponry like grenades in mind. Liz was with him. Her three cats were unhappy about travelling, but she'd had cat sedatives, and they settled quickly.

We reached Staines mid-afternoon. It had been a tiring journey, streets were clogged, and we had to make detours; we saw no one, but here and there, dogs slunk away from the sounds of our passage, and once, I saw a cat walking along a rooftop. Mic was ahead of me, and I saw her head turn to look. I knew she'd grieve for it, and for all the animals who no longer had a human to love them. Many would have died slowly, locked in a house or kennels. Those whose owners let them go would have ended in no better condition and probably worse; it would merely have taken them longer to die.

We got to Staines, found two sizeable adjacent vehicle parks, and lined up, switched off all engines, and climbed out to talk, stretch, and look about us. Where we were was solidly industrial, which, as Maureen commented, was all to the good; we wouldn't have to go far to start salvaging. Mic, who'd produced a small pair of binoculars, agreed.

"Take a look over there." She passed the binoculars and pointed.

Maureen took them and looked. "Oh, *yes!*"

I received them in turn, and discovered we were standing only a block from what looked like a shopping centre and mall, which was probably built to provide for local employees. 'That simplifies things," I said, keeping my voice low. "Look, let's have something to eat and drink; then you two go there and take a quiet look, I'll keep the binoculars and watch for you. If it's worth it, you signal, I'll bring my truck and get started while you come back for yours. Depending on what's there, we could be on the road home in another day."

Maybe it was because this area was industrial, the shops and mall probably drew their custom from workers, all of whom were going home in the evenings, and whom, when they died, probably did it in their own suburb or nearest hospital. Still, almost none of the places had been looted. We called Di and Liz over when we found not one but two pharmacies. One in the street, the other on a top floor of the mall. Even better, the top floor held a surgery for two doctors and a cosmetologist. Di and Liz chortled and started salvaging.

Mic had done a fast run-through and now directed us to footwear and clothing shops. One contained hiking and camping clothing and gear, in what was a large shop, plus more of the stock stored in a warehouse behind — we gutted all of that first. It had become custom that you didn't infringe on someone else's salvaging unless invited, so while Di and Liz worked on the mall's top floor, we started at the shops by the mall entrance and moved outwards.

I jimmied open a door from the street, stepped in, and found I was in a lobby. There was a reception desk in one corner, but there was no indication of what this place had been for. I opened the door by the desk and went deeper. A passage with a row of doors along that. I started opening doors. The locks were electrical and must have been on a different circuit because they were all off, although the lights were still working. Offices. Offices. Offices, a corridor. I went to the end, passed through another door — which would have originally been coded to open — and blinked.

There was a garden of some sort. Rows of plants, all alive, all thriving, and at the end were brief informational labels on stakes. I didn't recognise most of them, but I knew one. This had to have been official, experimental, and while maybe not specifically secret, it wouldn't have been known about by those who didn't work here. I headed outside again, doing my best to look casual.

"Doc, Liz, you need to come and take a look at this." They followed me and stared in turn at the rows of plants.

Liz nodded. "I heard a rumour about this just before the plague hit. My son had a friend here. They were investigating combinations of plants to make effective non-addictive non-habituating drugs. Apparently, they'd managed the first bit on several of them, they were still trying to sort out the other one."

She saw my confusion. "Not the same thing. You know what addiction is." I nodded. "Well, habituation doesn't mean addiction; it means that if you keep taking a drug too long, your body gets used to it, and the drug stops being effective at that dosage. You need more; then after a while, more again; eventually it gets to where that amount of drug you take to stop the original problem becomes dangerous in its own right." I got that okay.

"This set-up must be on a completely different electrical system. It's gone ten years, almost certainly without anyone most of that time."

"Could you take everything?"

Liz shook her head. "We could, but it'd be a waste of time and space. What we can do is take all the information, the notes, and records. Samples of the plants we don't know and can't find in our area or somewhere else reasonably close. Don't forget what we got from that house outside old George's town. We could duplicate this at about a tenth the size for a while, as long as we have the ecosystems. Maybe someone will join us who knows more; if so, we'll have all they need to build on it. If not, well we'll haven't overdone the effort."

They left the plants to themselves and joined Mic. If we got our three vehicles all loaded, we could then pack what the Docs thought was sufficient, first thing in the morning, and we could leave after that was done. With five of us, it wouldn't take more than an hour, and five vehicles was the minimum allowed for a small convoy running for home. We improved that later in the afternoon when I went down a narrow alley and found an electrical goods warehouse at the end, facing on to a different street. I called Dave, the electrician.

He'd come along with his two daughters, Bronwyn and Rosie, both in their twenties, good drivers, good shots, and sensible women, both also trained electricians by now. He took one look, and a broad smile spread over his face. "Oh *great*! Will you look at that? There's absolutely *everything*. Ecosystems, a mountain of spares, wiring, switches, generators, tools, long-life chargeable batteries... This lot will see me out and my girls can take over."

I grinned back at him. "And then there's Paddy."

Dave looked puzzled. "Paddy, he's a plumber; nothing here for him."

"Not here, there isn't," I said, my grin widening. "Want to go out the main door and look left?"

Dave obeyed, and I heard a whoop. He returned. "Want me to tell Paddy?"

"Yup, tell him to do what you're going to do, circle the block, park by the front doors, and start loading. We struck a motherlode of our own, and we plan on heading home day after tomorrow. We can't wait, but if you can load that fast, you can come with us without having to wait for anyone else."

Turned out they *could* load that fast. Much of what was in both warehouses was in bins, and there were electric forklifts that we charged overnight. Paddy's wife, Joy, had stayed home. However, his son Eddie and his daughter Marnie could drive, and between our trio, the Docs, and Dave and Eddie's group, we were eleven vehicles strong when we departed Staines a day and a half later.

We weren't wasting time either. We headed straight for home; we were loaded to the roofs, had no space to stop and salvage anywhere else, so we boomed down the main roads, running at a sensible speed that meant low risk, but also wasted little time. It was two day's drive home, and we planned to layover in a small place called Sherborne that was about halfway. Doc Di had been there a few times and said it had a big old house in its own grounds that'll be ideal.

We pulled in mid-afternoon, planning to have a reasonable forage about, then dinner since we'd have to go to bed before it was too dark. We parked around back where no one passing on the road would see the vehicles, descended, and stretched. Kaiser started sniffing about, and I watched him casually. I saw when he found something and stiffened. I yelled a warning. There was a shot, but everyone was already diving for cover, so it missed. That shot was the first—and anything but the last. Guns opened up on us, someone was yelling incoherently. There was a hiss, a trail of fire, an explosion, and Paddy screamed. "RPG, RPG."

I sat behind the wall where I'd dived for cover, Kaiser shivering beside me, while I was saying aloud, "A role-playing game? *What the fuck?*"

Mic, who was close enough to hear that, hissed back. "Rocket-propelled grenade, Hughie."

Oh, right, of course. Hang on, we had grenades ourselves. And a few other items too. I grabbed my machine pistol and let drive at an upper window that was spouting gunfire. Someone shrieked and the gunfire stopped. I switched to another window, then we were all shooting, the fire lessened, halted, and we heard a door slam in the distance, there was the rumble of motorbikes and Di called out:

"Cut them off."

Where we'd parked, we were in a good position to do just that, several of us ran for our vehicles, and since I was driving a car transporter, we pulled right across the front of the drive, blocking off all of the road in and out, plus much of the over-grown lawn on either side. Paddy added his truck to one end, Dave's daughter added her truck to the other, and as the bikes came roaring around the house, they found they weren't going anywhere. The riders sat there, eight bikes, sixteen people. Then five of those on pillion vaulted off and raced for cover.

The men they'd been behind yelled in what sounded like anger and outrage. Mic shot, and one fell thrashing and howling; it decided the rest of them. They spun their bikes, made off around the house, and out of sight. A female voice yelled from where the five had taken cover.

"If you let them go, they'll follow you. We were all prisoners."

Mic gave me a glance and nodded. "If we can take them, better they aren't out there."

Liz hadn't waited to hear that; she, with Di riding ahead were already peeling off down the drive. I heard later that the bikers had been slowed by tangled vegetation and had only exited onto the road again as the women came hurtling towards them. Liz didn't stop; she was driving an army truck with reinforced bumpers and sheet steel in a curve over the front. She hit the first two bikes side on. Bikes and single riders ended up in a crumpled heap as down the road. She slowed the truck, a quick back and forth as she turned; then she was coming for them again.

They hadn't expected that; they hadn't expected Doc Di either. She carried two shotguns, one on either side behind the bike's fairing. Most think of a shotgun as something that has half a dozen shells at most. Di hadn't wanted those of the sort that had to be constantly reloaded. While salvaging in Portsmouth, she'd found an opulent house, investigated, and found two shotguns in a cabinet. They fitted into the fairings in brackets, and they were nothing to mess with. The Kel-Tec KSG-25 bullpup shotgun stores forty-one shells in the actual weapon, and Di knew how to shoot.

The remaining five bike riders initially hesitated which way to go, then chose the woman sitting on her bike in the middle of the road as less dangerous, Di waited a heartbeat until they committed; then she started shooting. It took them another heartbeat to understand they were under fire, a third to begin braking, and all that time she shot. A steady drum-roll of death. Three of the bikers still had passengers, but this close, she'd been able to see two were terrified thirteen or fourteen-year-old girls, and the third was a boy of about fourteen.

Her shots took out the riders, hitting centre mass; the passengers remained terrified but unharmed. The bikes went down, sliding and skidding. Then slowly, silence fell, and Di stood there, legs slightly astride, as Liz's truck halted behind the fallen bikes. One girl, olive-skinned, brown-eyed, and slender moved cautiously to extricate herself,

"Gonna kill us?"

Liz spoke quietly. "Who are you? where'd they find you?"

"I'm Lexi Smith. Romany, my family split off to go to a farm we knew. I was collecting firewood. One of them came out'a nowhere, grabbed me, hit me, and next thing I knew, I was, I was…" she gulped once. "I was under him, and he was using me."

"Do you know where your family were camped when he kidnapped you?" Di was reloading her shotgun.

"Making for a place near Okehampton by the railway line." She glanced at the other girl. "She's Jess Ruxton. They took her from the line further in towards town. Boy too. Don't know his name. Raver got him before us, and we never heard him talk." Her face twisted with hatred. "Raver liked boys, an' he weren't no sweet an' gentle type."

Several of our group had arrived; Di had signalled them to stay back, and they had. Di walked forward; the boy hadn't moved, and she'd wondered why. Now she saw he was handcuffed to the bike. She frisked Raver, found the key, and removed the handcuffs. The boy looked up, his eyes and face blank.

"You're free. Raver's dying; hang on I'll just make sure of that for you." Di produced her .38, walked to where the man lay twitching, placed the muzzle in his ear, and pulled the trigger. He spasmed, went limp, and the boy smiled at her. Right, older than she'd thought. Maybe fifteen.

"Jess, Lexi, and you, boy, you're free. We're not dumping you here, unless that's what you honestly want. We're on the way home to Cornwall; we live in a village near Falmouth. We can take you to your homes and drop you there if you want. Or if there's no one for you, you can come on with us. Gran Mic will take you in her truck, and believe me, no one will try to hurt you with her there. For tonight, you can sleep in one of the vehicle cabs, together, apart, whichever suits. If you want to run away, now's the time; no one will chase you."

Di started walking back to us. Wandering, she said later, if the boy would run; she thought the girls would stay. There was a small sound from where we stood, and she half-turned to see the boy kicking Raver's body, over and over with all his strength, his lips peeled back in a snarl of hatred. Lexi walked to him, took his hand, and led him after Di, Jess followed, and Di signalled Mic who went to the children. She took the boy's hand.

"You need a decent meal, something to drink, a wash, and clean clothes. Let's do something about all that."

****

We spent the night in our vehicles; no one wanted to sleep in the house. It stank to high heaven; obviously the bikers had been there a few weeks. I won't describe the condition of the place; however, Mic went inside before we left and discovered there was a small cellar. We'd long since learned to look for those; it could be fascinating what some people had in them. Clearly, the bikers hadn't known it was there because it had shelves of first edition books, mysteries, many signed, bags of rice, powdered eggs, and milk, cans of tea and coffee, and an entire shelf of personal medication. One look, and Mic came for Liz and Di.

"I'd say they were an old couple. Heart trouble, high blood pressure, and so on."

Liz was reading labels. "All that and more. There's painkillers here, nothing suggesting arthritis; it may be that one of them had been in an accident." She walked down the shelving. "And one of them probably didn't live more than a year or so past the virus. The man from the name. He had a condition that kills you without medication for it. Medication doesn't have a long lifespan either. There are ampules here. Their use-by dates all ran out a long time ago. I wonder where the people ended up."

"I can tell you that," Mic said quietly. "Bikers never found that either." It had probably been created in our century as a panic room off the main bedroom. Inside, it was twenty feet by ten. There was a tiny bathroom at one end, two chairs, a portable Victorian writing desk on a stand, and a large bed fully made up. On that lay what remained of two people; the woman had an envelope in one hand.

What *was* it about people that so many spent their last hours leaving messages, final thoughts, or philosophical musing? No doubt one day, we'd find a sheet of original music and lyrics, titled "Dying alone and that's fine, I'm fed up with people anyhow…"

Di was reading the letter. "Yes, his medication stopped working; it wouldn't be a quick or particularly pleasant death, so they decided to go together. They were in their eighties, had no family, and all their friends had died. They say their neighbours came to tell them goodbye, they were going to family, and they were sorry the toddler had given them that cold thing."

She looked up. "Staph, most likely. Doctor gave them allodaxin, so they were immune. Not a great help for them. Too old to manage on their own for long, no relations to take them in, they stayed here until he started getting bad, and made their decision."

She went back to the letter. "She says, her husband had

an old spaniel. He shot it before he got too bad; they could see what was going to happen. They gave her cat some of his medication the week before this. They already had a grave dug."

She read: "*At the back of the property, past the Rhododendrons, there's our pet cemetery. If you find us, if you will do us a kindness, please, lay us there with them. We left a space between Wally and Ginger Spice, and we left the grave ready. It's covered, just move that off, put us in, and use the spade left there. All our gratitude to you.*
Jonathon Michael and Rosemary Denise Marli-Winton"
****

That occupied us. Not that it took so long. Dave's daughters stayed back to cook us all a meal, but the rest of us were involved while the three rescued children stood watching. We moved the bodies, if they could still be called that. Mic placed the bedspread over them, and we lifted mattress, bodies and spread together, carrying the bundle down the stairs, out into the garden, and past the rhododendrons.

The pet cemetery was charming. It went back several generations, and many of the graves had actual headstones with dates, and sometime a line beneath them. I noticed one; it was black, with a Bast-like cat engraved and picked out in gold. It said, "*Sekmet.*" Under that, dates, *Aug.2010-Nov.2027,* and the final line: "*A mighty hunter.*" Maureen's gaze met mine, and I could see we'd both had the same thought. It wouldn't be practical this way, but we could adapt it. I wouldn't mind sleeping with a cat or dog.

The grave was where they'd said, between the two small most recent ones. It had a tarpaulin pegged down firmly, and since the area was sheltered, there'd never been a wind sufficient to remove the cover in the years since. Paddy and Dave took the cover off, Maureen and I, Liz, and Di lowered the occupied bedding and smoothed it. Mic had stopped as we continued, picked sprays of flowers, and now she came up, dropped them all over the faded spread, and spoke a brief prayer from one of the psalms. She stepped back, and there was silence as we wondered if we should do something more.

And from where the three children stood, one of the most beautiful voices I had ever heard rose up. It sang, in a pure sexless soprano that riveted us all. Only two verses, but somehow when the last word sounded into the quiet air, we knew it was done, that what we'd done was all those who lay there now would need or would ever have wanted.

Jerusalem the golden, with milk and honey blessed –
the sight of it refreshes the weary and oppressed.
I know not, oh, I know not what joys await us there,
what radiancy of glory, what bliss beyond compare:
to sing the hymn unending with all the martyr throng,
amidst the halls of Zion resounding full with song.

The Lord is ever with them, the daylight is serene;
the pastures of the blessed are ever rich and green.
There is the throne of David, and there, from care released,
the shout of them that triumph, the song of them that feast.
To God enthroned in glory all our voices blend,
the dead forever blessed, by the Light that knows no end.

And as that rang over the graves of beloved animals and the two who'd joined them by choice, I saw it was the boy, that if he did not speak, it was because of trauma, but that almost certainly at some time, he'd laughed and talked with family and friends. He'd probably sung in a school or church choir, and I hoped with all my heart this would be the start of his healing. A new beginning where he'd find his own place.

We ate dinner after that, sorted out places for the children to sleep, and spent a quiet night. In the morning, I found Liz and Di had gone over the bikers and their gear, taken anything useful, and dragged the bodies into the long grass by the road. They'd left them there, and none of us felt inclined to do more. We drove away, three more in number; we'd return without them to take what was in the cellar, to lay flowers again, and to add items from the panic room. But we'd never forget yesterday or the voice we'd heard.

CHAPTER TWELVE

We reached the Manor at sunset the next day. The gates opened in welcome, and Di, who'd ridden ahead, gestured everyone back who was assembled at the gates, speaking quietly. They parted, letting Thorne behind her and our three vehicles, through first. The boy looked wonderingly at those who greeted us and drew back in his seat. I smiled at him.

"They're our people; they're happy to see us safe home. No one will hurt you here, but they may want to talk to you; some may want to hug you to be friendly. I'll tell them not to if you want." His look flicked to me, and he nodded. "Okay. I'll see everyone hears that. But if one of the smaller children forget, it isn't meant the wrong way."

Mic took him home to our house, while Maureen and I supervised the unloading of all three vehicles. Some of the items in our loads were for us; the rest went into the containers marked for general supplies. This last convoy had been the largest ever; it had continued for almost five months, and the field of containers was vast. Under Thorne's suggestion, we'd broken it down into five different places. Each collection of containers held a mix of supplies so that if any one of them was looted or destroyed somehow, the other four had the same mix and what we lost was mass not diversity.

One lot had gone to the secret installation, and Polwithin were told they could take from that, but — politely — they shouldn't go mad helping themselves. Hilla had agreed.

The fact was that anyone of intelligence understood everything we salvaged these days was finite. Once they were used up and gone, for very many items there would be no more, if not forever, certainly for our foreseeable future. One of those items was fuel. It was something that Dave, the electrician, had come quietly to Thorne and us three before the convoy started and mentioned something none of us had considered to date.

"You were saying a while back as how fuel'd be gone in a while. You ever thought about steam?" We hadn't. "Railway lines all over the place," Dave commented. "Okay, lot of those lines aren't used any more, but they're *there*. Steam trains run on those, too, you know. If we find a few of the engines, freight cars, carriages, and so on, we can go wherever the rails do. We can put weed catchers on front of the engines and go slow first time anywhere; that'll clear the lines most of the time without anyone having to go ahead on foot." He grinned. "And it doesn't have to be full-size engines. Lot of places like parks and zoos had miniature railways, an' you'd be surprised how powerful some of those little engines are."

We talked about that all through winter. Lexi and Jess had been able to tell us that both their families had been last seen in an area where there were railway lines. The boy said nothing; so far, he'd never spoken, nor did he seem to remember where he'd been when the bikers took him. He wouldn't go close to anyone, but Doc Di, Liz, me and Maureen, and Mic; he trusted us five to some extent, a little more as the months passed. From the girls, we'd been able to work out possibilities; however, and look at those when spring returned.

Once the weather improved, we went hunting for miniature steam trains. We found three within easy distance, got them off their own small circuits, onto main lines, and made maps of how far we could take them before we struck blockages, how much freight they could pull, and what was required to keep them working. A lot of the time, they'd be easier to fuel and quicker, too, depending on what we wanted them for. In Plymouth, there'd been a hobby group, with two full-sized steam trains plus four carriages. Dave pointed out that for what he called "passive rail-stock," anything could be pulled by a steam locomotive, so we added a number of the freight cars and open wagons. Mic talked to me that evening.

"None of that will last forever either, Hugh. Locomotives break down, so even if you have a line of carriages and wagons, with nothing to pull them, you're going nowhere. You need to regard trains as interim transport. Once they're gone, they're gone. In the end, we'll be back to horses, and anything that can be run on electricity. Even with electric vehicles, there could come a time when a future generation can't repair things and can't make them. Although we can hope there's an overlap. That by the time the last of them fail that were salvaged from before the plague, we'll have learned to make units from the ground up."

She was right, I knew it, and I could live with it more easily knowing that such a time would be well after the three of us were gone. But we were building for the future too. I nodded. "Dave and I talked about that. He thinks it could be already possible to build electric ecosystems from scratch. Over the last few winters, he's been looking at that; he thinks in another couple of years, he'll be able to do it with basic ones."

Mic lit up. "That'd be wonderful, but they do have some metal bits. What about that?"

"That's what he's working on. He says the prototype will be big, clumsy, and not long-lasting, but if he can make a working one without metal, after that, it's a matter of refining it, and that's just time and work."

I didn't mention the other discussion I'd had with him and Paddy; that while it was possible to mine metal, refine it crudely, beat it into necessary shapes, and use it, it was time and labor-consuming. We'd gone over, as a civilization, still more to various forms of plastics and resins, and those we couldn't duplicate. It'd have to be metal where we couldn't use something more readily to hand. While there'd be metal for generation, in buildings, vehicles, and other items around, that wouldn't be so forever either. There'd come a time where, if we had to have metal, or even wanted it, we'd need to mine. And by then, would those generations know how to, or where to look?

I said that Dave and Paddy looked at me and Paddy sighed. "All we can do is the best we can do. Make sure the kids learn to read, that the smarter ones can read the scientific and the mechanical information. That way, when the time comes they need to know, they can read and learn."

Dave looked at us. "I think we could go a fair way down before we start back up," he said quietly. "Just so long as new generations know it's possible, that it was done in their past, and that they could do those things again. Teach them what happened, that you need an educated population for some professions, that you can need numbers as well. Don't let the plague become a fairy tale. That way, new generations don't believe stories about the before times, don't accept they can climb back, and don't bother to try."

I went home and thought about that. I kept a diary; I knew Mic had one as well, in her case, a special one based on the one we'd found at Bremmers. Thorne had one, and most of the fifteen schoolchildren we'd had when this started. Others might have them too. If we laid hands on several of the self-contained publishing machines and supplies for them, if those diaries were collected, edited, and printed? If we had an archive of them? If anyone who wanted could have a copy of any they wanted? If we had a special day … a week, some fixed time when we read out of them, discussed what had happened and how? Made certain Manor children knew this had been our reality, and that it could be again if they worked towards it?

Mic came back from milking goats with the boy in tow. Maureen returned from helping with salvage, and over dinner, I raised the subject. My family were enthusiastic.

Mic grinned. "My diary's private. I followed the Bremmer system, and I've been fairly crude, really personal, or graphic in places, but that could be edited for general reading." Maureen nodded in agreement. "As for those publishing machines, when I was in London in thirty-seven, I spent time with a friend, Sian

Jones; she was running a small press using those. She told me how they worked and what you needed. She was in London, staying with friends, while she was looking at sizes and prices to buy two new ones."

"Where did she live?"

Mic smiled. "You'll love this; she was from Cardiff. And she wasn't the only one there who had them. So far as larger places go, there was the Cardiff University Press; hers was called Emphasis Press, and she said there were about five or six others. Most are in an outer city suburb or in a village just outside it, but somewhere I have her address, some of her books, and her letters and emails. I'd say I could point to where we could collect half a dozen of the machines anyway, and they'd have supplies there too." We took that to Thorne.

He listened, to how Dave had said we should make sure the plague didn't become a fairy tale, so people stopped trying. How we needed a literate population. How many of us had diaries, and they could be edited into history books. We finished, and he pursed his lips. "Have you also considered that we could replace books that fall to pieces because they're so popular and we can't find replacement copies? We could find an author here—*if* they knew that they could write books and see them published and read. We could have copies made of technical work, professional, and scientific papers. We could copy into bound books the diagrams, sketches, drawings, and useful writing we find when we salvage."

Well, no, we hadn't got that far. "We'd been planning a trip to Cardiff and Newport," Thorne reminded us. "We need to make it soon. This is one more reason and something else to look for when we salvage. Luckily, we hauled back all those papers from the Staines laboratory."

Mic nodded. "I think we haven't thought of publishing because so far, there's been multiple copies of most books. Past midwinter this year, though, will be the start of 2051. How much longer will machinery and papers still be working, readable, or intact enough be duplicated? Buildings are falling down; some side roads are becoming unusable. Those bikers, they were nomadic; they went wherever they could find what they wanted, they stayed until they'd used it, then left for somewhere else. But what we never asked at the time, was, how many of that sort are there?"

Maureen said three words: "Britain post-Roman."

Our faces all become thoughtful as we digested that. Yes, the Romans had brought a form of civilization, but when they left, the barbarians they'd kept out came sweeping in. Cities burned, and civilization to a great extent was lost again. It wasn't impossible—or even that unlikely—it could happen here and now. Thorne stood up.

"What we need is walled villages where people can retreat with their livestock. And again, we don't have a lot more time before the CBMs stop working or what we need to supply them is gone or useless. From now on, where we go, we warn people if they already have some sort of village or homestead with a number of inhabitants. We suggest, we can't enforce that, but we can tell them about bikers and nomadic groups. That they can be a danger to everything they have, own, and those they care about."

I grinned. "Messiahs in trucks."

Mic laughed softly. "A network of villages, places like us and Polwithin, who come to each other's aid, who have yearly markets. And there's Comsat; the Amcots went there." They had. They'd chosen that name too, half as a joke; it was an anagram for their family name, plus in a way, it was a satellite of the Manor, and they communicated. It had begun with the two families, but others had gone there and settled. It was fifty-three people now and doing well.

"Thorne," Mic said, "there's small places like Comsat, hamlets where everyone died, but there's still houses, buildings, and feral livestock. If we took the CBMs we have and walled, say two more of those to start with, if we suggest to some of the people, we find that they take over one of those places? If while we're in Cardiff and Newport, we pick up not just small cargo boats, but fishing boats, too, and come home in convoy with them, we could establish anther fishing port — down the coast towards Land's End — maybe two, one on either side, say Mounts Bay and St. Ives."

Maureen, who'd been sitting there meditating on I-knew-not-what, but I knew the expression, spoke. "If we went to Wales, using the steam locos, we wouldn't have to cross the Severn at the coast. We could go all the way up and cross at the bridge. Just us armed. No vehicles. Miniature locos could be loaded onto cargo ships to come home then." Now that was a seriously smart idea, I said so, and she grinned.

And it was decided; we talked it over with solos and families. We could also take Lexi, Jess, and the boy if we loaded electric bikes, plus two ecosystems, on the train; they'd be sufficient for us to reach the small places they'd been taken from and see if there was any family left for them to rejoin. Winter wore away as we made plans; suggestions were offered and accepted — or not. People decided if they wanted to go, and those at Polwithin having talked to us, Hilla was sending a contingent of expert sailors and fisher-people, on the agreement they could take some of the fishing boats found in good condition, and Polwithin people would also captain others to go to St. Ives and Mount's Bay.

Since from what we had found in various guidebooks, there'd be a host of fishing boats, or if not specifically fishing boats, then yachts that could be converted, we'd agreed and come to another agreement as well. The Polwithin group would be fifty strong, an initial two men or women per boat. They could choose up to ten boats for Polwithin. We could take more, with one Polwithin sailor per boat, and another two of our people. That'd be as many of thirty more; they'd be divided into two groups, one to be left moored or beached at St. Ives, the other at Mount's Bay.

Hilla had looked appreciative at that, and I was mildly

surprised. She saw it. "'Tis like this, Hugh. Fishing villages tend to marry among our own. If we have two other villages, we have better and wider choices, do you see?" I did. "'Sides, takes numbers to build boats, and yes, we know how, haven't done it since my grandfather's time, but we can. And anyways, with a good fleet as we'll have after this, we'll be getting in practice with repairs. We've a family that knows coopering too. Before that virus, they'd been making barrels mostly to saw in half for rich folks to put flowers an' lil' trees in. But they know how. They been collecting metal for strapping and all."

She chuckled. "We got a big line of containers filled with stuff just like you, and our people as are going along will be looking for any fisher-folk who'd like to come back with them. Reckon they may find one or two, and anyone's a bonus."

I reflected that everyone had an agenda these days; the main difference was that such agendas were mostly to benefit the clan rather than the individual. Hilla was adding something, and I paid attention. "Lads and lasses been told to look for some other things too, Weapons and ammo, bows and arrows count as well. Plus music. I told them to pick up any sheet music they find, musical instruments too, and any books or designs an' things on how to make those."

She said an abrupt goodbye when a son came in with something for her to decide, and I headed for the Manor, making mental notes that she was right about musical instruments and information on making — or repairing — them. We should gather those ourselves.

****

I mentioned it to Thorne, and he agreed. "Very fond of music myself, as you know, Maureen plays violin; you play guitar. I'm not bad on the piano, and Mic can do drums. I know others of us can play the pipes, trumpet, sax, and bugle, and we should consider an orchestra or at least official musical evenings with songs, dancing, and music interludes. I know we have them irregularly, just when someone feels like it, but we need to make music more official. It's always been part of Cornwall."

That he delegated, and a schedule was drawn up covering the year. Approximately the four times of older days, when people celebrated the changing of the seasons. Merr was delegated to make lists of who could make music, and found a surprising number at our Manor could play something, owned that instrument, and most of those had written music squirreled away to go with it. He discovered that Doc Di played a mean sax, was proficient on the guitar as well, and could manage a lap harp. Merr himself was capable on the clarinet as I knew. What I hadn't known was that he'd always wanted to play rock guitar. All of which lead to something I hadn't seen coming, but Mic noticed almost at once.

She said nothing, considering it no one's business but their own, until I found out by accident, was stunned, and told her, thinking it would come as a surprise. It didn't, which surprised *me*.

I'd been to ask Doc Di something; the door wasn't locked. I'd had my mind engaged on the problem, and without thinking, I'd walked in. She was there all right, with Merr on her sofa, and they were kissing in a way that even to me indicated it wasn't an unusual occupation. I backed out the pace I'd taken past her door, shut the door quietly, and went away. Mic was in the kitchen when I returned, and I spilled it to her, along with astonishment and maybe touch of disapproval.

"Hugh, don't be a Puritan; they're adults. Do you expect anyone who isn't married to live like monks or nuns?" I grinned wryly and mentioned church scandals of the earlier years. "Yes. Anyhow, it isn't as if this hasn't been a relationship for a while."

"What?" I said, stunned.

Mic's lips twitched. "Hugh, they've been lovers over a year now."

And all I could think of to say was, "But, Mic, she's much older than he is, and she's a doctor." My grandmother snorted. "What? Doctors can't have love lives? As for older, Merr was twenty-eight when he arrived; he's just turned forty now. The

Doc's forty-nine, *and* she doesn't look it." Well, no, she didn't, but ten years older? Mic shrugged as if she'd read my mind.

"Age is a number or so they used to say. Di's fit as a fiddle, healthy as a horse, and to complete the metaphors, if she wants to go at it like a rabbit, he's the buck she's picked. I wouldn't go telling her you think she's too old, or you could have trouble with the next injury you suffer."

I went to have a bath, and while relaxing in hot water, I made up my mind. It wasn't any of my business, Mic was right in everything she'd said, and if I broke a leg next week, it'd be better for me the doc wasn't annoyed at something I'd said. Just because Maureen and I had been twenty-three when we'd married, it didn't have to be the same for everyone else. Come to that, I'd never liked what I'd read about the Puritans anyway.

****

The winter crept along; now and again when the weather was less wet and windy, we made short forays to empty hamlets, farms, or company housing. Maureen and I took Merr, Liz, Doc Di, and Annie along, and we didn't skim. We deep salvaged, looking for any overlooked medications, first aid items, long-lasting food, musical instruments, or sheet music. We found a surprising amount. Not a lot in any one place, but over say, twelve to twenty houses, we sometimes filled a couple of trailers.

One haul delighted everyone. It had originally been an isolated shop at a crossroads. It had a single petrol pump, a charging point, and for where it was, it was quite a reasonable size. Probably everyone local there used it for top-up shopping when they didn't want to drive to town. What no one noticed up to this time was that it had storage cellars. Kaiser was with us, and he barked. He stared at the floor and barked again.

We investigated and found a fox den dug partly under the edge of the building, (complete with an inhabitant that left in a hurry) but in finding that I noticed something.

"Hey, I think this place has a cellar. I never saw anything inside."

That, we discovered was because at some stage, someone, possibly the owners, had moved the shop freezer over the trap door. It took two of us to move it back, pry the door up, and Merr produced a small powerful torch. "Let's take a look, could be empty. Owners may have cleared it out. Place was all shut up 'n' tidy."

It had been. But they may have assumed a quick trip to the doctor, they'd be back—and been wrong. The cellars were loaded. Everything from food—mostly in cans and packets of powder so it was edible still, to two shelves of small household items like vegetable knives, peelers, eggbeaters, fish slicers for lifting fish out of the frying pan, and sieves of various sizes. Deeper in were larger containers of washing-up liquid, laundry powder, disinfectant, plant fertilizer, other similar things, and an entire shelf of non-pharmacy medications, bandages, elastic strapping, dozens of packs of Band-Aids, ten hot water bottles with covers, seven thermometers, six plastic measuring cups, four sets of scales, two complete sets of matching towels… I was grateful we were absent the partridge; it would have made a hell of a mess over the years.

The cellar was watertight and may have been airtight, too, since there was no sign of insects, and it was dry. Really dry. So, with that, nothing down here had deteriorated in any way but past a "use by" date. Liz and Di had landed on the first aid shelves. Merr had found them a stack of flat-folded cartons and was turning those back to container shape and passing them down. The docs filled them, passed them back up, and he carried them out to their trailers.

I saw something—and said nothing. Yes, I know, but I wanted to see what might be there first. After all, Kaiser had given everyone this windfall. We finished loading everything, and as we went to our Landcruiser, I looked towards a hill and nodded at it.

"I think that's a farm up there, Maureen, and I'll go and have a look there. If there's one farm, there's others, and we've got space for more still." All quite true, and they headed away. I drove off, circled once they were out of sight and returned to the shop, parking when anyone coming back this way wouldn't notice us. Maureen waited until we were into the shop to ask why we'd come back.

"I saw something in that cellar. I'm not sure, but I thought it'd be nice to see for ourselves. Just you and me." Maureen grinned and followed me down the stairs. I went to the very back and pointed at the wall which had been made or repaired from old doors nailed onto a frame.

"That one, do you see any nails?"

She reached out, got a grip on the strips of wood outlining what would have once been a window at the door's upper half, and pulled. The door opened silently. It would have been part of the original cellar, but it had been walled off with the frame and the old doors. Now there was a strip of space, about three foot deep and fifteen feet long. Within that was — contraband. Not the sort of thing, or mostly not, that a general-purpose store should have. I guessed many of the older customers would have known inspectors would never find this, and newer customers wouldn't know to ask.

It was split into three sections, the middle one the smallest. The far one held alcohol. No beer, but two local brands of cider, both high alcohol for cider. There were spirits; I noticed types like Ouzo and most vodkas were missing. Yes, this was for those they knew, and they knew what was wanted. There was also brandy, whisky, gin, sherry, and shelves of other middle-to upper-class alcoholic drinks.

The next section along — the smallest — was tobacco. Cigars, cigarettes, and pouches of tobacco. I'd bet they'd never had a license to sell any of that either. In fact, as fewer and fewer used it, so fewer licenses to sell commercial retail were granted anyway. I'd bet there was a trailer-load here. The final and largest section was chocolate. Everything from Easter eggs and Easter bunnies to Father Christmases and elves, fairies, and a line of chocolate cats wearing Christmas symbols and Cheshire Cat grins. As well, there were tins. I felt my mouth water. Hot chocolate and cocoa! It might not be copyright, but it certainly was safe from thieves.

Maureen wasn't wasting time. "Help me pack the hot choc and cocoa. I'm not sharing those. Mic loves it, so do we, and it's pretty much out everywhere by now. Some of the cheaper alcohol the docs could take, disinfectant in an emergency, or to buck someone up if they're faint, whatever. We can give the tobacco to Thorne for trade. The other chocolate and booze can go to storage. Thorne can share it out however he wants, but grab the cocoa, hot choc, and the cats."

We did. I estimated that if we weren't pigs, the amount of two-pound tins of the hot drinks would last us years. The chocolate cats would make it only a week—or less. I added a carton of the Easter eggs and one of rabbits. We loaded the drinks and chocolate, carefully putting them under other items, rearranged everything on the shelves, and waited up the road. In my binoculars I saw Merr, and the doc's vehicles returning as they drove down the road, halting by the shop again.

They pulled up beside us. "We miss something?"

"Maybe. I remembered half-noticing something; it wasn't until a while ago it dawned on me what. I figured it wouldn't hurt to check."

I pointed out the unnailed door once we were in the cellar. Liz opened it; there was a lot of talk, discussion, comments, and when we left again, our trailers were all fully loaded as were the rear spaces in most of the vehicles. Kaiser had had a wonderful day; apart from anything else, we'd found an overlooked carton of cans of gourmet dog food in the back of the small office behind a cabinet. It had been voted his by acclamation, and he'd had half of one on the spot.

Our welcome home was considerable once the chocolate was revealed. The alcohol and tobacco went into stores, but the chocolate was shared out over the remainder of the afternoon and evening. I doubt much of it lasted beyond that night. We smuggled the cartons of cans containing the cocoa and hot choc-olate powder into the house and swore Mic to secrecy before we showed her. She groaned.

"It's not really right, but if we shared it, it'd just about give the place a cup each. So okay, my lips are sealed. Next time you go out, take a tin of each and bring them back for Thorne. Tell him you found them wherever you were; say it's specifically to aid negotiations." I can say that it did well for us on several of such occasions. It was surprising who loved the stuff—besides the three of us.

Winter departed, spring came and went, and it was early summer. People had backpacks filled with essentials, and, head-ing into one bright clear morning, the mini-locomotives got up steam, and we boarded carriages. Liz was our official doc. Thorne had come with us, but Mic stayed home. If anything hap-pened to Thorne, she and Jake would lead the Manor, and they'd have Doc Di. The mood was a trifle somber, so I started singing. Maureen and the others joined in, the song spread, and I found I was grinning. Like the Cornish of old, we went singing to what-ever we'd met, and it was good.

CHAPTER THIRTEEN

We ran at a moderate speed, but a locomotive doesn't tire, and we were using the three miniatures spaced as front, back, and centre. Twice we saw someone standing gape-mouthed as we passed. We waved, they waved back, and we went on. Even on rail with tireless power, it took time, but by that evening, we were at the Severn Bridge. We crossed over and rolled into Wales. There we stopped at the rail halt for a small village. No one was there anymore, but it'd had forty or fifty houses, a hotel, and a B&B. Thorne allocated beds; we spent the night with guards on watch. On my shift, I had Kaiser as well, and nothing disturbed our night. The next morning, we headed for New Port.

With us, we'd taken all three children. They'd petitioned to come with us, and Mic had taken me aside quietly.

"Hugh, what they want is to spend time with you and Maureen. If you find their families, they are far enough away from the Manor that they may never see you again. Then, too, if you do find their families after you've been in Wales, it would be logical for you to return via the railway, bringing salvage that could be used to help any family that might be in difficulties."

That made sense, and Maureen had already suggested coming straight back via rail once we'd seen the ships depart for Land's End. As she'd said, if there were any of us injured, Liz could deal with the initial medical requirements, but someone badly hurt would not do well spending days on a ship if the seas were rough. I hadn't considered the children either. So that was decided, and now they sang loudly, enjoying the atmosphere of anticipation. Watching them, I realised I'd miss them if we *did* find their families.

New Port was a wasteland. It had been a dozen years since the plague; it looked to have been thoroughly looted during that time. With any obvious supplies of food, drugs, and alcohol all gone, whoever had remained at that point had gone too. Not only that, but large areas had burned. We spread out in well-armed and watchful groups on electric bicycles. Food, drugs, and alcohol weren't the only things we could use. We found a tiny group of three shops down an alleyway; each had been broken into, but most of the contents of two were still there.

Apart from anything else, we had long since discovered that a surprising number of places — shops, houses, businesses — had cellars. They were often intact, and now we always searched for any indication of one. The three shops were of the sort with living quarters behind. Those had been mostly looted, but Maureen, Thorne, and I went over each building carefully. We found a cellar in one, and looking in the same area of the others, we discovered they both had cellars as well — dry, undiscovered, and well-stocked.

Thorne was first into the middle one. The shop above had been a corner dairy; above-ground, it had been emptied. The cellar was a different matter. It was filled with long-life food, including powdered milk. We gutted it. Thorne left that to others and headed for the shop around the corner, Maureen and I right behind him. That had been a bookshop. Much of the stock there had been left untouched, but the break-in had left the entire plate glass smashed, and the weather had ruined it all.

The cellar, however, was half-full, and everything was fine. We gathered books, reams of A4 paper, and cards in the same size by the armload, also transferred into the rear stock-cars; it left us with one empty. We turned to the final shop, heading for where the cellar entrance had been on the previous two, found that, and descended.

Thorne made a sound of astonishment in his throat, and we shone light on the contents. "What in heaven's name was this for?"

Upstairs, the shop had sold children's toys. We estimated some three-quarters of them to have been taken, and again, the break-in had let weather in so that over the years, anything remaining had been ruined. We'd expected more toys and would have taken a reasonable selection; what we saw, however, were emphatically not toys. Down one side of the cellar were shelves; they contained… "Bows and arrows, *spears!*" Thorne cried.

Our gaze circled the walls and shelving. It looked like a Viking armoury. There were shields of various sizes and shapes, throwing axes, chain mail and armour plate. That was the first two walls. The third contained books—I picked one up, then another; Thorne and Maureen were examining others.

"How-to books," my wife said. "Explicit, from the ground up stuff. With these if you had any ability at all, you could make just about anything down here from scratch."

I was paging through another. "Blacksmithing how-to. Horseshoes, wagon furniture, all the iron bits you need to put wood together to make a wagon, a carriage, even horse-drawn farm gear."

Thorne held up a book. "And household smithing, how to make or repair kettles, pots, churns, chains for cow bails or byres, and household knives, forks, spoons, ladles." He replaced the book on the shelf. "We take all of this. We don't need it now; we may not need it for generations, but a time could come when this is invaluable."

Maureen and I nodded. We would likely be long-since dead before the Manor needed smiths, but when the time came that the Manor did need this information, it would be no time to be trying to find DIY books. We'd talked about this; we'd see to it we always had a couple of people from the beginning who could make or mend and teach others, and this would back them.

"Okay, what's over here?" I asked

Three looms of ascending sizes stood sideways against the wall was what. Along with a high shelf of books on weaving, sewing patterns, knitting, and weaving, plus in spaces below that were spinning wheels, drop spindles, bobbins, and a stack of smaller items that went with them, all carved from wood. And in a niche by the stairs, were papers. The shop owner had been an enthusiast of old ways. He'd made additional income by demonstrations, lectures, and visits to schools. A copy of one of his letters in a folder explained a lot. Maureen read it aloud.

"...today's children, and even many adults, assume the people of earlier centuries lived lives that were ignorant, uncultured, and without any form of technology, and that this was because they were stupid. Showing the everyday things they had to make from scratch, and which often required skill to even use, teaches them that this wasn't so.

It shows if our civilization collapsed, anyone today would have real problems surviving. Children are habituated to Google, to Wikipedia, to specialist sites that tell them anything they want to know at the click of a mouse. I ask them how they will find out and where they will learn if none of that exists any longer? Who will teach them if no one is left who knows how to do something?

Hand-milking a cow is not easy. Still harder are building a house, a shed, a barn. Growing and reaping crops is exhausting work if you don't have powered machinery. Travelling real distances is time-consuming, expensive, and possibly dangerous if you have only horses. And if all you have is horses, how do you make wagons, saddles, bridles, reapers, hay-mowers, or how do you shoe your animals? People of centuries past might not have had computers, smart phones, or intelligent homes, but they were far from ignorant or stupid..."

Thorne grinned wryly. "Knew what he was talking about, didn't he? What was his name?"

I'd been flicking through the file. "Eavan Hughes." I unfolded a sheet of paper. Here's a genealogy. His ancestors got around. Bloodlines from Ireland, Wales, Denmark, and the fens.
"

Maureen straightened from where she'd been examining the looms. "Take everything, Thorne, put it in a special building, and call it Ayvan's Legacy."

We exchanged glances, and without a word being said, so it was decided. "Let's have a closer look at where they lived, "Thorne said, and we trooped back upstairs to the rear where the Hughes' living quarters had been.

The main bedroom contained bones, a man and a woman, from the tatters of clothing that remained. Along with a cat skeleton, and partly concealed under the woman's hand, an envelope of the sort used to preserve documents.

I read it. "I won't go into all of this, it's mostly a repeat of what his letter downstairs, said. She says everyone they knew is gone, they are on medications that aren't replaceable, and they're old, they chose to go with dignity and take Blackie—their cat; he's seventeen—with them." I read the last bit as it was written. *"Whatever of ours you find, take if it's needed and value it. Remember our names, and if you can, give us all three a burial together.*

Valda (Erwen) Hughes."

Our gazes met again, and once more we knew without discussion what we'd do. We shut the door behind us as we left. All of their cellar had been salvaged, and we'd be on our way again in an hour after we'd had a meal and gathered more firewood.

****

We headed for Cardiff once we'd eaten; the rail lines ran through and around both sides of the city, and to the docks. We went there first, finding cargo ships, tankers, and trawlers, while in a nearby marina were yachts and other sailing ships of that sort of size. There were beautiful private yachts only engine-powered, but we had no interest in those.

We checked all of the cargo ships. We wanted something that could handle moderate seas, but that also didn't demand a large crew, that we could fuel from what was available, and that either had empty holds, or that contained a cargo we could use. We found five. One, to our amusement, was filled with neatly stacked and tied down Ikea furniture.

"We'll take it," Thorne decided. "And the one with the barrels." They were filled with corn syrup, and as that was the largest of the five loaded ships, and it was *fully* laden; there'd be sufficient of that to see us provided with sweetening for years. It would be shared between our three villages, and those in charge there would have to decide its division after that.

The other three were mostly empty, apart from one which had a number of chests in one hold. They were, we found when we opened one, tin-lined, and filled with loose tea. Maureen sighed. "That won't have any flavour left by now, but the chests will be useful."

Liz, who'd joined us, picked up a handful and smelled it. "Tea's a very good fertilizer, it has nitrogen. Take it as it is." She smelled it again. "And I'll tell you something. I don't think this is as old as the virus. It's black tea, those chests are airtight, so it's been dry, no damp, no light."

The captain's quarters told a brief story where a diary lay on a cabinet beside a bed containing the writer. He'd been visiting a family member who had a tea plantation. When the virus struck, they'd died, but he and several of the crew had had the preliminary infection via the child of one of the crew. He'd stayed where he was until he became so homesick, he'd rather die at sea than stay on the plantation. He'd headed for the docks, found his ship, taken on fuel, several other homesick sailors had agreed to come with him, and he'd sailed for Cardiff eight years after the virus.

He'd taken the chests and filled them with tea as something he might be able to trade on arrival. He'd made it. The crew had leapt ashore and disappeared the minute the ship tied up. He'd never seen them again. He'd gone home to the suburb where his wife, his children, and his own parents had lived. There he'd found a brief note from his wife; she'd taken everyone to her parents' farm. He'd followed them and found them all — dead, with a final note from his wife saying she loved him. He'd burned bodies and farmhouse, returned to his ship, and decided he had no one and nothing left. And he had no wish to live on without all he'd loved.

Before he'd burned the farmhouse, he'd taken the painkillers his wife's mother had for her arthritis. He'd also taken the portable player his wife owned and several of their favourite disks. He'd loaded the disks, set it to turn off when they'd played through twice, and laid on the bed drinking a bottle of fine old brandy he'd found, while every couple of mouthfuls taking some of the painkillers. He would die, he'd noted, without pain, and to the sounds of the music he and his wife loved. His final thoughts would be of his family; his final hope, to see them running towards him, welcoming him back.

I had tears in my eyes when I finished reading that, and I think everyone else did as well. Liz sniffed once. "The tea is four years old; it's been double-treated and kept under optimum conditions. It should be fine, and any that's lost flavour can be used as I said. We've got three ships with mostly empty cargo holds. Let's start filling those."

We did. It took several weeks. We'd chosen smaller rather than the enormous cargo ships; they were short-sea trip, or coasters, but even coasters can carry a good-sized cargo, as one of our sailors explained.

"A standard truck takes about twenty-five tons; a coaster's load equals at least forty trucks, and on average between one and two hundred trucks."

This meant, since we'd picked a size around halfway for our five, we'd be taking a total of five hundred tons of cargo home. Thorne said to everyone, that in view of this, each person could take up to a hundred pounds of personal salvage. That was met with cheers and delight, as the next morning after his announcement, people scattered in groups of never less than five, armed, and all eager to see what they could find.

Cargo trickled back over the days. Everything from electric vehicles, ecosystems, footwear, books, medicine, and then we hit a factory that did double-layer and double-sealed sacks of flour, sugar, salt, and powdered milk, for areas overseas that had problems with humidity and storage. We emptied the place, filling one ship from that alone. One of the women arrived with a fanfare of sounds like nothing on earth.

Liz and I were at the gangway, counting people in and out, checking loads, and writing down information. We both looked up. Lily Tilliker had a cage in one hand, the sounds came from that. A sort of whooping with odd grunts. She marched up the gangplank and offered the cage for inspection. I blinked at the inhabitants.

"Beavers!" I cried. "Where did you get *beavers*?" Two of them. They were young, maybe not even completely weaned yet, and they were making it very plain they didn't like being in a cage.

Lilly made soothing sounds to them, then to me. "Their mum was dead. They were by her body crying. We've got beavers in Cornwall, so I thought I'd take them back, fened them, then when they were old enough, I could let them go where's there's others."

Liz looked at me; I looked at Liz and sighed. "Oh, well. Yes, take them to your cabin, but you're looking after them, and no making a fuss if they die."

I watched her carry the cage away and allowed a smile to surface. It'd been over thirty years ago now since a project in Cornwall had seen beavers reintroduced. Almost immediately, the project had seen improvements in flooding that affected a nearby village. During the virus, some of the project beavers had escaped. They'd come in our direction, and Thorne had issued a ruling that beavers were not to be harmed. He'd be delighted to see this pair, both probably from a different strain to those in Cornwall.

I told him when he returned three hours later, and he headed for Lilly's cabin. Over dinner with Liz and Maureen that night he enthused about them. "Lovely little beasts, just one thing though." We all looked a query. "Not sure what killed the mother. I think a single fox had trouble. A big dog maybe? What occurred to me was, if the beavers got out of the zoo, what else may have escaped — or could be some of the keepers, fond of their animals, let some go."

That thought had already occurred to me, along with: *It's amazing what you can get fond of,* and, *I wonder what animals were there?* I said that and Thorne nodded.

"Well, if it's dangerous animals, to make it to the Manor, they'll have to go all the way up to the river's headwaters, then all the way down half of England, whatever they are. No one will be giving a free ride to tigers or something like that."

Which was true, I thought, unless some later population threw up a Hannibal who liked elephants, but... "What about marine mammals?"

"We've got enough of our own. Seals, sea lions, otters, we probably wouldn't even notice a few new ones turning up on a beach."

"We'd notice polar bears," I said.

Thorne winced. "Good Grief, I hadn't thought about those. Hang on, Cornwall's a very temperate climate. If they'd got out, they'd head north. And it's unlikely the zoo had any. I think I read somewhere the only zoo with them in England was in Yorkshire."

Liz broke in. "They live on coasts anyhow, don't they? Why would they come as far inland as the Manor is?" We came to the pleasant conclusion that all things considered we wouldn't have to worry about polar bears. And if some large predator did make its way in our direction, sufficient to the time would be the problem — especially since it was unlikely to be in *our* time.

The beavers learned in two days that Lilly fed them; they learned in another day, that humans in general petted, scratched gently, and also fed them. Kaiser considered them and made advances which were cautiously accepted. By the time the holds of all five ships were filled, and we've split back into two main groups, the beaver babies were under the impression the human race existed for the convenience of young beavers.

However, as Thorne said firmly, no, we weren't looking for more. No, this duo would go free as soon as they were old enough, and no, we weren't going to the zoo to see if anything had stayed around. And as he said privately to Maureen, me, and Liz. He wasn't risking someone finding a baby tiger ... elephant ... or crocodile ... that needed aid.

We watched the fleet set sail for home. And once they were out of sight, we climbed back into our train, pointed it towards the bridge, and fifty of us started back, a faster, easier way with three children, all of us in hopes their families survived.

****

We halted at the Devon border with Somerset. Lexi's family had been making a place near the old railway line; she'd been there only a year previous and could guide us. We stopped at a tiny halt and, leaving over half of us to guard the train, the children, Liz, Maureen, and I, with another fifteen people, headed on foot to where Lexi believed her family would be camped about a mile away. We came through the screen of bushes, Lexi saw the expected vehicle roofs, screamed, and took off running, yelling names as she ran.

We ran after and caught up with her barely a minute after she reached the clearing and halted to stare in numb-faced shock. The family vehicles were there — windows broken, doors hanging from their hinges. Lexi bolted for the nearest, Liz behind her, and when she paused at the doorway, it was Liz who put gentle arms around her. Maureen and I looked past them. Bones on the floor. The fittings smashed, drawers and cupboards open; you could see from spaces where items had been taken.

Lexi broke free, running from vehicle to vehicle, gasping, shouting names, begging them to be there — and all through the circle of vehicles, there was no answer.

Liz caught her once she slowed. "Come with me."

Lexi obeyed, her face and eyes blank, her body shaking. I put our people on guard, spaced out some distance back, while Maureen, Liz, and I searched. It looked as if they'd been taken by surprise. I looked at Maureen and spoke quietly.

"Lexi was taken collecting firewood. I wonder if they saw

her walking, grabbed her, then realized there must be others around. Maybe the one that got her took her on a ways, while the rest of them hit her camp."

"Wouldn't bikers have taken some of what I think is missing?" Maureen asked.

"No, but there'd be locals, probably after rabbits. If they came across this, they'd salvage," I said.

Maureen made a sound like a snarl. "Pigs, they could at least have buried them." I agreed, we did in such cases, but that was our decision, that where we salvaged a fair bit, we buried the original owners. It felt right, but maybe whoever had found the Smiths hadn't cared. There was nothing here, nothing to be salvaged, and only death and destruction to see. But we could do Lexi's family a final service, and maybe there was something left. I'd read several books, by and about the Romany, and it was possible … at least no floors had been torn up.

Maureen and I, once I mentioned that, returned to the vehicles. There we studied the floors in the back living quarters. Maureen found a faint crack, produced the wicked little knife she carried, and pried. The square came up, and under that was a compartment. About nine inches deep and about one and a half by two and a half feet in width and breadth. I took the sack I had and shovelled everything into it. There were three vehicles, each had an underfloor compartment, and each of those was at least half full.

I took them to our carriage section, tucked them under our seat and returned, speaking to our people. "These bodies were Lexi's family. Who agrees they should be buried and given a decent farewell?"

It was unanimous. We took it in turns to dig a long single trench. Into that we placed what remained of the bodies, each with those from the same vehicle. The boy watched, his lips quivering, and finally, he went over and sat, his arms about Lexi who leaned against him. Jess sat on her other side while they comforted each other. While most of us dug, two went hunting for an empty farmhouse, with certain instructions from Maureen.

Once we had everyone laid in the trench, the two salvagers having returned, Maureen took what they'd brought and laid out the quilts and bedspreads over the remains. They were bright still, a brave show, and something that would be easier to remember. Liz brought Lexi and her friends, and they stood there, looking down. I saw glances in my direction, and I knew I should speak. I wasn't sure what to say, so I hoped like hell it'd be right when I opened my mouth and talked.

I don't remember any of what I said. Maureen told me later I'd had most of them in tears. Apparently from somewhere, I'd recalled Binyon's poem *For the Fallen and* recited it. Then I said Lexi was ours from now on, that she was Lexi Smith, daughter of the Manor, but then she should never forget her own either. Plus a few other things. Then, as he had once before, the boy took a step forwards and sang.

> *The Romani came to our Good Lord's Yetta,*
> *And oh, but they sang sweetly,*
> *They sang so sweet and so very complete,*
> *That down came our Lord's fair lady.*

I knew the song, although I wondered where the boy had heard it — perhaps from Lexi herself. I'd read it in a collection of papers from a Folklore Society. It was sometimes called "The Song of Johnny Faa," and the Society had believed it to be a very old song, based perhaps on a real incident. He finished, the final lines ringing into the silence. Liz took Lexi to the train, and one by one, we moved the rusted derelict vehicles to stand in a long line over the trench.

The rest of us went back to the train, fired it up, and left. Lexi fell asleep, into something that looked more like an escape than anything. We let her sleep until we halted near where we estimated Jess's family to be closest to the lines. We heated food by the fireboxes, woke Lexi to eat, and she had something, if not much. I produced my salvage from her family's wagons and laid it out for her on several of the carriage table tops.

"This is your inheritance. Whoever came to your camp to steal was cheated. They never thought to look where Maureen and I did, so we found this for you, to keep, to remember. When you see your family again, you will be able to say that what they valued, you had from them and valued too."

She went through it, item by item, pausing now and again to explain something. A shawl that had been her grandmother's, a knife that had come down the generations, and was said to have come from their homeland. A beautiful flute handmade from bamboo. She exclaimed at that when she unwrapped it from the handkerchief. "That's mine. My uncle carved it for my tenth birthday."

There were other things; tears trickled down her face, but they were tears of remembering, love, sorrow, and healing. And once she'd seen everything, they were stowed away, she ate a little more and fell asleep in Liz's arms. I had more wood gathered, set guards, let the engines' steam die down, and retired to sleep as well. It was likely that tomorrow would be another long day, though not as distressing, I hoped.

CHAPTER FOURTEEN

With morning, Jess was able to tell us where we were. "Our farm's five miles from here, that way," she pointed. "You can see it from the rise."

Five miles. I wasn't doing that on foot when it could be avoided. We broke out all of the electric bicycles, and in a column of three abreast we rode to the top of the rise, to where below we could see that our journey here would not have an unhappy ending. There were animals in the fields. One field was planted in what looked like oats, and smoke came from the farmhouse chimney. I also noticed that the animals looked thin, and the oat field sparse—my hand shot out to clamp on handlebars the second I registered occupancy.

"No, Jess. It's a year since you were there. If you go in screaming, someone could think they're attacked and shoot you. We ride in slowly, everyone stops a distance back, you get off the bike, and walk the rest of the way, shouting for your mum and dad. Let them have the time to see it's you and that you aren't a prisoner."

That was what we did, that was what they saw, and then two people in the forefront were the ones doing the screaming and running. After that, we were all but dragged inside the farmhouse, and everyone, including the dogs, were kissing us while people talked over each other, and the dogs barked us almost deaf.

Finally, things calmed down a little and Jess told what had happened to her, how she'd been rescued, how we'd killed her kidnappers, and how we'd brought her back.

Her mother stood up. "We owe you more than we can repay. If we have anything you would like, take it."

Liz looked at them. "I'm a doctor. If any of you would like me to check over you, I'd be happy to do that." She grinned. "No charge."

Since they'd seen no doctor since just after the virus killed theirs there was a happy mutter of acceptance, and while Liz started cheeking patients, I took Jess's oldest brother aside. "Mr. Ruxton, how well are you doing here? Really?"

"Call me Rowan," he said absently. "And tell you the truth, not so well. This place's been in the family for six generations, and it never was that fertile. My grandmother brought money into the line, and that kept us well enough until my generation. We bought fertilizer, lime an' such, and we managed. Now we've no money to buy, it isn't there if we could, no one can haul it here anyway, and why would they when we can't pay? It's been getting worse since the virus, and I dunno what to do."

I smiled. "Mr. Ruxton. I know where there's good fertile land, no one owning it. I knew people who'd help you move there, and about the only thing you couldn't take is the house — and the one there is larger and comes with cottages."

We stayed three days, talking, discussing, and looking at maps I had. The Ruxtons would grieve to leave their house. They'd miss the familiar, but Rowan and Mrs. Ruxton sat them down, told the truth, and after three days, they all agreed. During times like these, they couldn't afford to cling to sentiment and starve. We'd continue our journey; then we'd return in a couple of months. By then, they'd have most of what they owned gathered up. We'd come with the train, pack it all into that, and they'd start a new life near the Manor.

Jess was ecstatic. Still more so when it was decided that to be certain it was the right move to the right place, her brother, Vail, and her mother, Shanna, could come with us. They could look over empty farms, read the dairies of Thorne's family — most of which continually mentioned the weather, and after a month, they could go home and report to make a final decision.

They joined us the fourth morning. The train pulled out,

heading for where the girls had been certain must be the area of the boy's farm, or village, or home in some way anyhow. It was between Bodmin and Saltash. We stopped after what was quite a short trip—engines don't tire, and the lines in this case were more direct. The boy looked about and shrugged. If they were right, he remembered nothing, I wondered if that were true, or if he didn't want to. However, we mounted bicycles and set off in groups of half a dozen, leaving the girls and some of our people on guard at the train.

We had no luck to begin with. Place after place, where their occupants denied knowing the boy, and he showed no recognition. Not of anything. Then we came to a hamlet, twelve houses, a single shop, and what looked to have been an inn or B'n'B of some sort. There the boy calmly dismounted from his bicycle, walked to a door, and used the knocker. A woman opened the door, stared at him, and then started to close it again. He shoved back.

I hastily intervened. "Do you know this young man?"

"Sorta."

"How?" I demanded.

"He were kid to my sister's husband. Been married before, her man had. All but this 'un caught that virus and died. We didn't want him. Next thing we know, he's gone anyways. You found him, you keep him mister, 'cause he weren't nothin' but trouble and expense, and we ain't taking him back." And to the boy, "You heard me, Kerry, let go'a' that door, and clear out."

Then, for the first time we heard the boy speak in a clear, quite educated voice." I don't know why you wouldn't want me, you found me so *useful*, you worked me like a dog, fed me *just* like one, and I slept on sacks in the washhouse. You stole everything my parents owned, including my mother's jewellery, dad's car, and everything they had with them. You said my dog was useless, and you shot him. I want everything back if I have to leave."

The woman had gone red, white, and red again in turns. Now she spluttered wordlessly as Maureen walked forward with Liz at her side, both carrying guns. Liz looked Kerry's step-aunt in the eye.

"I believe him, and so does my friend here. You'll give him everything that belonged to his parents, and he goes with us. He'll live with me and with Lexi; I'll be their Aunt Liz, and he'll have a family again. An aunt and a cousin, and one day, I hope what you've done to him happens to you."

Maureen took her up. "Open that door, lady. We'll walk through every room. You heard us. Kerry, anything you see that honestly belonged to your parents, you pick up and bring out."

"No," the aunt tried again to shut the door.

Maureen levelled the gun. "Shut that another inch, and I'll shoot through it if I have to. Now, get it open, let us three in, or you'll get the first shot anyhow."

It didn't take long. Kerry knew everything that had belonged to his stepmother and his father, scooped it up, and walked on. The main bedroom was left until last. I was on the women's heels, and I saw how Maureen circled it. They went there finally. Liz marched to the dresser, opened a leather covered box, and held it out. "How much of this belonged to your mother?" Kerry sifted out about half and stood holding it. "What else do you know they had that isn't here — apart from your dog?"

He sent a look of hate to his aunt. "They had cash, she took it all, got their cards, and got as much more as she could from the money machine. Spent it in the shop, got trolley after trolley-full. She took my step-mum's clothes, and Dad's too, and his computer."

"Right." Liz picked up the jewellery box, handing it to Maureen. "We'll call what's left in this as even for the money." She marched to the double wardrobe, whipped open the door, and smiled slowly. "As for the clothes…" She took a leather coat, a fur coat, walked to the next bedroom, turned to the drawers, and added everything in Kerry's size up to two higher Most were new in original wrapping, Underpants, shirts, t-shirts, jumpers, trousers, jeans, and track pants. "Fair swap for the clothing, I bet you never paid for any of this anyhow. You'll just have to go looting again, won't you?"

She walked out of the bedroom, heading for the front door, while Maureen kept an eye on the enraged aunt. Kerry was grinning. The look of someone who's getting his own back to a level he'd never have expected.

No one, if there were others witnessing this, did anything to prevent it. Not that this surprised me. If she was like that to others, they were probably enjoying the show almost as much as Kerry. Liz and Maureen swept out, Kerry between them as they reached the outside. They carried what they had to the bicycles and distributed it between several trailers. Then Liz looked at the aunt where she stood in the cottage doorway.

She spoke formally and in measured cadence. "A curse on you, may nothing you eat nourish you, may nothing you drink ease your thirst. May you be treated as you treated Kerry, and when you die, may you be food for the birds and beasts. I curse you, by a straight line and a crooked, by sea and by land, by earth and air, from the scalp of your head to the soles of your feet, may you die in pain, in fear, in misery, and alone."

She stepped onto her bicycle, Kerry on his bike beside her as they started down the road. As I reached for my own cycle, I saw that the aunt was shivering violently. I hid a grin. Heaven alone knew where Liz had got that from, but the aunt seemed to believe in it, and I knew if somebody did believe, a curse could be surprisingly effective. The remainder of our people fell in behind us as we returned to the train. Mission accomplished, if not as we'd hoped, still it seemed to have satisfied the boy we now knew as Kerry. That'd do nicely.

****

Once back at the rail line area closest to the Manor, we disembarked. People took their own backpacks home, while several of us carried Kerry's reparations to Liz's cottage and surgery. I made a mental note to add a couple of extras to it, for storage and bedrooms. Then I left her to sort out her expanded family while I trotted to see Mic. She'd been on the ship to shore radio and looked up as I came in.

"They'll be in Falmouth tomorrow mid-morning, barring problems." I hugged her hard. "What's that for?"

"For not being Kerry's aunt?"

She grinned up. "Maureen said something about that. Now that you're here, you can give me the whole story."

Over a meal, we took in it turns to do that, and once we were done, Mic sniffed. "I can see both sides, I suppose. She got landed with a boy who was no relation; it sounds as if he's different from her family in practically everything, and she felt him an unfair responsibility. I'd think he made no attempt to fit in either. Don't assume you two, that it was all on one side. And there's something odd about the timeline too."

I sat up. "Hell, yes, that never dawned on me. They only had him a year or so before that Raver grabbed him. So where were his parents and what were they doing up to then? Turns out he's fifteen."

"Exactly. Don't ask him though, Hugh; get Doc Di or Liz to talk to him. Just the occasional question. Let it come out as naturally as possible. But we need to know." I raised my eyebrows, and my grandmother added, "Just in case. Some lies or things left out are harmless." Her voice hardened. "Some aren't. Not knowing can be dangerous."

A number of possibilities flashed through my mind and, from the look on her face, through Maureen's as well. I'd been automatically seeing Kerry as the complete victim because of the circumstances in which we'd found him. He quite possibly was, then again … I'd talk to Doc Di and Liz about it, and see what they said, what they could discover. And without making a song and dance about it, I'd talk to Thorne as soon as they got back, and he had a spare hour.

Meanwhile, while we'd been gone, those remaining had been putting in another storage unit, a large underground place disguised as a hill, with a scatter of larger and smaller boulders over it. They were partially embedded and designed to prevent outsiders from riding or driving over the hill. It had been started before our trip, and the Manor people worked on it when they had time. Now it was almost complete, and we could start filling it when the ships landed.

The ships came into Falmouth when expected, and we were incredibly busy for several weeks. I found time, as did Mic and Maureen, to take Jess's older brother, Vail, and her mother, Shanna, over the surrounding countryside, empty farmhouses, and fields. I saw them noticing the fertility of the land, and the feral livestock. Shanna queried that.

"I've seen cows, horses, goats, a few sheep. Don't you do anything with them?'

"What?" I looked at her.

"Catch them, shoot them for meat."

"Anyone farming has all the farm stock they can handle. We do shoot a few for meat, usually yearling males if it's for us, old animals for the dogs. But it's Thorne's policy to leave them mostly alone. He says they're a bank. We don't need the land they graze, and if our numbers increase, then we can catch the young quality ones and domesticate them again at no cost apart from the work."

Shanna nodded. "Sense," she commented, and dropped the subject to pick up another. "Before the plague, we were living in three places. What if we want at least two again here?"

I shrugged. "Pick them. If you can farm the land, no one cares."

And so, when they reported back, the Ruxtons gathered everything they could move, apart from the old rambling farmhouse, and came to join us officially. Vail had often taken an electric cycle, one of those with fat deep-tread cross-country tires and using that, he'd gone, or so I believe—looking for a specific spot—and found it. I never told him, but it was the one we'd had in mind for them. The Ruxtons emerged from the train, were driven to the Manor, met Thorne and the Manor Council, and put their case.

Our council at that time comprised Thorne as head, Mic, Maureen, and me, with Jake and Annie, Dave, the electrician; Paddy, the plumber's wife, Joy, and either Doc Di, Liz, or both, depending on who had time to attend. We had supplemented that with one girl and one boy from the older children. The limit was twelve to eighteen. They often thought laterally and could ask questions that hadn't occurred to us adults.

Thorne started. "This is our reference map, within the blue line are the lands of the Manor area we claim directly. Beyond that, marked in green, out to the red zone are the lands we count as only to be settled by friends. Those have a claim on us for assistance. Beyond that, if you settle in the red zone there, you owe us nothing, but nor do we owe you."

"Owe? As in?"

"Assistance, basically. If you settle in the green zone and you're attacked, send for help, we'll come. Suffer a devastating fire, we'll help rebuild. If there's a drought or flood and we can do something for you, we will."

I saw that sink in. Shanna looked at her son, Rowan, and he nodded. "If we choose a place in the green zone, do we owe anything for the land and the buildings already there?"

"No. In fact, once you'd chosen and settled there, it's likely one of us will call for an aid day. That means," he added as he saw the question in their faces. "That you can make a list of work that needs to be done as fast as possible. We'll post that on the community noticeboard. Some of our people will — as they choose–no obligation on either side — gather tools and materials and come to your place for a day or possibly two, to help you get that done." He smiled at Shanna, who smiled back. Thorne took in a breath. "Now, have you chosen a home, and where?"

Shanna produced a crudely drawn map of her own and placed it alongside ours, placing a forefinger on a small circle. "Here. Vail's gone over it a couple of times. He says, from what papers he could find, it was bought back in the early two-thousands by a family from Hampshire. They pooled their money and liked the place because it had a main farmhouse and three cottages. Cottages are far enough out of each other's shadow so those in them have privacy, but close enough to be comfortably near family."

Thorne studied both maps. "How much land do you estimate?"

"Original farm was two hundred acres"

"And now we're going back to lighter electrical machinery and more hand-power; that's about what you can manage." He met her look directly. "You had a larger family than we knew, Mrs. Ruxton?"

"We did. When you came that first time, I had some of them nip out the back and stay away. Didn't know who you were, then you gave us back our Jessie, and we thought you likely to be good folks, but times aren't what they were, so I stayed cautious. I make no apologies for waiting to be certain."

There was a concerted chuckle from the council, and Jake spoke. "No, we think the better of you, first that you were careful, and then that you trust us a bit more now."

"Then all's well. Now…" Shanna said. "I'll tell you who's who and a little history so's you know us. I'm Shanna Ruxton, mother and grandmother to my family. I wed early, my husband's long dead, accident near thirty years ago, but the farm we had was mine, anyway. I was an only child. Mum and Dad both had some money; they came of farming blood, and when they wed, they used their money to expand the farm. When my grandparents died, they left the farm to them officially, and some money they had as well, and my parents bought more land." She smiled. "As my dad used to say, 'They aren't making land anymore; buy it now.'"

She waited out the amusement before continuing. "A year before he died, my husband won a fair bit of money in the pools, and we used that to add a bit more land and upgrade some of the stock and farm machinery. By then we had two hundred acres. I had children. Rowan, my eldest, stayed to farm. My

Maisie and her family died in London start of the plague. We had a final zoom call from them. Said our goodbyes, wept for our kin, said how much we loved each other. Maisie had pills they could take. We watched them lie down, all together, and we sang them to sleep." I could imagine it and felt sorrow.

"After Rowan and Maisie, I had twin lads, then another girl after I wasn't expecting any more. The boys were still playing the field, but Jannie was engaged. Her fellow was a nice lad; his mum wasn't married, but she did later and had two more kids, older girl, younger boy. They got the early sickness."

Ah, that explained the small group I'd seen onto the train. A woman in her early twenties, a man of similar age, but the two children with them were around eleven or twelve, and there was no way the older pair were their parents. No, the kids would be his younger siblings. But what happened to their parents? I heard now.

"Kids got that infection, but they were away at a camp. Camp took such things seriously. Parents signed a consent form, camp took the kids to the local surgery, and they had allodaxin. But by the time they came home, they were right over it." We understood the unspoken part after that. The children had survived; the parents had died. "About that time, one of the local kids got it too. Jess picked it up from them, Jannie's Alex was staying, and we all got it. His parents died when the worse plague hit. He packed up the kids and brought them to us, went back with Rowan, Jannie, and me, and farm trucks, and brought back everything they could move."

She produced a sheet of paper. "This is how we figure. I'm taking the main house with Rowan—he was divorced. His wife phoned when she was dying, and he went and got his kids—that's Gary, Trix, and Hamish. All well into their teens now. That'll be us five in there. In one cottage, Jannie and Alex, with his brother and sister." She chuckled softly. "Parents may have thought it funny, but they're Joe and Jo, Jonas, and Josie. Cottage two are my lads, forties and still not wed, and now it may be unlikely. Vail and Ben—short for Benjamin."

She sighed. "Then there's our Jess. Best to be truthful here, but I'd thank you to say nothing in front of her or the others. Rowan's her dad, although she thinks he's her oldest brother. She's never looked at dates and years nor when my husband died. After his divorce, Rowan had a fling with a girl on holiday. Went on the two weeks she was about, then she went home. A year later, she phoned, said she'd had his daughter, was getting married, and her fiancée didn't want some other man's bastard. Rowan drove over there, took the baby, brought her home, and she's been mine ever since. Whatever, she's Jess Ruxton, born and bred, and she's *ours.*" Her eyes were fierce, and Thorne nodded.

This meeting, as sometimes happened, the junior twosome wasn't here, and I thought that was good. Kids can be cruel to other kids even here, and it would be better this wasn't known to children who might lose their temper and taunt without thinking.

"So," Shanna summed it up. "We have a spare cottage for whoever marries next. And right now, there's twelve of us, thirteen really, I guess. She'll be living with me. That's Peaches. Found her walking along the road about a week into the plague. Far as we could tell from what she said, she was sort of an unwanted kitten; you know how city folk can drive into the country and just dump them?"

We all nodded, and Doc Di glared. "Bloody townies, dump a cat convinced it'll be fine. Seen enough dying to know they're often wrong."

"Yes. She'd have been about five, we think. Probably brain damage when she was born, she looks completely normal until you talk to her a while. Then you see. She's a sweet child, always kind, happy, and good with animals. I guess her family decided that she'd be too much of a burden when things went to pot, and they took her out into the country and dropped her off."

Shanna looked as if she wanted to spit. "'What the eyes don't see,' as my granny always said, 't'heart don't grieve over;' no imagination as to what it's be like for Peaches probably. She had a little pink backpack with a spare pair of socks, and under-pants, a tin opener, and a few tins, couple of meat-paste sand-wiches, and a bottle of coke and one of homemade lemonade."

Doc snarled. "And when she'd finished that, she could just lie down and die quietly. Or be picked up by some man who'd think all his luck had come at once, no law, and a little girl with no parents to yell about it."

Shanna looked at her. "Yes. I've a fair idea where Peaches lived. If I ever get over that way, me and Rowan and my lads would really like to—meet them." I had a definite feeling a "meet-ing" wasn't what she had in mind, and the family who'd dumped Peaches would regret it—if Shanna or any of the Ruxtons ever *did* make it over that way.

We ended the meeting with Shanna's family in agreed possession of the land and buildings they'd chosen. They were about seven miles from the edge of Manor land, and we'd start moving them there in the morning. Again, it was a busy week or so, but the Ruxtons settled in, and we had thirteen more allies, should anything bad happen. On the reverse, they had around a thousand, and I know Shanna was happy about that.

****

Winter came, the year turned over, went around several times, and we celebrated the twentieth year since the plague. Mic had been sixty-one that year, now she would be eighty-one. Life and death went on. Merr was still with Doc Di, although his adored cat Mally had died five years ago. Kerry and Lexi had married, had a cottage and ten acres, and had set up a system of keeping track of livestock breeding, and between what they grew and raised, and what they got in payment for records, they were managing very well.

Kaiser had died, and we missed him, Mic most of all. Her cats were still with her, cats usually live longer than large dogs, and Kaiser had managed a very good age for his type. But Jason was going, another year we thought, and we'd mourn him too. Willow had been a kitten when Mic took him in and he might have another three years, more if we were fortunate. Doc Di had had two cats when she joined us. Happily, they had been quite young, now Spitfire and Merlin were in their twenties, and it was clear to everyone that they, too, would be crossing the rainbow bridge soon.

There'd been other pets gone as well. It had become a custom, if one wished, and if your pet had been particularly loved, to take a fruit tree or nut tree sapling out of common stock, dig a deep hole, place your pet in that, then plant the sapling over them. Sometimes the tree was on the person's land, sometimes in the communal orchard. But the custom had grown to where many loved pets were remembered that way. Kaiser lay under an apple tree, Willow and Jason, when their times came, would lie under walnut trees.

****

A year later, we knew someone had moved into our vicinity. Whether by accident or they'd known something, they were well outside the Manor's lands *and* beyond our friend zone, too, so we ignored them. If they cared to come to the Manor gates, we'd greet them pleasantly; until then, we didn't care that much. That changed abruptly the early morning that Jess came riding in, eyes desperate. Our two guards saw her coming, knew Jess, and saw it was urgent; they had the gates open before Jess reached them. She thundered through, was off her horse, and grabbing my arm as I ran up to ask the trouble.

"Peaches, she's gone missing. She went out to pick blackberries yesterday afternoon, she never came home. Hugh, she's been gone *all night*."

That could be an accident, some sort of animal attack, or Peaches had picked until the was tired and fell asleep in the sun. It had been a warm night, too, and she could be just now waking up to head home. On the other hand, like pretty much everyone, I liked Peaches, and then, there'd been Jess...

Jess was shaking my arm. "Hugh, what if it's like me?"

That was the other thing that had occurred to me. "Come

in. I want to see on a map where you think she went." Maureen had come to see what the fuss was about and heard enough, better not to waste time came to my mind. "Maureen, call out the Manor Guard. Ask Liz or Doc Di if they can come, and make sure everyone in the guard is well-armed — just in case. Oh, and put a hand-guard on the gates." *Hand-guard* had become common slang for five men with a sixth in charge.

She went off at a trot, and I took Jess to Thorne, a quick explanation, and we were looking at a map he pulled out of the map cabinet and flicked open across the table. It showed Manor lands and those out in a circle to about a hundred miles of us.

Jess put her finger on their cluster of farmhouse and cottages. "We're there. Peaches, if she goes blackberrying, usually goes that way." She traced a line with a forefinger.

Doc Di had come in. "I'll be coming with you, Now, Jess. Is Peaches the only one that picks?" Jess shook her head. "If it's been a number of you, would there be that many berries left in that spot? If not, where would be the next place she'd be most likely to go?"

Jess looked stunned. "Never thought about that. No, I'd reckon we've about picked that spot clean. There's a couple of other places, but..." She frowned and thought. "Peaches doesn't know them well; they're a bit tricky to get to, and one's dangerous. If she was going to another place, this is most likely where she'd go." She indicated a place on the map about five miles past their holdings and lower down.

My gaze met Thorne's. That was on the boundary between friend zone and into red. Beyond it, there was that group who'd moved in. Our people, our council — and Thorne — weren't idiots. We'd scouted them, we knew exactly where they were — they'd never seen us — and we knew there were eighteen of them, give or take one or two coming and going. The thing that had struck Maureen and I when we went quietly to scout them one evening a month after their arrival, was that there seemed to be no women, not a single one. Either it was a commune of gay men, or — something else.

Thorne, who'd heard what we thought at the time, looked at us. "Jess, you go and chose another horse. Yours is probably too wiped out to go back immediately, more so if we're in a hurry. Go now, get his saddle and gear off, sort out a replacement, and saddle it ready." She went, and he sat looking weary as his door closed behind her

"If one of them picked up Peaches, he probably thought she's ordinary to start with. By now, they'll know she isn't. And since she's in her late twenties, and it's a long time since the plague, that means — if any of them have thought about it — someone's looked after her all this time, loved, and cared for her. In which case, they *will* come looking. We have a choice to consider before we move out; do we ride over, just a couple of us, and ask if they're seen her or…"

Doc Di cut in. "Won't work. If they didn't take her, they won't have seen her, and that's what they'll say. If they took her, they still won't stand there and admit one of their people kidnapped her to rape. Probably for gang rape. Either way, we don't get the truth, and don't know if they have her. We have two choices. We don't go to them, instead we hunt all over for her, and if we don't find her anywhere, we accept she's gone by some accident, and walk away."

Both Thorne and I hissed through our teeth, and Doc Di grinned. "Thought not. Then again, we have two choices. We take fifty guards and say politely that we're there to search the place. They can stand aside or fight; if we find Peaches, they're packing up and leaving the area. If we don't. we'll pay generous reparations." Her smile was savage. "How they react will tell us a lot. If they don't have her and genuinely know nothing, if they're smart, they'll smile and let us in."

"And if they have her or worry we'll spot something, that tells us that," Thorne concluded. "They'll try to put us off guard, then attack once they think we're fooled."

We rode out in an hour, seventy strong, not counting the Doc, and Kaiser's several times grandson. The first female in the line had been a Staffordshire Terrier, the much loved and gentle dog of a family who'd joined us in the third year. The one with Doc, six years old now and named Vilhelm, had been trained by Doc. He lived with his family usually, but for search and rescue, he was her partner and had proved his value more than once. He rode comfortably in her electric cycle's trailer until he was needed, and from his tongue-lolling grin, he knew this was work. Those of us who rode were armed to the hilt; it was work for us too.

I glanced at my windup watch — salvage from the Police Lost Property in Brighton years back. It was just after ten, a cool cloudy morning, a good day for a fight, and if this group thought we wouldn't take them on, they were much mistaken. Thorne had given clear orders; we'd made a stop on the way that could make some difference, and if the fortunes of war were with us, this bunch should all bend over right now.

We reached the area where the group lived; we had scouts well ahead and all around us as well who reported there was no one about on the land near us, but ahead at the sprawling pile of buildings, men were outside. As the scout said:

"Don't know if it's us they're expecting, but they're expecting someone."

There was a chuckle that ran through the whole group, and someone commented dryly, "Good, wouldn't want them disappointed." That raised a louder laugh.

We were a mile from them when Thorne signalled. Jess and ten of her family rode ahead, down to the buildings at a slow walk, a white flag on a pole flying from where Jess held it. Doc Di had dismounted, and now she and Vilhelm quartered the land in a circle around the buildings, far enough and behind enough natural cover that they wouldn't be seen. Vilhelm worked in two ways, loud or silent; today he was silent, but we all saw his reaction, as in a line with their gate and the clump of blackberries four miles back where Peaches had almost certainly gone to pick,

Vilhelm jerked to a halt.

He sniffed, moved a pace forward, and sniffed again. Doc called him to her softly, rewarded him, and looked up at us sitting motionless.

"She's there."

Thorne nodded. And to us, his voice was low but clear. "Pass the word. We wait to see if they tell Jess and her kin that Peaches is there. If they deny it, our plan stands. Wait, we attack only if they attack the Ruxtons or if the Ruxtons return and say they've been told no one in that place has seen Peaches or knows anything about her." There was more to it of course, and we prepared. The Ruxtons' Jess and her flag in the lead were on the way back. Our scouts spread out to watch, and Jess cantered up.

"They swear they've seen no one of Peaches's description. Not ever, they regret her loss and hope she is found safe and well." Her fierce eyes met ours. "What do you say?"

Doc Di spoke then. "Vilhelm sure he says she came walking towards their gate. He doesn't say she went through because we can't alert them by coming that close. But for myself, I'd point out one thing. That if she got so close as that, then they saw her; when they say they never saw her, I believe they lie."

Thorne spoke. "You have your orders. Plan B. *Now!*" The last word was a hiss, which carried to all of us, but little further. We obeyed; below if all went well, they'd swallowed that those who'd left, went believing. And we didn't fight battles for glory, for trumpets, and flying flags. We fought to win. We held our positions out of sight and waited for a signal.

CHAPTER FIFTEEN

The signal came, and we moved forward. No hurry until the enemy raised their alarm. I was surprised how long that took. Did they all go to have tea and cake once the Ruxtons left? Were they *that* satisfied they'd fooled them? Or was it that they never bothered to keep proper guard? We were halfway down the slope when someone within their gates yelled. It was all we needed. In a complete circle around their rotting stronghold, we closed at full speed. Two of us hit the gates with the ram we carried between our mounts—and went through them as if they were paper. In fact, as I saw later, the state they were in, paper might have resisted more.

Doc Di had Vilhelm on a leash, nose to the ground; he was following the trail through the gates, ignoring everything else. Yup. No doubt Peaches *had* come, or been brought, here. He was running hot, and the guards watching over him and Doc Di were hard put to keep up. We'd dismounted, left our horses to those whose job it was to hold them, and, forming a flying wedge ahead of Di and Vilhelm, we went forward as we slashed and shot our way. Through the main door before it could be closed. We were in.

CHAPTER SIXTEEN

I don't know how much experience they'd had; maybe they were more used to hit and run tactics, or to flitting out of the night to kill an unprepared family before they were sufficiently awake to defend themselves. Or, and more likely as part of their strategy, they were used to having the numbers. Here and now, they had none of that. We were awake, we had the numbers, and we were used to fighting separately or as a body. Moreover, there were few there who hadn't met and liked Peaches, we knew what she was, and outrage fuelled our determination.

We fought, we killed, we left the dead, dying, and crippled behind us, and as we moved deeper into the building, a chant arose led by Thorne and picked up by all who fought with us. "*Kernow, Kernow, Kernow bys vyken!*" It was a chant we knew, but it had never been used in battle before. Here and now, it was a declaration. "Cornwall, Cornwall, Cornwall forever!" A statement, that we would not allow evil into our lands, that we would fight to drive it out. And we did fight.

Until there was no one in front of us, until Vilhelm halted at a locked door in a far corner of the place and gave forth his own triumphant cry in canine of, "I've found her, I've found her, she's here!" And Billy Harker raised the battleaxe he preferred for close combat and took the door down with a single crashing blow against the lock.

Vilhelm had been right. Jess flung herself past Billy and was on her knees beside the bruised and bloody woman lying under the shuttered window. "Peaches? Peaches? Say something to me." The swollen mouth opened.

"Wot you wan' me to say, Jessie?"

Jess hugged her. "I just wanted to hear your voice. Oh, we're all so happy you're alive, lovey."

"Thirsty?" Someone passed a waisted bottle forward; it was common knowledge Peaches was a fiend for Coco-Cola. Shanna only let her have the sugarless type usually, but I think we all felt this one time, something else would be acceptable. Peaches drained it in five gulps. "Good." She leaned on Jess's arm and staggered to her feet. "Knew you'd find me. They said no one would come. I tole them they were stupid. Gran Shanna says it: 'You never leave family behind.'" And in those words, I could hear the echo of Shanna Ruxton's voice.

Jess was handed a wet piece of material and slowly, carefully cleaned Peaches's face. "There, you look a lot better. Who hit you, lovey?"

Peaches being Peaches, she took this as a request to start from the beginning and did. "Went blackberrying. Near bushes were all picked out, I knew where next big patch was, so I walked. There was this man when I got there. He said he knew where there were much better blackberries, lots more and bigger, better taste, real juicy, said my family would love them." We were listening, and I could feel a wave of fury growing and thought it not unique to me.

"He brought me here, said he'd get some coke for us before we went picking. Once I was inside, he grabbed at me. He hurt, and I bit him. I bit him real hard, Jess. He yelled, and two other men came running, I dunno why they said something about teaching me. Rowan teaches me, he learned me to count to twenty, to read those books you got when you were little, an' to milk Bet an' Honey. They weren't doing that. So I bit him, too, and I kicked the other one." There were murmurs of approval, and amusement.

Thorne asked a question and gave an order, and half a dozen of us, Doc Di and Vilhelm in tow, went looking. We were successful after we tossed out any loving kindness. When we came back, our three captives yelling, demanding to be let go, and then falling silent as they saw Peaches who stared back at them.

Thorne spoke gently. "Peaches, which man brought you here, and who were the other two who hurt you?"

She pointed without hesitation. "That man, he lied, there weren't blackberries here. An' the other two, they tore my clothes. I bit that one, too, an' I kicked *him*." Her forefinger singled them out in turn. All three broke into a babble of protest.

"She wanted to come here."

"I never touched her."

"She's a liar, you can't believe her, she's a..."

Jess's fist cut the final words or words short. "She's my sister. And if she's a liar, why do two of you have her teeth marks in your arms? And you, where'd you kick him, Peaches?" A forefinger shot out again; Jess stepped forward, knife in hand, and grabbed the folds of trouser and sliced. Wrenching so a whole of the worn material portion tore away.

Someone whistled. "Got him a good one; that's a real recent bruise too."

Thorne nodded. "Hugh, you and Maureen are the only council here today. How do you both say?" Maureen's gaze met mine, filled with a sick disgust. She moved to hide her signal and looked at me. I repeated it, and her look was a grim approval. We turned to Thorne and both of us gave our verdict. Thumbs down.

"Take them outside." They were removed, even as they started yelling again.

There was the sound of footsteps, and a man entered our portion of the corridor. He had black hair going to silver at the temples. He was tall and had probably been lean and hard-muscled a few years ago. Now he'd started going to fat, and his face showed signs of self-indulgence. "I'm Douglas Southen, leader of this place. Now, who are you, what do you think you're doing, and once you've explained and apologized, you'll leave."

Thorne faced him. In a few sentences, he made plain what

had brought us here, what we were doing, and that we certainly would be leaving, but there were things that would happen before we did that. Southen opened his mouth, and Thorne looked him over in a way the produced abrupt silence.

"You had no more than twenty men here. I would say that over a dozen are dead, and the remainder are dying, or crippled. You have an hour to get any alive assembled outside your main gates. We'll allow you to take sufficient carts to remove the living together with food and drink for ten days. Before you ask, you're going north ultimately. Some of our people will go with you until you're far from our lands. Come back, and you'll be buried alive."

"Our clothing, our possessions…"

"Stay here."

While Douglas Southen tried to change Thorne's mind, we did as he'd told us to do. We scoured the buildings, bringing out bodies, those living we laid in a wagon. Apart from Douglas Southen, we found only two others of his men besides the three we held, and I doubted either would see another day. The bodies we stacked in the front room of the building and left them there.

Then we salvaged; much of what we found brought an enlightenment we could have done without. Doc Di found the only other survivors, or rather Vilhelm alerted her to their existence. He whined at a corner where the floor had rotted into a small hole. Di went on her stomach, shone one of our salvaged lights into the gap, and used a couple of words I'd rarely heard from her.

She stretched an arm down and came up with a cat. She must have been a large powerful cat once; now she looked like a skeleton with matted fur, and her eyes were already dulling as she lost her fight. Di said something worse, reached again, and produced a single kitten.

He'd been sired by some male still left of pedigree stock, I thought. Possibly British or Russian Blue, He too showed signs of being a large cat—if he lived—and while thin, he wasn't the skeleton his mother was. His fur was groomed, a rich silver-blue all over, except for white slippers on his front paws. His head was broad, his eyes a clear amber, and in my opinion, he'd be around five to six weeks old. He looked up at Di, then wobbled to his mother and rubbed his head against her. She licked him feebly, and Di scooped them against her.

"See if they have any non-cow milk in the kitchen, will you?"

I went there, found a small packet of soy milk powder, made that into a jugful, and warmed it against me as I hurried back. "Here." The kitten wasn't quite sure how to manage, but after a few minutes, he was hungry enough to lap at it. His mother didn't want it, didn't want anything but to lie in warm arms, under stroking hands. I nodded to her.

"She's known people."

"Maybe one of them liked cats and brought her here originally. Maybe he got killed, and after that, they just ignored her. She's starving, but there's no injures I can find." We took them outside and wrapped them in a blanket, just as Thorne was speaking to Southen.

"Get going."

Southen swore, gave him a vicious look, and flicked the horse into motion. Ten of our people went with him.

I spoke quietly to Thorne. "You know he'll come back, don't you? He'll go just as far as he needs to find another bunch like that, he'll feed them a long tale about how we're rolling in wealth and women, he could even claim it was all taken from him, so it'd be right to take it back. So long as he's alive and has what he'll regard as a right to this place and a grudge that you took it, he could come back any time."

"*So long as he's alive,*" Thorne repeated my words quietly.

My look met his, and I understood. Somewhere along the road, Southen would die. A hard decision to make, but for the sake of the Manor's people, he'd made it. But who would do it? I saw no one going with the man who'd be happy to execute him in cold blood. Thorne saw me wondering.

"He demanded good food and drink to take with him for the ten days as I'd promised. He's a greedy man, so I saw to it that our people had a large tin of hot chocolate powder, I said they should share it, at least one cup for him at night, but no more. He also has a tin of hot chocolate powder in his supplies as well, the more expensive type that's pre-sweetened and has milk power mixed in. He won't touch that so long as our people share theirs, but once they leave him, he'll drink that day and night until it's gone—*or until he is*." He emphasised the last four words, and I understood. He'd had something from Doc Di and mixed that into the powder.

"How long?"

"Di says his time will run out before the powder does. So it'll depend on how fast he drinks it, but what's in there is cumulative. And, as I said, he's a greedy man."

I'd seen Southen's rooms, the hoard of valuables, the items squirreled away. I'd bet he'd tucked a few into his clothing, no matter how he'd been watched. A windfall for whoever found the body. I nodded slowly. "What goes 'round, comes 'round. A smart leader stops trouble before it starts." We stood a moment, both understanding each other, until I remembered the cats and Di.

"Oh, and Di found two cats, I don't think the mother will make it, but she had a kitten." I looked to where Di cradled her foundlings. Thorne walked over to look at them.

"Dear Heaven, how long has it been since they ate?"

"Days at least," Di said sadly. "I think it's been several days since she could feed this kitten anyway."

"Yes, at his age he should look like a fuzzy little ball of fur; instead, he's, well, the word that comes to mind is 'lanky.' More like a teenage kitten." Di grinned.

"Perfect name. I'll call him Lancaster. After all, I've got Spitfire and Merlin already."

****

That led to a conversation with Kerry and Lexi several days later. "Why'd you call him Lanky?" Kerry asked as he teased the kitten with a feather.

"Because it matches with my other two."

Lexi looked puzzled. "I wondered about their names. I mean, Spitfire I got; any cat's a bit of a spitfire. But Merlin? And now Lanky? Am I missing something?"

Di nodded. "They came from long before your time, or mine, come to that." She went to her bookcase, took down a book, and laid it open on the table. "World War Two started in 1939 and continued until 1945. One of the main war machines were planes. One was the Spitfire. Spitfires had a higher victory-to-loss ratio during the war. In the Battle of Britain, Spitfires killed about two planes for every one of them shot down, and people remembered that. Pilots loved it, and it wasn't only used as a straight fighter. It could be a photo-reconnaissance, fighter-bomber, and trainer, and it kept being used years after the war was finished.

"The original plane was designed to use Merlin engines." Both children developed looks of sudden understanding. "Yes, that's where Merlin got *his* name. The Spitfire was so well built, that as it was it kept being used with more and more powerful Merlin engines for years after the war. Up to the plague, there was still over seventy of them still flying." She turned a page and pointed to a photo. "That's the Spitfire."

Kerry looked it, and his face fell into sad lines. "We'll never fly again, will we"

"Not in my generation," Di agreed. "Not in yours either, maybe not even in your grandchildren's. But the day *will* come again. That's why we have libraries, why we make new books. We have all the designs for planes from the start of them. One day we'll build them again, and we'll fly. We'll look down on rivers like thread on the land, seas like ripples, and forests like green fur."

"They really look like that, you saw them?" Lexi gaped.

"Yes, they were, and I did. Before the plague, probably almost everyone had been on a plane. All it took was money and booking a seat." She explained the process of booking. Kerry fell about.

"Wow, so you asked someone to put your name on a list, then you went to an airport place and just got on a plane." Di laughed. "Yes, it was simple." *Well, it had been,* she thought, *if the plane wasn't overbooked, if the weather wasn't really bad, if some other stupid problem hadn't come up.* In fact, she shouldn't complain; it'd been a stupid problem that'd saved her. She'd been booked to fly from Cornwall to stay with friends in Texas for five days. The plane had been *overbooked* in error—as the airline had put it—she'd let a mother flying home with a sick toddler take her seat. And while they waited, she'd cuddled the baby to let the mother use the toilet in peace.

The plane had left, the mother hugging her in gratitude at the last. Di had caught the next plane six hours later, a two-hundred-dollar voucher in hand for her generosity. She'd had a great time in Houston, but on the third day, she'd come down with a virus. Her friend's doctor had given her Allodaxin, and, doctor to doctor, discussed how effective it was. Back home again, Di had made inquiries about it, and a specialist friend had arranged for her to get some of the first generally available.

The delayed plane and that toddler had given her one half of the equation, the specialist friend the other. And the discussion with the Houston doctor had given her the impetus to obtain the drug, too, and then see that everyone around the Manor and in her practise was given it when the minor infection flared up a fortnight after she got home. Di stared out of the window; life was what happened while you were making other plans, and sometimes what life sent you was better, despite what you might think at the time—she'd been annoyed about the infection catching her in Houston.

"Doc Di? What about Lancaster?" Lexi was demanding, and Di turned the pages to point to another photo.

"That's the Lancaster. It was a four-engine heavy bomber developed just before that war. They wanted one for use everywhere, one that could carry a torpedo inside, and make shallow dive-bombing attacks." There was a pause while she explained some of what she'd said, adding, "The Lancaster had Merlin engines too."

Kerry paused in tickling the purring kitten. "You call him Lanky most of the time though"

"I do," Di laughed. "And Lancaster pilots often called their planes 'Lankys;' it was an affectionate nickname they used."

"Oh, I get it. So when Thorne said he was a lanky kitten, that's when you thought of calling him Lancaster?"

"Exactly."

The kitten fell asleep on Kerry's lap, and Di's smile was sad. They'd saved his mother, who'd been called Mum Cat, for the five more months she'd lived. Di believed the long period of starvation when she'd put everything she had into her kitten had damaged the cat's heart. She's been so happy however, with humans again who loved her, sleeping on their beds, with her kitten growing stronger by the day, and good food to eat.

But Di had seen what would be. And when one morning, she'd rolled over in bed and found Mum Cat unable to move, she'd cradled her in her arms for the hour it took for the cat to cross the bridge while Lanky lay beside his mother, and at the last she'd summoned strength to lick him, then Di's hand. She slept under a pear-tree sapling in the communal garden, and when his time came, Lanky would sleep beside her under another.

Di got up and went to start dinner. It was a price you paid. If you loved something, particularly a shorter-lived animal, sooner or later, you'd grieve their loss. She'd been asked by a patient once why she'd get another cat if she was so sad about losing that one? She'd given the only answer that had ever made sense to her: "Because the love I'll get will be worth more than the sorrow."

And, she remembered, her patient had gone away looking thoughtful. The next time she came, half a year later, she'd proudly shown Di photos of her new cat, a retiree from an Ocicat kennel. Old Meg Samuels had gone a year before the plague started. Her cat, Tai, had died only days before her. At least, wherever they were now, in Di's belief, they were together. She banished memories, dished up the food, and called the children.

****

The ten who'd escorted Southen north returned, and Jess reported to Thorne.

"We took him across country as far as Taunton. We stuck around a while and salvaged there since we'd come so far. No one about that we saw. Southen holed up in some fancy hotel, found someone's stash of food, and lay about eating that and drinking hot chocolate he got from somewhere, may have been in his supplies from us. I don't know. But that was all he did, eat, drink, and lie around. After a week, all the space anyone had available was full. So we decided to go the next day.

"I went to tell Southen we were off, and there he was, dead. Hadn't seen him the last couple of days, so I can't say when it happened. I dumped everything from his supplies that was open. Some kid might find it, and if it'd gone off, they could get sick. Didn't bury him. Didn't owe him the work, and the others agreed. We took him downstairs, tossed him in back of the hotel and left him. Dog packs will do the cleanup. That's it."

Thorne nodded. "Thanks, Jess. Here's a voucher each from the general stores for you and the others."

She left, the vouchers in one hand, while Thorne looked after her. He rather thought she'd guessed. There'd been the faintest emphasis on how she'd dumped out all of the open food or drink. But then, considering what Southen had been responsible for, Thorne doubted he'd hear more on the subject, no matter what Jess might, or might not, suspect.

****

The next three winters were wetter than usual. The Manor being well up from the coast, had few problems. The same applied still more for the village of Comsat since they had the oak forest in a semicircle about and above them, while the tree roots helped prevent washouts and took up much of the water. Polwithin flooded; the stream running by the village edge came over the banks, and a fall of earth on the uphill side gave promise of worse if it wasn't cleared quickly.

One of the Manor gate guards came hammering at our door. "Mr. Hugh, Polwithin's in trouble. One of the women rode to ask for help." I threw on a coat and went to listen. I heard about the overflowing stream, which wasn't so bad. I didn't like the sound of the earth fall though. I called out the militia, transport, and tools, and led them to the village that was our ally.

Hell! The earth had come out in a wide shallow scoop that banked downhill of that. The hole was filling rapidly, and once it was high enough, it would wash out the downhill dam, and the whole mess of mud and water would go straight down through Polwithin. I yelled for Paddy, who took one look and starting giving orders. We dug. It would be a race against the scoop filling and the dam collapsing. Paddy had started a trench up from the beach and over to one side of the village. If he could finish that in time, break through the dam, and let the water go, under control, it would be fine. If not…

I started the evacuation. Hilla lent her authority, and in less than half an hour, we had every child tucked up in the big building they used for village conferences. That was on the furthest side from the most probable path of the water, if or when, the dam went. Hilla yelled more orders, and the strongest of the village joined Paddy and dug to save their homes. It was a very closely run thing—as I think Wellington said about Waterloo—but Paddy's son, Eddie, now a powerful man, was standing by the dam with a plastic pipe in one hand, and a sledgehammer in the other. He placed the pipe into the dam about half of the way up, and, as the trench connected below the pipe, he slammed the pipe end a powerful echoing blow. Half the pipe vanished into the dam, and he hit it again.

His father, standing over the scooped hollow, called for a third strike, then, "Out, Eddie, out, water's swirling."

It was. The pipe had emerged in the temporary lake, and the water was fighting to head through it downhill. Hands hauled Eddie out even as the first jet of water shot twenty feet out of the pipe end and roared down the trench. It was digging that deeper with every minute, but that was all to the good. We stood wearily watching the dam empty. And once the water fell below the pipe end, Paddy removed the pipe, inserted it lower, and Eddie hit it again, standing thigh deep in water.

The pipe went home. We had Eddie out so fast; his feet never touched trench sides, and the dam emptied itself in great spurts as the scooped hollow added more earth to the outpouring. Hilla came walking up the hill to look.

"Helluva job, lads, we're grateful. Come and eat now, an' ease your bones. I'd say you'd be the better of a rest and a meal." We were, and once I'd eaten, I took Hilla aside.

"Tail end of winter, so after this, if luck's with you, there won't be another storm like that one. But the last two winters have been worse than usual; no telling about the next." Hilla pursed her lips. "An' I know where you're going with that, Hugh. Scoop up there could fill again, or we could get another over a bit. What in your mind to do?"

I explained. Hilla thought it made sense, although it'd be a sorrow to everyone. Still, it'd be far greater sorrow if what had almost happened this time, did occur next winter or any other one, and there were things that could be done that'd make life better. I said if she talked to her people, I'd talk to Thorne and our council, and so it was agreed.

****

Winter ended as peacefully as any time of cold and wet. Spring came, and with that we arrived on Polwithin's doorstep and planted saplings. A new breed of fast-growing pine that had just been stabilized the summer before the plague—now over twenty-five years behind us. Maureen and I were fifty-two that summer, Mic was eighty-six, and Thorne, who'd celebrated his birthday with us a few months before the plague had started, would be seventy-five next month. I had that in my mind as I planted across the hillside. Some things needed council discussion once we'd settled this problem

It had been fortunate that so long as the roads let us pass, we'd salvaged. We'd gone to London and Staines a second time ten years ago. From papers we'd brought back the earlier trip Liz had found a reference to the pines. She'd come to show them to us.

"You know Loblolly and Scotch pines can grow three feet a year? Well, there's a government institute in Staines that's been working on improving them for quite a while. It's got Scotch pines now to where they're full grown in ten years. They planned to use them to stabilize hillsides, they can be grown from seed, you can plant them in squares, and harvest one in four around each square every eight years or so, replanting those you take. They bred for disease and drought resistance — although they were fairly good on that one already — and initial growth in the first five years is accelerated."

We all liked the sound of that. "So," Liz commented. "If we did a plantation, we could harvest it for wood every year, carpentry or firewood, and we'd get wood for that a lot faster, not such good quality as the longer growing, denser, more attractively grained woods, but very useful." That pretty much summed it up, so on our second visit, we trawled our way through Staines until we found the institute mentioned. Their automatic system had died a while back and so had the saplings, but they had seeds. Glory, did they ever have seeds. We took the lot.

In a year, we had plantations. A big one to the east of the Manor, smaller ones by our villages, and the Ruxton enclave. Children gleaned the pine cones for kindling, and the trees, harvested as a tenth every year — and replanted — were becoming incredibly useful. But we made sure to have seeds on hand. A lot of them. They stabilized hillsides wonderfully, and, like the beavers — who'd increased considerably in numbers — they also helped in flood prevention.

Now we planted the slopes above Polwithin, Hilla, too,

had talked effectively, and the village, as they did when she talked, had listened. Summer came, mild, and almost windless, so we converged on the fishing village. Some of the houses could be jacked up and moved as they stood. Some, all, or a part of them would be lost as the homes they were. But by the end of summer, Polwithin rose from the earlier disaster to a safer place, with all the hillside above it planted with growing pine saplings, and, when you have several hundred people combining to get something done — it *gets* done.

Some of the trenching machines, or ones which could be used that way, had been employed to dig a long curving trench some seven-foot deep. We'd filled that with stones mortared together, then gone upwards from there. A twelve-foot wall shielded the village where it now stood. Houses stood on concrete platforms four feet above the land as well. If a flood of water-only came, it would wash around the footings, and the houses would be safe.

It took all summer. In autumn, the other fishing villages having seen what could be done, had petitioned for similar improvements, and the year after, both Mount's Bay and St. Ives had walls. Ruxton's, Comsat, and the latest village that had begun when two families wanted something no one else did, and which they'd named Honan, informing us that in Cornish it meant "Stand Alone," asked then for improvements too — and received them — while the summer after that, we sent out a convoy to any larger village or town we could still reach.

It was amazing that after all this time, we could still find building materials. It appeared no one else had wanted them, and here and there, we found good-sized amounts yet. They were gathered up, brought to the Manor stored in dry caves, containers, or underhill warehouses, and Thorne heaved a sigh when I went to tell him that all the materials expended had been replaced short of about fifteen percent.

"I had an idea too."

He glanced up from the list I'd placed on his desk and grinned. "Don't tell me, Hugh. I had the same one, I suspect. Cardiff?"

I nodded. "Cardiff. We are still so used to vehicles; we think of them first. But add the three fishing villages together, and the five cargo ships we have tucked into that fjord down the coast, and we could start doing runs up the coast. I don't think the cargo ships will last in decent shape much longer, and I wouldn't want to be caught in a real storm once they're deteriorating, but I think we could do another two to four trips."

The council came in on that discussion. Mic was almost ninety but as clear-voiced and minded as ever, and she was for it. We had a larger council, a man and a woman from every village that was ours, or an ally, and we hashed out possibilities, where to go, someone asked would we bring back settlers, and what if we were attacked? That last produced some amusement.

Jess Ruxton sorted. "If we take all those who're fit, can fight, and want to go, we could be boarding a couple of thousand." She was right, I guessed, over time you, tended to forget how numbers rose, the more so as another village was started, so there didn't seem to be a noticeable increase in the numbers around you. Although, come to that, it'd been a year or so since we'd walled in another section of Manor land. And Jess had mentioned how Ruxton village had expanded.

And about those who were fit, could fight, and would want to go, I'd be one of them, and so would Maureen. A thought saddened me. Mic might want to go, but there is no way she could, not at her age, and while she was fit enough for her years, it wasn't *fit* in general terms. The discussion went on for days, and it was decided. We'd go once the spring storms subsided. We'd take all five cargo ships, about half the fishing sleets and led by Thorne in *The Gosling*. It was the largest of the five, and Thorne on this trip would be acting as Commodore in charge of all the fleet. Each ship would have its own captain, and before we shipped out, we'd write a list.

We'd salvage what was on that in preference. Anyone going was permitted to bring back either one item, or a set weight of items as personal salvage. And that would be adjudicated by the captain of whichever ship they were on. I had a mental picture of someone wanting to bring back an army tank, a baby elephant, or something that while being one item, weighed several hundred pounds and would turn out to be a waste of time.

We thrashed out details for weeks; almost everything was settled, and then two days before we'd leave, the bad news landed. On me and Maureen. We were sitting back with cups of tea after a good dinner when Mic mentioned that she'd be coming. So was Doc Di and her current dog, Karl, from Kaiser's line. The dog was fine; I'd have no objection to Doc either. She was in her sixties, her dark brown hair mostly silver now, but her green eyes remained sharp, her reactions good. She could hit what she shot at, and a doctor would be essential on the trip like this.

It was the first bit that registered. "Mic?"

Very blandly. "Yes, Hugh."

"You aren't coming, not at your age, I'm telling you, you aren't. There's no way Thorne would agree."

Mic smiled. "Thorne has already agreed. I'll be on *The Gosling*."

I stared at her. "Who'd you have to kill to get him to agree to that, or do you know something he wouldn't want to get out?" I was only half-joking too.

"Neither, Hugh. You know Thorne better than that." Her face turned serious. "Look, lovey, you're right. I'm old. This will be the final trip I'll ever make. I had friends in Cardiff, I visited them often, and we're going to Swansea first and back via Cardiff, not just there and back. I had friends there too; I stayed with them a month or in the late twenties, going everywhere, seeing everything, and listening to people who were born there talking about the place."

Damn, she had a point. What she knew could be hugely valuable to the fleet and our people. And she was fit and healthy enough if we made sure she didn't work too hard, push herself too far. I'd found an electric tricycle, one of the last made for pensioners, around fifteen years ago and given it to her as a birthday present. It had a large basket in front—I could line that with metal and add fairings for greater protection—it had a trailer at the back too.

I grinned, at Staines last time Maureen had found Kevlar cloth and made that into a couple of sets of coats and leggings. Mic had never worn them; now I'd use those for blackmail. It worked, and Thorne, when I told him of Mic's armour, grinned at me.

"Good, excellent, I feel a lot happier, make sure there's extra batteries for her tricycle too. Her official title is going to be 'Mediator.' She'll settle arguments, quarrels, talk to anyone we meet— out there—and generally arbitrate. People know her and trust her to be fair, and mentally, she's still as sharp as a blade. The Kevlar is a great idea, oh well, Hugh, my lad, we sail morning after tomorrow. I hope you and Maureen are ready too."

We were; we climbed up the gangplank on a windless, overcast morning, looking over what I could only call a genuine fleet. Five cargo ships and twenty-seven fishing boats, and while we didn't have the 2,000 salvagers Jess had said when this started, it wasn't less than fifteen hundred, and I suspected some fishing boats carried a couple more than those listed. That way, if they came across any fishing boat in good enough condition to be salvaged and brought back to their village, they'd have the sailors to sail them.

I swiped tears from my eyes. I'd worried about Mic being with us every minute we were gone, and yet, she'd been so much a part of everything that had happened. There'd been times, too, that we survived because of her. Under me, I felt the ship stir to the tide, and excitement blew through me like a gale. Minutes to go now, only minutes.

CHAPTER SEVENTEEN

The sun rose, someone on our ship blew a whistle, and Thorne gave a quiet order. Majestically, boat helms over to take us out, we sailed from where we'd gathered for days beforehand at St. Ives. One of our last and possibly our greatest convoys was underway. The fleet fell in behind us, and we were voyaging. While *The Gosling* lifted to the waves, Daisy Blake stood up in the bow and sang. Not the original song, but the version Mic had written a decade earlier, a song to match *our* time.

Daisy's voice rang out in the salty air; the song ran from ship to ship as she sang full voice, her clear powerful contralto carrying across the waves. She sang, and we who listened or sang with her, knew what we believed in, what we would do, and who we were, now and always.

Weapons in a steady hand!
An honest heart and true!
The future here shall understand
What Cornish kin can do!

Yet do they know the where and when?
And shall our Cornwall die?
No! Here's twenty thousand Cornish kin
Will know the reason why!

Chorus:
And shall our Cornwall live?
Or shall our Cornwall die?
Here's twenty thousand Cornish kin
Who shall say NO, nor lie.

Clear spoke our leaders brave and bold:
A proud strong group they be
If all the lands against us stand,
We'd keep our Kernow free!

We'll cross the ruins land to land:
The rivers are no stay:
With Kernow blood and hand to hand;
There's none shall bid us nay?

We have our own in keep and hold,
"We're Cornish kin," we cry.
And if you come against us then '
'Tis you who'll lose and die.

Chorus:
And shall our Cornwall live?
Or shall our Cornwall die?
Here's twenty thousand Cornish kin
Who shall say No, nor lie!

And has become the custom since first that version was sung. We took a breath, then shouted three times the cry that had become our own. That was heard as an affirmation, a defiance to fate and anything that came against us in these changed times.

"Kernow bys vyken! 'bys vyken Kernow! Kernow bys vyken!"
Forever Cornwall, Cornwall forever, and let it be so down all the
years to come.

We'd talked about a decision only days before we took ship, and it had been decided. we would go direct to Swansea, standing, if the weather was good enough, out from the coast so we should not be seen. The weather *was* fair, and anyone in the city would have had a shock as our fleet came charging into the marina out of nowhere at first light.

Swansea might have been the second largest city in Wales when the plague struck, it had a population then of near a quarter of a million. But they and Cardiff had taken a beating right at the start. One of them being that for some unknown reason, the medical staff in both cities had been some of the first to die. Which meant, in turn, that many who might have survived with the right care — didn't. That had produced rioting, murder, looting, and arson. And as that accelerated, many ordinary people scrambled to get out of the city.

Farmers in the mountains had taken in many families; some parishes had tried to help, and often been overrun by those who, desperate, took, rather than gratefully accepting what was offered. As Mic had commented when we heard that:

"Gratitude goes out the window when you're starving, and you see those who offered you dog food feasting on bacon and eggs."

I don't know if that ever actually happened, but it summed up a greater truth. That if there is a finite amount of food, it won't help matters to share every crumb so that you *all* starve. I believe someone called it "the lifeboat principle."

Others of those starving had headed for nearby towns and villages and used sheer force of numbers to take whatever they wanted. Which produced some brief but brutal battles. So ultimately, most of the population of Swansea and Cardiff had died — from the plague, more or less naturally from various causes, been murdered, or simply gone fast and far to somewhere empty where there was just enough food to keep them while they learned to farm.

We salvaged Swansea to the hilt, and then some. But that had been a decision too. As we'd done with our great land convoys, so we'd do now. With two of the cargo ship holds crammed, and ten of the fishing boats, they separated from us and sailed for home, all sails set on a brisk wind, cargo ship engines hammering, not quite red-lined but not too far below it. They'd unload and return while we continued our salvage hunt.

We did well, even by our standards. The entire fleet made two trips, and the fishing villages had added three boats each, plus nets and other gear when they departed on the second re-turn. The best salvage so far as Thorne and Mic were concerned, was living. In the course of Mic's zooming about on a tricycle that being electric was silent, she happened on a litter of kittens. The mother fled, the kittens being only about four or five weeks, sat there blinking at a sight they'd never seen before.

Mic arrived back with a muttering fabric sack and exhib-ited her salvage. The five kittens were tabby, the fur thick but only slightly longer than that of an ordinary tabby, However, while you only had to look at them to see their age, they were massive, broad heads, big paws, and bodies that suggested thirty pounds of cat at full growth. Thorne blinked at them.

"What on earth breed are they?"

Mic produced one of her smiles, the sort when she's been both clever *and* put one over on you. "Scottish Coon."

We all stared, first at the kittens, now sucking on rag teats and warm milk that cat lovers had rustled up, and then at Mic, who'd taken the most comfortable seat and held the largest kit-ten. Doc Di came in to listen and was passed Mic's kitten and his milk. Mic looked around the circle of interested faces.

"I had friends in Scotland," she began. I snorted quietly; the thing about people in science fiction fandom is that they have friends all *over* the bloody place. My gran, before the plague, had corresponded by zoom and email with people in nine countries. Her pal in New Zealand was older; Mic said once she was grateful her friend had died before the plague. She'd turned ninety, was crippled, had a lethal medical condition, and as it was, she died with friends around her, her ashes then quietly — and illegally — dropped in the local river.

"Friends in Scotland," Mic repeated, giving me a stern look. "Their grandparents bred cats as a hobby. In the sixties, they had Maine Coons; one of the females got out and bred to a Scottish wild cat. The kittens were huge, gorgeous, and not *quite* as un-tameable as the pure-bred ones. So she kept them all and bred them back to Maine Coons again."

I looked at the kittens and got the idea. So they bred the friendliest to the friendliest… "

"And the biggest to the biggest," Di said thoughtfully. "Did they ever apply for breed recognition?"

Mic sighed. "Yes. The year the plague arrived, they pretty much got there at the same time. The Scottish Coon would be provisionally registered as an 'experimental breed,' and could be shown in that category at cat shows."

Thorne considered a purring kitten. "But here they are in Wales?"

Mic shrugged. "Provision Registration only, doesn't mean they can't be sold, and cat fanciers who'd be interested mostly had already heard it was going to be granted. I heard from Mhari that they'd got good prices for four of the boys and two girls; one family took a boy and a girl. There's one thing about Scottish Coons; they like people; they'll get on with just about any animal that respects them. But if a dog—say—attacks one, he can get the fright of his life. And if he's slow on the uptake or the getaway, he'll get the beating of his life as well."

Di stroked the kitten in her lap which purred sleepily. "Not surprising if they're thirty pound as adults. I wonder how Karl would feel about one." She gave a low whistle and he ambled through the door, moved up to sniff the kit, nosed it gently, and the kitten woke, sat up, and looked at him. The massive black dog developed the soppiest look I've ever seen on a dog, ran out a long tongue, and washed the small creature—which promptly brought up its paws, clamped one on either side of the dog's head, and wrestled him.

I almost choked, trying not to laugh too loudly. "I think we can see how Karl feels about the kitten,"

"And," Thorne added, "How it feels about him."

I had a feeling we'd acquired five kittens as crew, and I was right. They got into everything, were tripped over on a regular basis, were cuddled by practically everyone, and by the time we headed home, their ownership had been settled. As Mic said, she had found them, they were her salvage, so it was for her to distribute them.

And, Mic having informed us that it was the original breeders' custom to name the boys after Scandinavians, the girls after Scottish characters or places, Doc got the biggest, the boy she promptly named Sven. We took the smallest girl, and Maureen named her Iona. The remaining three went to Paddy the plumber's son Eddie, Ollie Tilliker, and the Berenson twins. Both had married, but they shared a big house, and they'd happily share a kitten too, they said.

We arrived back at Polwithin, took a week to restock, checked engines, sails, hulls, and decking, relaxed until we stopped feeling the ground under us still rolled, and found caretakers for the kittens. The five Mic had weren't the only ones that joined us. Once her kittens had been viewed, a number of others had gone ashore on electric cycles and sneaked around alleyways. Two more had found Scottish Coon kittens bedded down while mothers hunted, made a grab, and come back in triumph.

So, spread now over our lands, the fishing villages, and the Ruxtons, we had a total of eleven kittens. And looking at them against those other cats we all had, I thought it likely that in another few generations—of people that is—what we'd have all over would be something mostly like a Scottish Coon, in size, colour, markings, and temperament.

****

A week later, we headed for Cardiff on a day that was annoying because of the light wind. We had three more fishing boats this time; the fishing villages had sent one of their previous ones in good condition, while they restored the dilapidated ones taken from Swansea.

We picked to arrive in Cardiff at dawn again. This time, someone saw us, and when we docked, we were greeted by a large armed crowd. They shook weapons, shouted abuse, and screamed threats until, at Thorne's orders and ship by ship, our people assembled on the decks. That produced an abrupt silence as they paused to count numbers and came to a realization; they were threatening a ratio of some four to one — in our favour.

At which point, an old man came forward, walking to the part of the dock closest. "Greetings. Why are you here and is it in peace?"

Mic strolled to the closest bit of deck and called back. "In peace for preference. In war if you demand it. We have a doctor with us, and she'll happily help anyone who asks."

We saw faces brighten at that. Few in the group were idiots; they'd survived and wanted thing to stay that way. And at current odds, they wouldn't if those facing us were silly enough to attack, and they understood that too.

So we parlayed. In the end, everyone was sensible. Few of them lived in the city proper. They'd long since moved out to farm, to raise crops, livestock, and children in cleaner air and where rats didn't swarm. Our smallest cargo ship made a fast run for home. The rest of us mixed with the people here and salvaged. It became clear we'd retained more of a civilization than they had; probably the way the plague had hit them accounted for most of that, and we shared fairly all we found.

The cargo ship came back, bringing saplings for fruit trees and nut trees, vegetable seeds, and slips from berry bushes. To the delight of many, it also brought flower seeds. Then we opened the hatches and led out thirty yearling Nubian goats, plus five adults, four nannies in milk or kid, and a billy. Thorne handed out information on each as the families chose, discovered that one family at least knew how to milk, and had buildings where goats could be housed at night over the winter.

Mic handed out more information, including half a dozen copies of *The Goat Owner's Manual*. We were feasted. Three weeks later, we left Cardiff, loaded to the gunnels, in a haze of goodwill and friendship. Our people had spread out to the various family farms, made suggestions that proved to be useful, given physical help at need, received gratefully, and Doc Di had been a major hit. She brought with her medicines, copies of herbals — seeds to go with them — and treated half the population. If we'd been royalty, we couldn't have been more regretfully farewelled, and we promised, if at all possible, we'd return. Then once more, we sailed for home.

It was a quiet winter. I noticed Thorne seemed depressed and mentioned it to Mic, who scowled. "I know. Something been bothering him since we got to Swansea. I'll maybe have a word with him." She did and came back looking almost as depressed as Thorne.

I looked her over. "Mic?"

"I can't talk about it. Yes, Thorne talked to me, but only on condition I said nothing to anyone. I can promise you, Hugh, it's nothing that's a danger to us."

I left it lie. My grandmother had given her word, and I know her, but I talked about the possibilities to Maureen who came up with something I hadn't even thought about. "Maybe he's worried about who takes over after him?"

That hit me like a hammer. Truthfully, it'd never been anything I'd thought about, but I should have. In the world we'd lost, and because of our deal with Thorne, if he'd died, and the distant cousin who was legally his heir because Thorne had never married, had then inherited, not a lot would have changed most likely. We had life rights to the house we had, we had life rights to our share of the school profits. And all three of us had healthy savings and bank balances.

Even if the heir dumped the school, and settled back to be Lord of the Manor, he couldn't toss us out, and dumping the school would be a stupid move. We'd never anticipated the pandemic. But my wife made a very good point, with that everything had changed. Thorne's heir was almost certainly dead, and even if he wasn't, he'd lived in the Hebrides; he was very unlikely — after thirty years — to show up here ready to take over, even if there was some way we could get word to him when Thorne died. Apart from that, we had our council, and I suppose I'd assumed that would take over.

The census we now held every second year, and which had been done last summer after we'd returned from Swansea and Cardiff said that those directly under the Trelenwold banner, now numbered a handful over two thousand people spread over six sites. Adding in our allies, and we had solidly over three thousand who looked to us if things went pear-shaped.

Nor was that remaining static for any great length of time. For most of the thirty years since the plague, there'd been a steady trickle of those who came to our gates and asked admittance. It was known that if you were a good, hard-working person, if you kept our laws and customs, you could be accepted, and thereafter, you'd live in far better—and almost certainly more peaceful—conditions.

And as smaller groups found it harder and harder to live any kind of civilized life, as of late, we'd several times had entire groups of up to thirty asking to live under our Banner. That and our birthrate being larger and far more mothers and babies surviving, thanks to Doc Di and Liz, their nurses, and apprentice doctors, was how we were up to five villages, with talk of establishing and walling a dozen more *soon*—before our two Computerised Building Machines—and salvaged supplies to provide the walls—failed.

****

Spring came in a rush of constant showers, warmer weather, an explosion of greenery, baby creatures everywhere—and preparations for a voyage again to Swansea and Cardiff. Annie died that spring. Doc Di told us later that there'd been indications, and Annie had forbidden her to tell us. She wasn't going to die young, she'd said, and that would do her. She left a magnificent herb garden at the Manor, but smaller ones now existed in most villages, and so did Annie-trained herbalists. And more and more often, as the civilized drugs were no longer available or had passed their use-by dates, Doc Di and Liz fell back on carefully created herbal drugs that saved many lives.

We'd be sailing in greater numbers this season too. The five cargo ships had been overhauled as well as we could. St. Ives, Mount's Bay, and Polwithin had combined to set up a boat-building yard three years ago and produced a boat for each — they had sent those along the coast up the Thames to London. Each was crewed by thirty armed fighters, towed a barge, was prepared to take risks, and those boats and barges — now known at Artics in combination, or if the boat only, then as a Seabird — had returned filled with salvage. We might no longer be able to reach many places by road, but the seas remained open, and the Manor had it in mind to make a similar trip to hunt out wall materials once we'd been to Wales.

The time for that trip came. Five cargo ships, the three Artics, and ten ordinary fishing boats from each of the three fishing villages. We sailed on a quiet sea with a fair wind and reached Swansea in a single day. No one appeared. So, we went ashore and headed for the sites Mic had noted on the last voyage. She'd stayed home this time; it had taken her weeks to recover completely from the last double trip, and this time I'd put my foot down, first with Thorne, and then both of us with her. She'd grumbled but complied without much protest, and I thought, knowing my grandmother all my life as I had, that it wasn't a good sign.

Liz, too, had stayed behind. She was now eighty, and while she remained lean and fit, Doc put her foot down there. I only found out the day before we set sail that Doc had taken Mic and Liz aside and begged both to look after the other. Happily, they did and had expanded on that to carry out some of their own plans. However, we had Doc Di, half a dozen of the nurses she had trained, and two *interns* as she called apprentice doctors. We had an electrician, Amy, Bronnie's apprentice who was almost out of her apprenticeship, and Gayle presided over clerks to keep track of what was loaded, what was wanted, what wasn't yet found, and what areas had been checked.

As I said, Swansea was empty. However, twice, someone found a body, and not one dating from earlier times. After the first one, they called Thorne. He looked over the remains, called in Di, and got an estimate.

"Last year, probably sometime over early winter." There was a pause as she investigated further; she looked up, her eyes worried. "He was killed, Thorne. Looks like some kind of a large knife."

"I see." Thorne came to find Maureen and me and passed this one. "All right, it may have been a quarrel between two people, a squabble over salvage perhaps. But the place is empty. We knew there were at least a hundred people living around the city when we were here last year, could have been two or three times that. They never came near us, but we saw glimpses of them all the time."

I nodded. "I'd tell everyone if they see anyone alive, or anybody that doesn't look more than a year or two old, to call you and Di." Maureen nodded agreement.

There were no sightings of anyone live, but two more bodies were found before we had sufficient ships loaded for them to start the run home and return to meet us in Cardiff. Both those bodies, too, were recent; one, Di estimated to be only a few weeks dead. She talked to the three of us in the captain's cabin while Thorne supervised the loading of twenty electric motors and nineteen complete sets eco-electric systems plus all spares, found at the back of a warehouse that had specialised in making them, and which items had been well mothballed so that Amy was sure the motors would still work.

"I don't like the look of any of this." Di said. We looked at her and waited.

Thorne shifted in his seat. "All right, why?"

"Because there don't seem to be any remaining alive here. Which suggests either the living all packed up and left, or that those who were in the city last year, were killed. It's possible a disease cropped up. Something like measles, whooping cough, mumps, any of those can have a high mortality rate, particularly if those who catch it have depressed immune systems or are malnourished. But if a disease was responsible, I'd expect us to be finding graves, or bodies where the person had clearly died from a disease. So far, the only bodies we've found have died by violence."

"What do you think we should do? Should we assume it's disease and leave?" Thorne frowned as he spoke, and I could guess he didn't want to leave yet but didn't want to take stupid chances with our people either.

Doc sighed. "In my opinion, it isn't disease. Ask our people to watch for fresh graves for reasonably recent bodies, and signs of live people. They report any of those at once."

We didn't have to wait long. Five reports of graves and two more of bodies came in a day later when we'd shifted to salvaging an area further north. Di attended each as fast as possible, balanced with care in inspection. She reported to us that evening.

"Violence, in a couple of cases that's *all* I can say. Crushed skulls, both of them. Several more were shot with bullets, others suffered major slashing or stabbing." She considered. "I'd say none died earlier than the start of winter, and none died later then just past the middle of that. If you want an educated guess, I'd say a bunch of people came from the north, went through the city, killed every adult or older child they found, took anything they had, and moved on."

Thorne sighed. "Second generation bandits."

Maureen and I nodded. We could see it. Some lawless or lazy bunch who'd found it easier to take from those who'd spent their time gathering. If that was what they did, however, they'd have to keep moving. They killed those who did the work, so they had to find more. It hit me then.

"Thorne, if that's how they're operating, do you think it's more likely they went along the coat towards Dyfed, then north again to Aberystwyth, or would they have gone the other way — straight to Cardiff? And when?"

Thorne looked horrified. "Vicious or lazy doesn't mean

stupid. And there's still maps to be found; we've seen them ourselves. Okay, thirty years since the plague, but they could have someone who reads maps. It isn't unlikely they came down the coast from Aberystwyth anyhow. If they can read a map, the logical place then *is* Cardiff."

"So should we drop everything and go there now, or do we finish salvaging for the walls, send those filled ships off, and rendezvous with the first lot that left? If we stand out to sea a bit, we can pick them up short of Cardiff."

There was a discussion, a report from those salvagers tasked with finding and loading all wall and building materials… it was their estimation they had found sufficient to load two cargo shops, all three Artics, and a dozen fishing craft, leaving us three cargo ships, if we picked up the returnees in time, plus eighteen fishing boats. While we talked, the materials were loaded, their carriers set sail for home, and Thorne made the decision.

"Anyone wants something in particular, they have the afternoon and evening until dusk to collect it and come back aboard. Get a good night's sleep, people; we sail at first light." We did, we hung off the coast, saw our smaller fleet coming, gathered them in, had a day's conference with dinghies rowing to and from, and agreed. The sea was calm and clear of other shipping these days. We edged into Cardiff well before it was light, so that by the time dawn showed, we were almost into the marina.

We anchored or tied up, depending on our draught, and for the first time, became aware of an odd sound coming from the city. It was blurred, but after Thorne signalled to wait and listen, it gradually became individual sounds. Screams, yells, gunshots, Thorne took in a deep breath.

"I believe those who destroyed Swansea have arrived here."

Before he could continue, a harsh voice rose up from within a crowd at a gangplank. "Bandits like them killed almost everyone I knew. and in a shriek that soared up. "*Kernow bys vyken!* Kill them, kill the bandits, *Kernow bys vyken!*"

CHAPTER EIGHTEEN

That was all it took. Many of those we'd taken in over the years had lost friends or kin to this sort of group. Others had seen everything they owned taken, women raped, dogs slaughtered for trying to protect their humans. They'd seen friends and family starve. They'd come to us so it wouldn't happen again, and now they expected we'd make a stand.

Thorne did. The *Gosling's* gangplank slammed down, and Thorne's small electric tank-like vehicle, designed for times like these, went down it, spun to a halt, and he stood up in the open hatch on top, megaphone in hand.

"Form up by crews, only the most able-bodied, the best with weapons. Ship's second in commands remain to guard their ship. Captains, take charge of your crews." There was a pause as people scrambled to obey. Then Thorne's voice rang out: "Advance at a walk." We did, Maureen and I behind him on our electric tricycles—better stability for shooting.

"Advance, trooooot." The sounds were individual now; we trotted up a slight rise in the street we were on, and Thorne paused at the top. Down the slope they were fighting. Guns, swords, tire irons, and bats from different games. Thorne waited for a few minutes until everyone had caught their breath, then he lifted his hand. "Pass this word back: No shouting, no firing until we're within a hundred yards, or until they fire at us." We heard word pass.

Thorne lifted the sword his many times great-grandfather had wielded at Waterloo. It had never been standard issue; it was beautifully hand-crafted, made for the man who first carried it. Belted about his hips, Thorne carried two handguns, Russian brands that were each a ten-shot, given to his father when in Russia. Thorne turned to look down at those who fought and died. Then he swung his blade to point at them, and his vehicle took off. We went with him.

Behind us came a thousand of our people. Riding electric motorcycles, bicycles, or on foot, running steadily and silently. We were almost within the distance Thorne had given when one of the combatants saw us. His mouth fell open, but before he yelled, Thorne, fixed him with a stare and shouted, "Cornwall Forever! *Kernow bys vyken!*"

The man's mouth opened; it was no warming he shouted, but an acknowledgement then, encouragement, and information to those of Cardiff who fought and died without hope that day.

"Cornwall with us. Cornwall for Cardiff."

The battle exploded as we crashed into them. Thorne had given earlier orders, and specific crew took to side streets, surrounding the battle, cutting off any bandit who would escape. What we had seen as we crested the rise had been uneven to say the least. My estimation as we'd paused there was that the attackers numbered at least two hundred. Whereas Cardiff, as of our visits the previous year, would have had a population of twice that. The difference was that those in Cardiff would have had perhaps a hundred effective fighters while the bandits were mostly all in that category.

Our arrival changed the odds from two to one against Cardiff, to almost five to one against the bandits. It was a massacre, and there was no mercy in us. Our people had completed the encirclement manoeuvre before any of the bandits thought to run. Then we, and our Cardiff allies, closed in—tighter, tighter, until they were in each other's way as they fought, and every third blow, struck one of their own. The noose tightened until they were a score or so struggling more to breathe than to fight. The last of them fell, and Thorne called:

"Step back."

We did so, and some of our people began disentangling

those who lay over or under their own side. Now and then, one groaned, writhed, or moved without purpose, and a gun fired, or a sword or knife came down. And while that continued, Doc and her medics went from one to the other of Cardiff's fallen, helping where they could. The final outcome, once we had done all we could, was sickening. Of some 390 people who had remained here, of whom around one hundred would have been fighters and adults, some two dozen of those remained alive. Most, Doc Di reported, were so injured they would die in the next week to a year, nor would they be able to care for themselves.

We told them the truth, gave them the choice, and they understood. To remain among the living was to draw out the grief, to burden friends or family unbearably with the extra care and work to keep someone alive, and at the same time, to do without that person's assistance. Gently, too, they were told we could not afford the time, the labour, ourselves. Many would require almost round-the-clock care, and we didn't have painkillers, so whatever remained of their lives would be agony hours upon days upon weeks.

They made their choice. One by one, they said their good-byes, accepted a mug of something to drink, and lay back as the pain drifted away — as did they a short time later. We buried them, those who died in battle and those of their choice, in honour. Then we gathered their comrades who lived. Most were determined to remain in the city or on their farms outside it. In some cases, of a family, all the adults were dead, and the remainder were small children. Those, we agreed, should return with us to become our kin. We had just agreed to that when a woman came walking quietly.

"I'm Meg Price," she said to Thorne, Maureen, and me. "I was hunting salvage, I watched them come, go into a hall by shops to the west, and not all came out again."

Di nodded. "Did you get any impression of who stayed?"

"I did, they had small children with them, and a few women; none came out."

Thorne stood up. "Will you lead us there?"

"I will." She turned, walked away, and quietly, as Thorne indicated to us, some fifty of us followed, including Thorne, we two, Doc, and several medics.

We found the hall, surrounded it, and peered through gaps in the boards. Meg Price was right. Inside were nine women, all armed. But with them were almost thirty children, sobbing quietly, staring blank-faced at the walls, or sleeping.

Doc moved us away and spoke softly. "Those women may have orders to kill the children if anyone tries to take them. For myself, I'd say they were loot from Swansea, see the canvas bags heaped in the far corner, one has a name and a Swansea address. We need to decoy the women away so we can get between them and the children."

Meg Price rose silently to her feet. "My man and my little brothers fought and died. These," she spat. "I was hunting and came back to find my sister and our children dead. Mine were too old to be wanted; they'd have remembered. Hers, she was from Jamaica. I have no one and nothing left. Watch, now, and be ready to save these here."

She was moving, then at the door, swinging it open and racing through to the back of the hall; there she turned and shot, and again. She'd have been a good hunter. Both shots went home; a third arrow flew, injuring one so that the woman screamed, causing more confusion. Then we, too, passed the door, throwing ourselves between the armed women and the defenceless children.

The women, finally seeing what was happening, attacked us, all but one who was engaged against Meg. She was the younger and stronger, and Meg went down. The remaining seven, one staggering, were never going to be a match for us, and they died. The last being the woman who'd attacked Meg. We soothed screaming children, removed bodies, and Maureen and I with Doc went to Meg, who lay against the old stage.

Meg smiled up at Di. "See to someone else, woman. I'm dying, and I need no doctor's help to do it."

"Are you in pain?"

"I am, and that's well enough; so long as I am, I'm alive. Listen, we lived, all of us in a big house at the edge of the city. They came that way, likely why they killed my family first. But we had beasts, pets, two sheds with gear, and a cellar." Here, to our surprise, she winked. "Go to…" she recited an address, groaning softly. "To the four of you, I give all that was ours. Take what of it you want and share the rest. But if you will and can, take me there, too, and once you empty the place, leave me there, and fire the building. I'll not be worm-food or meat for the rats."

Her grin was more pain than amusement then. "You'll not need to fear it spreading. The wind blows from the city out across the fields; the house alone will burn. My kin lie in the building already, so I'll have no distance to go to meet them." She moaned, and her breath went out of her in a long quiet sigh that seemed to me to be one of satisfaction. She'd avenged her family, told us everything she wanted us to know, and now she could let go.

We did as she wished. Thorne took most of those with us back to the ships to do whatever was to be done, but Doc, Maureen, and I, with Meg's body laid on the back of a trailer, went to the address. It wasn't easily found, but we did, and Meg had told the truth. It was a big house. I thought it had belonged to someone wealthy once.

Long ago, it had been landscaped; the sheds Meg spoke off were large, well-built, and had, as she'd said, harness and gear. Much of that in the first shed was of the best quality, the gear being mostly hand tools, which by the look and quality of them, had been made by experts some generations ago. There was also a line of barrels containing nails, screws, and items like locks, taps, and window catches. All were expensive quality. And an investigation of several tarpaulins hanging against the back wall, found, stacked behind them, a hundred and forty bags of cement and four long large bundles of steel reinforcing rods for concreting. *Those* would be useful; like the cement, they were one of the buildings' items we were looking for. Thorne would be delighted.

The second shed held a large wagon in excellent condition, two pony traps, harnesses for the three vehicles, plus saddles, bridles, halters, horse and pony covers, grooming gear, and a portable forge with the tools, bags and bags of fuel, a stack of bar steel, and another of ready-made horseshoes.

Doc whistled. "If she said all this was just 'gear,' I'll be interested to see what they had in the cellar. Let's lay her with her family, check the livestock, get everything out of the house in case of anything happening. Then we can see to them."

We started by finding the pets. A cat that came to meet us meowing. We all knew that tone. I found cat food in the kitchen and fed the cat, which earned me an approving purr. She was, I estimated, about three, and a possible mix of Tonkinese and Ocicat. After her came the dog, a little more cautious, but a nice animal. A mostly Rottweiler wearing a collar with a small silver shield and the name *Brutus* engraved on it. I doubted the collar had been his originally; maybe the family called all their dogs post-plague the same name to match it. Both animals had clearly been well fed, well treated, and loved. I fed Brutus too.

We walked outside to the fields beyond. There were a four-mare team of Suffolk Punches, right, for the big wagon; ten ponies all of around fourteen hands give or take an inch, and about half cob-types. (For the traps and riding.) With them were twenty goats — of three breeds including five Nubian — an in-calf Jersey cow, and a dozen sheep of the easy-care variety. We all beamed at that lot.

We returned to the house, left Meg lying with the woman she'd called sister — probably her sister-in-law, and, surrounding them on beds we pushed together in the largest bedroom, the bodies of the seven children. Then we sought out the cellar. It was well concealed, the bandits hadn't found it, but after some hunting, we did.

Doc was down the stairs first. We arrived to find her speechless. Our gazes followed hers, and we, too, gaped. Meg and her sister must have known every expensive shop in the city and got to many of them first. I wasn't surprised at the drugs, which was logical, although Di was all but crooning over them — and the crate filled with packs of tampons, the bins of multi-vit-amins, and first-aid items. It was the entire section filled with faux fur coats of every length from ankles to waist. The racks of dresses all made from expensive materials, bins of underwear, shelf after shelf of boots, flats, sandals, and shoes, all real leather, and that was only the women's items.

After that, another section held clothing and footwear for men. Along with condoms, shaving kits, packs of razor blades, leather strops, and about fifty of the old-fashioned folding razors. There were needles, thread, pins, and bolts of expensive materials, all carefully packaged so they wouldn't be attacked by moths. And to help that, there were a lot of set and baited mouse and rat traps, some minus the bait and with a body. Doc found the first set one by stepping against it, then leaping into the air when it went off. There were also a gross of new ones in packaging.

The cellar, unlike many we'd come across over the years, was actually as large as the entire ground floor. It was strutted, pillared, and matched by attics that had a similar spread. They, too, contained an incredible assortment of things. I looked at one lot and couldn't believe how stupid the Prices must have been, it was all inflammable, and if that lot had caught, Meg would have had her wish — to an incredible degree. I know attics can be dry, but it still isn't a good idea to fill them with matches, can-dles, fire-lighters, and a hoard of similar flammables.

Maureen heaved a loud sigh. "'Empty the house,' she said. 'Take what you want and share the rest.' We can choose what we want, but the rest is going to have to come back and be shared out at home. It's the sort of thing a lot of people won't appreciate not getting a chance at."

I may add that was what was done in the end. It filled two

cargo ships, and an Artic once we had all the goods and the animals aboard. And once home, there would have been few families who didn't get at least one item. However, when we had the house, sheds, and fields emptied, we waited for the right wind again, sang *Abide with Me*, and Thorne stepped up and lit the fuse into the house. It went up like Guy Fawkes night. We sang another song, Doc recited a poem, and we left.

The ships had all been loaded — including those of the second small convoy which had returned. We slept that night, and by first light, we were sailing, except one brief holdup as Merr came flying to the foot of the gangplank with an unconscious male strapped into his passenger seat, and a feral looking girl of about seven or eight in the back seat. She had a deathly grip on the man's hand, so that it was difficult to get him up the gangplank, but we managed.

The *Gosling* weighed anchor and led the fleet out to sea. I looked back, seeing the glow of Meg Price's home, and knowing we were unlikely to ever return. Thorne had it in mind to sail past London next year. We wanted all the building supplies we could gather, and it was getting closer to the time when we'd have electric vehicles and could sail, but other fuel would be irreplaceable, either gone or adulterated. From here, we'd had the cream of the salvage and need not return, plus we'd also had the cream of an unexpected other crop.

With thanks to the bandits, if that was the right expression, we'd gained thirty-nine orphans ranging from babes in arms to around ten years old. They had no adult family alive; of those families staying, none were related; none felt they could afford to take them, and since we were prepared to do so, they were formally handed over. What we didn't know, until two days later, was that some of the crews had fallen victim to weeping and begging and quietly taken aboard eleven older children, ranging from fifteen to eighteen. They *would* probably have been taken in where they were; they were old enough to work hard, but they'd heard tales of the Manor, our better conditions, and, as Doc said, once they were discovered, they were old enough to make their own decisions. They'd just have to live with them or leave on their own, since we wouldn't be taking them back.

They all fitted in unexpectedly well; they *loved* our conditions and our mostly-democracy, and over the next few years, they became more fervently Cornish than many who were born and bred. In 2075, most having married, they formed the nucleus of a new village that went into partnership with Comsat, specializing in spinning, weaving, knitting, and crochet, using a mix of easy-care sheep and alpaca wool.

****

The sadder thing on the way home was the suicide of one of the girls, all of eight years old, who'd been rescued from the bandits. We'd guessed some had been abused if the bandit who took them had time and inclination. It turned out that of the thirty-nine, only six had been molested. Four were too young to fully understand what had happened to them. With love and time, they'd recover. Elsie was one of the other two. Her fellow sufferer was blank-faced, never spoke, and went to a farming family whose own children were almost adult. There, she was loved, cuddled, talked to, and given a kitten. One day, about a year later she "woke," and it was as if nothing had ever happened.

Elsie was different. She cried constantly and silently. Any time I saw her, there was a tear or two sliding down her cheeks. One of the children said Elsie's family had all been killed by the bandits, and Di thought that to have been done in front of her — as a beginning of the atrocities. She added that the child wasn't eating properly, refused to talk about what had happened to her, and had no friends despite overtures from other children her age. We dropped the St. Ives people off at the village along with their share of salvage and two children who wanted to join them.

We were there three nights before we sailed again, and all of that time, Elsie remained weeping, disengaged, and eating less and less. Di was keeping a watch on the child, but not close enough. After all, watching her twenty-four seven wasn't practical, although one nurse took up a lot of the slack. Until the night when the man Merr had brought aboard had a fit, Di and the nurse were distracted, and anyhow, the girl was asleep, and it was the early hours.

If she'd been asleep as everyone thought, it was then she woke up. We were moving along briskly on moderate winds and a choppy sea; tomorrow we'd dock at Polwithin, and everyone would split up to head for the Manor and villages. It was 3:00 a.m., the moon was up, and Elsie sat up, got out of bed, and headed for the door. She opened it.

Of the other five girls in her cabin, one woke up at her movements. "Elsie? Where are you going?"

"For a walk."

"I'll come with you."

"Don't want you."

This roused the other younger child's curiosity. She waited until Else was out the door, then followed, silent in bare feet. Elsie walked to the rail, looked down, squeezed between the upper and lower railings, and simply allowed herself to fall. The child went to look down. There was no sign of Elsie, and — as many of them were — inured to odd events and behaviour, she wandered back to bed. It wasn't until morning when the nurse came to check on Elsie that we knew.

"Where's Elsie?"

The one who knew nodded. "She's gone."

"Gone? Gone where?" The nurse's voice was sharp with fear and annoyance, and the child went dumb. "Rose, where did Elsie go?"

"Dunno." She stuck to that until Doc arrived, sent her colleague away, brought out a small chocolate bar, and coaxed the tale out of Rose as the child savoured small bits broken off the bar and handed to her.

"So, Elsie got up and went outside?" Rose nodded. "Good girl for telling me. It would be clever if you followed her and saw where she went. Did you?" Another cautious nod. "Okay, have another piece of chocolate. What did you do when she left?"

"I got out of bed, and she was by the rail." She licked the chocolate while Doc waited. "Then she went swimming. I looked, but I couldn't see her, so I went back to bed." She got the rest of the bar, and Doc came for us, recounted the story, and Thorne swore.

"No hope for her. If it was when Rose says, we were standing well out to sea. It was windy, choppy, quite rough in fact, and she wouldn't have lasted five minutes. Not even any use to go back and search. Tide was setting, the body will be well out by now, and it's turned again since; she could be anywhere."

Doc agreed. "She had no family, no friends, and anyone sad about her will be so more intellectually than emotionally. We'll have to keep a closer eye on the young ones though. I'll let anyone who takes them in know that this is a possibility."

We sent word to Mount's Bay, told those at Polwithin when we arrived, and Elsie was looked for in the months that followed. She was never found.

CHAPTER NINETEEN

The man Merr had found was recovering. His head injury had left him unconscious for days, but the child attached to him — often literally — gave us some information. Her name was Lia, and she was a rather undersized nine, not the seven or eight I'd thought her to be.

"Granny used to call him Draynen; she went away. Mummy called him Dray; she died. Granny said she came to our place because it was worse where she lived."

"Did she ever say where that was?"

"Aberystwyth, well, not there exactly; she lived on a farm. She told me stories about there before she left us."

"How old were you when she left?"

"Four, I think. Daddy said she'd gone back to her farm. Then Mummy died."

"So, it was just you and Daddy?" Lisa nodded. "What did Mummy die from?"

"She had a bad pain in her tummy. She cried, then she screamed and screamed; she said it hurt so bad. She was sick, but Daddy gave her something to drink, and it stopped hurting. She went to sleep, an' so did I. In the morning, Daddy said she died, and he was so sad. We went out into the country, and we buried her. We put lots of flowers on her and Daddy sang a song before we went home."

"Do you know the song?"

To our amazement, she sang, *"For this is my Eden, and I'm not alone. For this is my Cornwall and this is my home."* She considered and added, "I dunno Cornwall, but Daddy sings that song an' another one a lot."

I blinked and looked at Thorne. Doc Di glanced over at Merr. He nodded. "I can tell you something that may go with that. She says her Granny used to call her father Draynen." He paused. "That's Welsh for thorn" He grinned teasingly. "Don't suppose you had any hot affairs about thirty years ago?"

Thorne's face shut down. He rose slowly and walked out the door while most of us gaped. I didn't, though. I remembered the year before the plague. There'd been a charming girl, busking her way through Cornwall. Thorne was still hurting from his divorce, and I'd suspected when she stayed a week at the Manor that there was more going on than, as Thorne had claimed, her listening to his Cornish songs collection, and copying some of the music and lyrics. I also remembered a letter he'd had when the plague started; that was the night he got drunk and stayed that way for almost two days.

I followed him out. "Ynys?"

He sank down to perch on the railing. "Ynys. It lasted a week, and I've never forgotten her. She wrote to me before the plague hit, said she'd had my son; she'd loved Cornwall for a few months, but where she lived was her heart. If I wanted, I could visit now and then. But she'd never wanted to marry, never wanted to live anywhere else, had a career, and I had to accept that. I wrote to say it was her right to make her own decisions, and I accepted that. Just, tell me about my son, send me a photo now and again, and maybe when he was old enough, he could visit."

"Did she write back?"

Thorne's grin was painful. "She did. I got it the day we heard how bad the plague was; it was all over, millions were dying, I knew my ex-wife and my kids were dead, and it had hit particularly hard along the borders. Parts of those areas in Scotland and Wales where they bordered England were almost wiped out. I got drunk."

My smile was equally wry. "I remember..."

"Yeah. So do I, at least I remember the hangover I had."

"What did she say about the baby?"

"She said he was healthy, a happy baby, hardly ever cried, that he had her grey eyes and black hair; she thought he'd have my build, my brains, and she sent a photo." He fished in a pocket. "I went straight to my study when I sobered up, put that on a file, and printed out a bunch of copies so I'd never lose it."

His eyes were sad. "I thought, with everything, that he and Ynys and all her family—The Trehernes—were dead. I tried to phone; they said there were no connections. I wanted to drop everything and see if I could find her, but you know what it was like then, Hugh. I was needed at the Manor, and I was ninety-nine percent certain they were dead. So, I stayed—and they weren't. She survived; she and my son ended up in Cardiff."

"And I doubt she ever left," I said slowly. "The kid says 'Granny left. I'd say Draynen found her dead early one morning; the kid was four and loved her granny, so he and the kid's mother took her out and buried her. I'm guessing, but I think it likely he buried his wife beside or near her."

Thorne considered that. "Likely. Anyhow, this is *all* guessing. Just because of his name and that he often sang a couple of Cornish songs, doesn't make him my son."

I shut my mouth on an answer to that. I'd met Ynys a couple of times, and I thought I had her measure. When "Dray" woke, I'd bet he had proof. He was probably waiting until Lia was old enough to make the dangerous, tiring journey from Cardiff to Cornwall, and he'd think about even risking it at all; there were no guarantees Thorne would be alive, to start with, and to finish, no guarantees a bastard son would be welcome. It was over thirty years, now; Thorne could have remarried—or died—with the latter more likely.

I drifted quietly in the direction of the boat's ICU, a single bed where Dray lay sleeping under sedation. I slipped through the door and went straight to the single locker that would hold his immediate possessions. Clothes? Yes, jacket, jeans, t-shirt— and a thin package of papers in a carefully stitched pocket. I took them and reversed my steps, ending in Maureen's and my cabin.

There, I opened it without leaving traces I'd done so. I checked. Birth certificates. Two, Her's and Dray's. Copies of three letters, hers to Thorne, and his to her. There was a photo. One I thought to be a copy of the one sent to Thorne before the plague. Then the final item, a picture, amateur but competent, her work from the initials. It showed her in her sixties, Dray beside her, mid-to-late-twenties, and between them holding their hands was Lia—looking about three, so this would have been done a year before Ynys "left." Maybe she'd had a warning and wanted to add that as a final item.

I sealed the package again very carefully. Then I took it to Thorne who was in his cabin now and handed it over. "It was in Dray's gear. I thought your Ynys may have been smart enough to provide proof so you could be certain. And one other thing; Doc Di knows how to do blood types."

Thorne stayed in his cabin until we reached Mount's Bay; he was busy there seeing their portion of the salvage was properly unloaded, and that all the right things were said. We left the following morning, and I only knew because I'd watched, that Thorne had visited his son five times so far. Standing, looking at the sleeping face and trying to see himself—or Ynys—there.

Dray stayed unconscious, although Doc was more and more optimistic, and then we sailed into Polwithin, and all was hustle and bustle. Dray was unloaded first, and he, with Lia, Maureen and Doc started for The Manor. We'd be there in two or three days once we got the massive salvage we still had to be sorted and on its way to storage there.

****

Dray and Lia were bedded down at the Manor. In a spacious, often sunlit, pair of rooms on the ground floor and to one side. Lia gaped at her room. Both eyes and mouth open.

"It's *my* room, honest?"

"It's your room," Maureen assured her. "And the books and toys in it are yours, too." We already knew she could read.

About six-year-old level, but she loved books, loved reading, and took to improving that skill like a hound to the trail. We'd put several toys on a shelf for her, no sense in overwhelming her, but Maureen had noticed Lia was an animal-lover, and once she'd settled in, my wife and my grandmother took her out to meet the Manor's cats, dog, and horses.

She was taken first to our home where she met Iona, the Scottish Coon. Lia wasn't afraid, but she *was* awestruck. "She's so big, she's lovely; look, she likes me." Iona was purring and head-butting, a clear indication she's taken to Lia.

"Yes, she does. She says you could be a good cat-person," Mic commented.

Lia's eyes widened. "I could have a cat like *her*?"

"Yes, but we'll have to wait until there's one looking for a home." Not that it'd be long to wait, the female originals who'd stayed at the Manor were all due to have kittens shortly, and I was sure Mic had one of Iona's in mind.

Thorne spent time with the child too. She followed him like a puppy as he walked his lands, telling her how the Trelen line had started, how a king had given them the Manor and its lands, and in turn hearing more about Lia's gran and her daddy. They bonded and Thorne said privately that he was certain she was his granddaughter, and that if his son woke, or was unfit to hold the Manor, then it would go to Lia. He was teaching her, although she never realized, teaching her to value honour and fair dealing, to love the Manor and her lineage, and to under-stand people and the why of what they did.

She was bright, not just superficially but all through. We found her a tutor and she learned, information and abilities in great gulps. Dray had roused slowly. First with movements, then with the occasional word which he never stayed awake long enough to hear an answer to, But then he'd wake for an hour at a time.

He wasn't completely lucid at such times, but he knew his daughter, and always his first words were to ask if she was okay, if she was fed, her bed was comfortable, and was she warm at nights. She'd assure him she was, and he'd eat food if it was offered, drink water or milk, and be gone again.

This lasted all of the winter, but spring seemed to wake Dray too. Iona had kittened at the end of autumn. Mic had offered Lia her choice, and she'd taken a male, a boisterous bundle of energetic tabby fluff Lia named Vali, Norse for strong. He was, too; he went where he wanted to go, even if the humans couldn't believe some of the places he reached.

I suspected Vali had a paw in Dray's increasing wakefulness. The kitten was determined that no one slept during the day unless he did. He pounced, bounced, and demanded acknowledgement. Privately, Doc Di said it would do Dray no harm, so we minded our own business. And one morning, as I was passing the door on my way to give Thorne some information on orchard plantings, I saw the kitten pounce — and Dray roll onto his back, scratch Vali's ears, and speak.

"Yes, I know, all energy and nothing to do with it if I stay asleep. Where's Lia?"

I moved just enough for him to recognise someone nearby and looked at my watch. "Lia's having a reading lesson at the moment. She'll be back in her room in about a quarter hour."

Dray absorbed that, his eyes sharpening by the second. "She could read already?"

"Of course, but she's got more books for an older girl; she's doing math, and learning to ride. Once you're well enough to get out of bed, you can do all that stuff with her."

His face brightened. "Good. Um, where am I? How'd I get here, is this kitten really hers, or does Lia just look after him?"

I answered the last question first. "My grandmother Mic's cat Iona had kittens, and Lia chose Vali. He's a boy, a Scottish Coon, and he's hers. He won't have it any other way. Merr, one of our people, found you unconscious after a fight with bandits; you'd crawled under a building with Lia, you didn't wake up, people in Cardiff had no way of caring for you, so we took you home with us, we have two doctors, two interns, and a number of nurses, we were in a better position. And if you died, we'd have taken care of Lia." I saw relief in his face at that.

"Now, where are you? Short answer or long?"

"Short first. Then long if I stay awake."

I grinned. "Okay, short answer, In Cornwall in the upper lands above the coast more or less in the triangle between Truro, Dalworth, and Redruth—if that means anything." His eyes were drooping, but I saw it did.

"Is the Trelenwold Manor near here?"

I grinned down as his eyes closed. "Oh, it's here, don't worry about that, and Thorne Trelen is still Lord of the Manor. Ask for him when you wake again."

I saw him fight to wake again, *now*, and fail; his breathing shifted to the pattern of sleep, and I went to find Thorne. I had news, and not just about the orchard planting.

****

Dray woke again around mid-afternoon. Thorne was waiting, talking to Lia about Comsat village and alpacas. Dray stirred and spoke her name, and his daughter was there, clutching his hand. Dray looked at her.

"Is that Mr. Trelen with you?"

Thorne strolled into the room, picked up a chair, and sat by the bedside. "It is. Glad to see you awake and clear-headed. Welcome to the united and allied villages of Cornwall, and welcome to Trelenwold Manor where you are now."

Thorne, telling us later, said that Dray's gaze changed then. "Lia, sweetheart, go and play, come back in a couple of hours, okay?" Lia nodded and vanished; Dray turned to Thorne. "You're Thorne Trelen?" Thorne nodded. Dray spoke softly. "Do you remember a girl, more than thirty years ago now? She was a singer, busking her way around the U.K. Her name was Ynys?"

Thorne's gaze met his squarely. "I'll have been dead long years before I forget Ynys Treherne. I loved her; we had one single week together before she had to go home. We'd been careful;

then I had a letter to say she'd had a son of mine, but that she wouldn't return. She had her family, her home, and her career, and she loved them all more than Cornwall. I could come and stay in a year or so if I wanted, and when our son was older, he could visit. I write back saying I'd not try to force anything on her; they were her decisions to make. Then the day we heard here just how bad things were, I had a second letter. It had a photo of our son. Since that day, I've never been without it."

The demand was fierce. "Show me!"

Thorne reached into his pocket and produced the original. He'd known this time would come. He showed it. "And then I have this too."

Yes, his Ynys had been a singer. Mostly she'd sung at Welsh festivals, weddings, funerals, and parties. Folk songs, with three records, most of their songs in Welsh. One had been good enough to make the Best Seller list in Wales. He had copies of all three. And from a ruined record he'd found in Polworth, he'd taken her face from the cover and put it in a silver locket that had belonged to his grandmother. Now he lifted that over his hand and placed it, too, in Dray's hand.

Dray spoke quietly, still looking at the locket and photo. "I always wondered if you'd even wanted me. It wasn't for some years she told me how bad it had been. Only four of us survived. I got the first sickness from her friend's toddler. I gave it to her and Gran and Granda. Everyone else died, and the grands were sick for weeks. Ma said we couldn't leave them; we couldn't make it to you either. And where we were on the farm, it was isolated; no one much knew where to find us."

He sighed. "Gran died when I was ten, and Granda nearly two years after that. About five years after that, Ma said we could leave now. We took the pony and cart and walked a lot of the way until we got to Cardiff. We'd have cut over the Severn, but there was trouble there, fighting, and Ma said we should wait it out in Cardiff. We found a place, edge of the city where farmland was cutting in there. Living all her life on a farm Ma could manage.

She knew a lot of stuff, taught me, then Lia.

"I was about twenty-two, I think, when I met Lia's ma. She was eighteen; she'd been really sick. Her parents kept her alive: her ma was a nurse, but she was always weak. They never told me how weak. We married." His face twisted. "Well, we made a ceremony ourselves and had her parents and a couple of her friends there to witness. Ma sang. Lia came along only seven months later. And Lia's ma was sick for almost a year. Said to find another woman; she wasn't any good. Told her I loved her and that was that." A single tear rolled down his face, and he flicked it away with one hand.

"Ma had a heart attack, or that's what I thought it was when Lia was almost four. She told me it was her warning. That some of the women in her line died that way, about every third generation, and she was that. They usually got the one that killed them maybe six months later or thereabouts. She said we'd leave Lia with a friend and go looking for the right place. We found it; Ma said she wouldn't mind lying there and I went back a while later when it was drier and did what she asked. I dug her a grave, put a board over it, found salvage, a real bright pretty quilt, and put that away."

"Then you found her dead one morning?" Thorne said quietly.

"My wife did. She came and got me. We took Ma to where she wanted to lie, wrapped her in the quilt I'd kept, and we buried her. I had an eye on a rose bush in a garden near our way; I dug that up later and planted it over her." Thorne said he noticed throughout this discussion Dray never once called his wife by name and he wondered.

"And your wife?"

"Appendix, I think. I buried her by Ma, and while Ma had that rose they call Peace, I put one on my wife's grave that's pink, I think it's called Mount Tillier."

And as Thorne said, at that moment he understood why Dray never said his wife's name. As they'd wondered when Lia talked about her death. He met Dray's gaze, watched it slide away, and said gently. "An appendix can be painful, but when it bursts, when you don't have a hospital or even a doctor, when you know they're going to die, and you know they'd dying screaming, sometimes for hours. Then you call it mercy."

Dray looked up. "You know, don't you?"

"Lia told us about her mother, that she screamed and screamed, you gave her something to drink, and she stopped hurting; in the morning, she was dead. We all guessed, Dray. You did right. To make someone live hour after hour in unbearable agony just to keep your conscience clear is plain cruelty. I'd have *that* on my conscience, not giving them mercy. And there would be no way I'd let anyone I cared for die that way."

"You don't think I was wrong?"

Thorne shook his head. "I think you'd have been far more wrong to let her die screaming until she had no voice left, until all she could do was make rasping sounds like an animal in a trap. I heard a fox once like that. Local poacher caught it on our land. I was out with my father. He killed it mercifully, told me to run home, call the police to come out. He had his phone with him; in those days, you could take moving photos with one, and my father did. When the poacher came, he got excellent footage of him taking the fox out of the trap. Dad headed home, the police got there, and he took them to the man's house. The poacher had just got back; skin was there and traps. Dad laid charges."

Dray looked interested. "What happened?"

Thorne smiled unpleasantly. "Local animal-lovers all saw the photos. Poacher got jail time for killing a fox on private land, more for using a trap where they were banned. Then the animal-lovers got involved. They went to his landlord's home and demonstrated outside all night for weeks. The guy gave the poacher notice when he could legally; he took all his possessions to a storage company and left them. Poacher got out, landlord told him where to find his stuff, and when the poacher went there, he had to pay storage."

"Where'd the poacher go?"

"Away. No one in our area would rent to him. He had to empty his bank account to pay storage, so that was it. Someone said they saw him on the main road with his thumb out." Thorne had to backtrack at that point to explain the customs of hitchhiking.

He met Dray's serious gaze. "I was seven when that happened, but I've never forgotten the sounds that poor damned fox made. My dad told me a while later that sort of cruelty is one of the worst, that the man didn't care. He had a good job; he just wanted that few extra pounds, and for that, he would have casually tortured an animal to death."

He reached out and took Dray's hand in his. "You did the right thing; you showed mercy. If she walked in that door now, she'd thank, not condemn you. And nor would anyone here. We've mostly all been there and done that at some time or another these days. We know. I should leave you to sleep now; I suspect you're a bit wrung out."

"Thanks."

Thorne understood. "No problem, and one more thing. Welcome home, son!"

CHAPTER TWENTY

Lia and her father fitted in at Trelenwold Manor. There's no other way to say it; it was as if for thirty-two years, there'd been a Dray-shaped hole, and for eleven, there'd been a Lia-shaped one. Now the holes were filled with those who'd always been meant to be there. And without anyone, but Doc Di, Mic, Maureen, and I, knowing Doc had done the blood typing. Dray was Thorne's son; Lia was Dray's daughter and Thorne's grand-daughter, and we had the signed witnessed statement to prove it. Just in case someone down the track challenged his will that stated Dray's inheritance, and Lia's later or at need.

Dray improved week by week; that week, he'd first made it to his en suite toilet safely by himself. In another two weeks, he was walking slowly to sit on a comfortable seat outside to talk to those who went by, if they had the time or inclination, and many did. Lia spent a lot of her time catching him up on the people, their activities, families, and preoccupations. It took little time for us to note he was interested in all that, *and* he remembered it. It did him no harm either that Vali was a regular companion, and that other cats and dogs liked him too. Nor, that once he'd improved to where he could add the activity, that he was a good rider.

Lia had been started on a light .22 rifle and a bow within weeks of her arrival. She had a natural eye, and, or so it appeared, it was an inheritance. Dray could shoot with a rifle as well as any soldier — and probably better than many. He picked up a bow as if he was born to it, and Thorne chuckled to me in the first months as winter passed.

"Dad said it ran in the bloodline. Archers from way back we were." I knew Thorne in his time had been a champion; so had

Gerald, his father. "And now for something completely different…" We grinned at each other; Gerald had so enjoyed the Monty Python films and TV series.

"Okay, what?"

"The Thames and London." Thorne sobered. "It's like this, Hugh, my lad. None of us are getting any younger, outside, the cities are crumbling, and the salvage window is close to shutting for us. If we don't move in the next year or two, many places will be closed to us, I want to do something in particular before that happens. You and Maureen did well in Cardiff, finding all that cement and steel reinforcing rods. It gave us, along with what we had left of other salvage times in storage, enough to put up another wall for a village. *One* village."

"And you want to put up more, expand the Manor lands, maybe some of the established villages?"

"Yes. That's not the only thing though. It'd depend on how much of the supplies we'd need to do it, but, it's like this. Hugh, most think things can't get any worse than they are now. I think they can. I think in another three, four, or five generations we'll be into the new Dark Ages. I could be wrong, in which case we'll spend a lot of work and materials for very little; but if I'm right, I don't want everything we've built up to now, everything we've saved of civilization, to go down in fire and night. I don't want our people to be lost."

I looked at him. "Nor do I, Thorne. It wouldn't be just the people that die, although they're what comes to mind first. It's the heritage plants we salvaged, apples that go back hundreds of years, walnuts, berries, herbs, and spices. The animals, Scottish Coons, Welsh cobs, Arabs, and Suffolk Punches. We keep a section of anything pure to breed back at need. How long do you think anything will stay that way if everything falls in?"

"True, then there's reading, writing, logic, and no superstition. How long before we're worshiping the sun, burning any old lady we think is a witch, before books are to light the fire, how long before we're back to counting on our fingers?"

"Some still do," I pointed out.

"Some, not many, and it's a convenience, not a necessity," was the retort. "And how long before we live in a heap of bracken tied together and hollowed out? How long before we all have fleas, lice, and every damn disease we fought to eradicate?"

"Thorne, I know. What I don't know is what you have in mind to fend off that."

He paused. Took a long breath. "You know Hadrian's wall?" I nodded. "That's about seventy-three miles long, built by hand. I have in mind a wall, built from Fowey to St Austell; it's only sixteen and a half miles, and we have the CBMs."

I stared; then understanding sank in. Damn, it *could* be done. We *could* do it – and we would too.

CHAPTER TWENTY-ONE

Thorne talked to me, Mic, and Maureen, all that summer. We'd intended to go to London this year, but if we were really going to do this, we should make better preparations. Instead, we headed for Cardiff again, tied up at the marina, and went salvaging, not just for more wall materials, but going over all of the cargo ships, those a size or two larger than the ones we had. Last time we hadn't taken them because the larger a ship was, the more fuel it used. Now the point on that was that fuel was vanishing; leaks in tanks, and water in the fuel. Next year could be the last year there'd be usable fuel.

And on the outskirts of Cardiff, in a heavily fenced compound, we thought there was usable fuel still. It had been an army installation. It held an emergency supply of fuel in specially vented tanks. Most didn't even know it was there, but in one of our explorations, we'd come across information in the town Hall. It was vague, but if you read between the lines… Now we'd gamble that the fuel tanks hinted at, were there, intact, and that the fuel in them was still good — if it really did exist.

It took most of two days to break into the place. And while that was going on, Maureen had gathered every ancient business directory for the city and was trawling through them. She found places we hadn't known about, and small groups went to those and salvaged where they hadn't already been emptied. One of them was a cement works, and from that, we filled two of our cargo ships and sent them scuttling back home.

"No steel reinforcing rod though?" Thorne looked like a cheated gambler.

"There's other options for that," I pointed out.

"True. Now how are we doing for ships that could still be used for one more season?"

I smiled. I'd had the latest update on those only an hour ago, and it was favourable, or moderately so. "The Berenson twins have been running that. They say that so far, they've got two ships that, if they're given an overhaul and clean-up, are ready to go. The original cargo ships we took from here were a 100-ton and 125-ton cargo loads. The two they have are two hundred tonners. They'd found a third that's half that again — three hundred tons. That needs some work, but they think they can get it back to working again, maybe for no more than two or three round trips, but..."

Thorne finished that, "But it's a lot better than nothing. Tell the twins to get started on cleaning up and overhauling the three ships they have, but keep some of their group on looking."

We spent a month in Cardiff. Towards the end of that time, some of those we'd known arrived, asking after children we'd taken and friends they'd made. We held a banquet, handed over gifts we'd brought, did a little trading — where they could tell us of a place with salvage, they'd been unable to access, but we could, and we accessed and shared. Merr and Doc Di vanished into the increasingly ruined city centre and business areas, and returned with fourteen Scottish Coon kittens to the delight of our people, and then we were about to leave.

Old Jack, seventy and a survivor of the bandit battle, came to see us, and spoke quietly to Maureen and me. "You won't be back again, will you?" Our gaze met his, and we shook our heads together. "I thought not. Will you do me a favour?" I saw the mix of hope and fear, and I nodded.

"If we can, we will."

"I'd like you to take something of mine back wi' you. The Lord's given me advance notice. I reckon I won't see the year out, and I dunna want what I care about left wi' those that may not treat them as I do."

We returned to his home, a small place on the edge of an

outer suburb. He'd hoped, and in case we agreed, he'd seen to it we wouldn't refuse because things would take too long. He had two bookcases. Both at a guess, five feet long by four feet high, they were neatly filled with books. I glanced over those and nodded. Those would be useful, I could see a number I knew we didn't have,

Some of those were a set of six on glass-blowing and moulding. Thorne had said to me quite recently we should look for something on that subject. With them went four cartons of what looked like genuine Tiffany lamps, glass shades, with the actual lamps made from bronze, copper, brass, and one from steel. He'd packed those in wooden crates, using quilts and feather pillows as packing. Those on their own would be useful.

He saw that lot would be acceptable and turned to a cupboard, bringing out three large square containers. One was open at the top, and I could see they were filled with sealed packs of tiny pills, each pack probably holding a hundred pills, and with as many as fifty or more packs in each container.

"I had a friend when t'virus started. We'd been at school together. He never wed, but he were a smart lad, went to pharmacy school, and got all his qualifications. Had his shop only around the block from here. When things started, he told me later, he'd gone to local doc as he usually dealt with. Found the place shut up and guessed doc were gone. Went back to his shop, got his van, knew where doc kept the key, and he came back and cleared out the place." His smile was hard.

"Found containers locked away and an invoice. Being what he was, he could read all that medical stuff, and he knew what was in there. From the National Board of Health, saying they were trialling the contents, special Welsh project being done at Aberystwyth, an' tied up with the new euthanasia laws. There's those here as know I have a liddle can of them; they dunno I had all these."

Maureen looked at him. "Why are you giving them to us, not your own people?"

Old Jack's lips twisted momentarily into a snarl. "Since I was sick a coupl'a month's back, I been asking around, quiet like. No one wanted my books, nor the lamps; oh, they'd have grabbed these pills, but the other items, they wouldn't touch them. I decided, I knew you for good people. An' I reckon in the end, your place may be the last wi' the lights still on. Then, there's these."

He opened a door. "That's m' granddaughter, Seren. M' only daughter died having her a few weeks back. I had milk powder from my friend's pharmacy, kept her alive, but those around made it pretty clear; they won't take her in, not related to them, too long before she could work, take a lot a' extra food. Said I should give her to you; you took the others." He smiled, a grin with a razor edge. "I decided since they thought that, it were only right my other stuff went wi' her. Last thing's in here."

He opened a door and pointed to a cane basket. Inside a Scottish Coon nursed four-week-old kittens. "This here's Bella, found her lost 'n starving when she were six weeks old, an' took her in. She's five now; she loves an' trusts me. *They* said I should just let her go, she'd be fine, she'd manage." He spat. "Mebbe, so, but that's not how to treat sommat that trusts you. You take Seren, Bella, and her kits, and t' books, t' lamps, and those pills are yours. And I can tell you sommat else."

We waited. Old Jack sighed. "My friend, his family come from Aberystwyth, he guessed where that place making these pills was. I can give you directions. You been wanting that steel rod for concrete, 'S a place there that makes it. Off on a side road five mile out of the town. Town were hit hard and early; go there, an' I'd say you'll profit from other things besides them."

In the end, we took all Jack offered. We would have anyway, but there was another factor. Thorne's Ynys had come from there. He wanted to find her farm and take from it anything in repairable condition still to give to Dray and Lia. The possibility of good salvage, and the wanted steel reinforcing rods was sufficient reason to go anyway. We'd found three larger cargo ships; two of our smaller ones had gone home with salvage. None of the fishing villages had sent any of their own boats this time, but we had some of their people as extra crew.

Now we had eight cargo ships, and we sailed for Aberystwyth on a fine morning's tide. We wrung Old Jack's hand at the last and swore Seren, Bella, and her kits would do well and be safe with us. Then we boarded, and as we swung out to sea, we waved, and he waved back until we could no longer see each other.

Aberystwyth was all Jack had said, and a little more. We filled two of the smaller ships not only with the rods we found stacked in bundles in a warehouse, but invoices found in the office that mentioned a place that made cement. It was a day's travel into the country, but we made it, gutted the buildings, and brought the bagged cement back to completely fill one of our cargo ships.

Thorne found the Treherne farm, and yes, in locked cupboards, there were items still in reasonable or repairable condition. There was also livestock gone feral, but good animals, and we captured as many of those as we could. Only the younger healthy ones, but we believed Dray and Lia would be delighted. We sailed for home after that, pausing a day to salvage at any promising-looking village on the way.

That added forty-three people to our population. Over and over, we'd find one or two families — often related or old friends — who'd finally realized they couldn't live forever on the salvage of their village; they'd endanger their families by interbreeding, and there was always a scattering of solo people.

Seren, Bella, and the kits seemed to enjoy the voyaging; none of the kits fell overboard, Bella purred at crew who petted her, and Seren was a good baby, placid, happy, and well-named, we thought, since Seren is Welsh for Star. But all voyaging ends; we left the ships we'd never loaded moored in Mount's Bay and made port in Polwithin the day after.

It was a busy time then. Dray and Lia were delighted with the livestock from his mother's old farm. Jack's lamps were shared among the council with one of each being placed in a library room along with the books on glass-blowing. Maureen and I took one of the bronze ones, and we gave a second to Mic. Seren, Bella, and her kits went to the Ruxton village. Jess's son and his wife wanted her; married six years and no child, it looked likely this was a good way to acquire one. Three kits would return to us once they were weaned, but Bella and the Ruxton's choice of kit would stay—just as well since she was loved within days, and within about the same time, Jess and her son had settled on keeping the brown tabby-marked girl.

We warehoused the cement and steel reinforcing rods. It was decided that we'd hold it. Once we'd salvaged what we could in London, we'd know how much wall we could build. If there wasn't sufficient for our wall, then we'd use it for new villages and enlarging older ones. If there was sufficient, then that would go up first.

In fact, after a winter's discussion with one of those who'd come from a village during our last trip, and who turned out to be knowledgeable on specific items of history, we could see the sense in what he suggested. We only hoped there'd be enough of what we'd need. And with the assistance of another family who'd joined us and who were all builders, we were able to work out parameters, material required, and ways to fudge some of that if it turned out that we were short of the reinforcing rods.

CHAPTER TWENTY-TWO

By the time spring came around, we'd celebrated the beginning of 2072. Our voyage to London was planned out, lists of materials wanted and of those going had been made; we were taking all eight cargo ships, all three Artics, and the fishing villages were each sending four fishing boats. Dray was coming; Lia was not and was vocal about it. Doc Di and Merr would come; as she said, she was seventy, but it'd probably be the last major trip any of us would ever make, and she was going. Maureen and I were sixty, but we felt the same way.

We set sail for whatever remained of London at first light in mid-spring. Twenty-three ships and boats, twelve hundred people—all heavily armed and experienced—twenty trained dogs, with half a boatload of weapons and ammunition of wide-ranging types. A number of the armoured vehicles we called tanks, and, once we'd gone ashore briefly at Margate and Ramsgate and searched for them, a large stack of business directories, maps of London, and others of the city's suburbs from town halls, and information centres. Maureen and a group tasked with the job went through those minutely. We knew their value from experience.

And valuable they were. Telling us how far one place was from another, giving us alternate paths between them, and noting places that could have been overlooked if not specifically known about. We sailed up the Thames and came to the great tidal barriers. They were there, but more than thirty years without maintenance had brought them down. It wasn't easy with our largest ship, but we squeezed by, and found without the barriers London had flooded. Not completely, but parts of the city nearest the river, and into low-lying areas. We moored our ships, set guards, and in the morning after breakfast, we set out to see what time and tide had left of a once-great city.

London swarmed with rats, both two and four-legged. Twice, groups of the two-legged ones attacked a convoy of our people heading for a factory or warehouse. The first time, I allowed us to be driven away, while our scouts went in and watched. Thorne was incredulous at the reports.

"You're saying they attacked, but not to defend anything, not to salvage before we did? Why then?"

I grinned at Thorne. "It's a territorial thing," I told him Thorne stared. "It could date back to gangs, where territory is something almost mystical. It's their castle, their lands, it's where they live, and anyone coming in without some sort of agreement is counted as attacking them. Jodie Talisker and Cassius—and you know how good that pair are—went in after dark, got right up close and listened. She says so far as she could tell from what was said, we challenged to take their territory; what happened was their reaction."

Those of the council who'd come on this trip considered that and made two decisions. We'd salvage first in any area that didn't seem to be "owned." And, if what was on the short-list couldn't be found there, we'd take in larger convoys; if we were attacked, we'd defend ourselves, but we wouldn't chase them. It could be that after a couple of attacks, they'd realise if they left us alone, we'd ignore them. It worked in two of the territories. We found factories there where what they'd made and some of which they still had, we wanted. After several abortive assaults on us, that group understood if they didn't start anything, nor did we, and while they always had someone watching, they left us alone. That worked for the next territory too. Then Maureen came in with Doc and Merr. I sat and listened. Thorne who'd been with me had gone to his cabin on the ship.

"Next place we want to go had a combined medical centre," Doc said. "Hospital, health clinic, dentists, and all three were teaching places as well. They also had a few other clinics like physiotherapist, but they didn't take students, and we have all we need from others of that sort."

"Teaching places, so they'd have textbooks, instruments, and all sorts of useful stuff like charts, diagrams, and other information." Doc nodded. "But you foresee a problem?"

Maureen, who'd come in with them, nodded. "Yes. That area also has a literal street of factories, right down the far end where the land rises; there's one that made cement and has a massive great warehouse. Thorne will go there, and no one and nothing is going to stop him. And, around behind that and down the street, there's another factory."

"Okay." I waited for the second shoe to drop. It did so with a resounding clang.

"They made tungsten rods there; once they'd done the rod in lengths, it was cut into pieces for all sorts of stuff from ladder rungs to gates that needed to be extra strong."

I mulled that over. The one thing I knew about tungsten was it was far stronger than ordinary bar steel used in concrete. Thorne would know that, too, or he'd hear fast enough. After that, he'd be going to see how much there was, and as the poem said, "*I'll come to thee by moonlight, though hell should bar the way.*" I looked at Maureen, and she looked at me; we both knew the only thing to do, and I did it.

I tapped on the cabin door. "Thorne, we're likely to be in battle tomorrow." He sat back, made it clear he'd like that expanded, and I did so. As we'd expected, Thorne was going to have any cement we could use, and if the factory doing tungsten rods had retained a stockpile, he'd have every last one of those as well. That went for ladders and gates, too, plus any other useful items they had.

****

We moved out in convoy next morning, having waited until full daylight; the enemy had been watching. Leaving at half-light would be more a hindrance to us than them. We used every vehicle; all had at the least a driver, someone riding shot-gun, and two people at the rear, whenever possible. After that, it was war. Unfortunately for them, we were better, we were fitter, had better weapons, and dogs. We fought our way to the tung-sten factory first; we could return via the cement place.

The factory was a treasure house. Yes, they'd made ladders and gates, they'd also made taps, they added carbide or other metals and produced drill bits, grinding burrs, lathe cutting bits, saw blades, cutting wheels, milling bits, wire pulling dies, and ar-mor-piercing artillery shells. Most of that we could use since their warehouse was about sixty percent full of the rods, with the other forty percent filled with other such items — we had no interest in the considerable number of golf clubs.

Thorne took one ecstatic look and gave his orders. We threw a ring of guards around the factory and warehouse, gath-ered up over that day everything we could use, including infor-mation on tungsten. And Doc vanished into the factory's office block, reappearing with cartons of one-off items, including a fab-ulous knee-length leather duster she gave to Merr, and a consid-erable selection of plates, cutlery, and cooking utensils. I won-dered why she bothered until I took a closer look and realised this had probably come from the management's dining room. It was all top of the range and would have been expensive as hell. Which struck me as not something to be ignored.

I collected Maureen, hissed that information, and we slipped away to forage. I found the dining room, went further back, and Maureen yelped as she opened a door.

"Bathrooms and bedrooms." Aha. Management for the use of, if anyone needed to stay the night. All the rooms were fully stocked with the best in toiletries, soaps, towels, and flan-nels, and in the bedroom, there was riches. Bedding, linen, mag-nificent beds and other furniture, and in several cupboards, there was a sprinkling of casual clothing. We went back to where our vehicle was — complete with trailer — and loaded every last item we could cram aboard. Then we mentioned it to Dray, who saw to it that the remainder of the furniture was gathered up and loaded. People kept arriving at our gates, and the thing they most often didn't bring was furniture.

The sniping from whoever considered it "their" territory had mostly stopped. We made the run to where the cement factory was, checked it wasn't empty — on the contrary — and settled there for the night. Come morning, we set up and guarded a direct route to the ships, and over the next two days, we loaded cement. Meanwhile, Maureen's team had found several more places that would produce fruitful salvage if they weren't already emptied. Some weren't, and loading was on the schedule again.

By the time we'd been there ten days, about half the cargo ships were full, and they weighed anchor. We moved to another area of the city and started all over again. But that seemed to be the final straw for the inhabitants. We settled around another cement factory, had most of the contents loaded on another ship, and that night, they hit us. I think one of them must have watched the ships sail and assumed half of us had gone with them. People at the manor would unload, and we could need fighters here. We did, and then, too, the enemy continued to underestimate our training and good dogs.

Doc Di and Merr had settled for the night when Gunther growled softly. They looked at each other, quietly threw on outer clothing again, selected weapons, and while Merr went to tell Thorne we could have trouble, Doc and Gunnie headed in the direction he insisted they should investigate.

It was a considerable surprise to the lead male in the line of intruders. Gunnie had him by the throat before he realised there was a dog about. Di moved to where she was half covered by the bend, produced her Bullpup, and started shooting. There'd been twelve of them. In around thirty seconds, there was one: the last in line who had quick reactions and great common sense.

He left as if he had attached Jet Assisted Take-Off units to his backside. Unfortunately, in rocketing across the area between where they'd entered via a drainpipe, and leaving the building, one of the guards saw him, shot, then yelled that he should halt. Since the intruder was already dead and flat, he'd done so. The guard inspected the body, yelled for someone to remove the man, and to let Thorne know.

I will say that while they may have been mostly short of brains, most weren't short of courage. Six more groups tried for us over the dark hours, Again and again, the dogs let us know, and we were waiting. I don't know how many, or even if any, escaped. But by daylight, we counted over fifty bodies. We laid them out in the factory courtyard and rolled off down the road. After that, they left us alone and word must have spread because that applied wherever we salvaged in the city after that.

The business directories were invaluable. And as we got into the outer fringe of the city, we saw people of a different type. One elderly woman approached us.

"You tourists?"

Thorne's voice was gentle. "No, we come from the south-west. We have homes, schools, and doctors there, but London had some useful materials."

She stared and assimilated that. "You've got schools, an'… an' *real* doctors?"

"We do. Do you need a doctor?"

"Not me, my daughter. Last two time's she was pregnant, she lost the baby. Now she's pregnant again, an' we're all worried."

"All?"

"Me, her two brothers an' sister, and their kids."

"Bring her here. Doc Di will take a look at her."

She came, along with the family who wanted to be sure their kin were properly treated. She was, they heard about our home, and the next small convoy home had passengers — nineteen of them, since several friends had also liked the sound of our lands and our offers. One returned, went forth and preached, and by the end of that autumn when we made our last run for home, we'd gained a hundred and four new settlers.

Thorne considered our ships, talked to what experts we

had, and we gambled on a second year. We found more cement, more rebar, and two sets of massive sheet steel gates that appeared to have been made to keep dinosaurs in—or out. But that was it. Two of the small cargo ships broke down on the second trip back; we shared out their loads, crammed everything in, including crews and personal possessions, and decided that the ships still in London would be fully loaded and come home to stay.

They did, along with another three hundred plus settlers from the originally middle-class, respectable suburbs. These older residents hadn't forgotten what a civilization could be, but ours was still far better that the anarchy they'd had for the past thirty-plus years. To our joy, we found one of the families had done glass-blowing—as a hobby—but they knew the basics, and, provided with a house, food trees, a vegetable garden, and the offer of a cat or dog, they settled in with whimpers of satisfaction. They accepted a girl Scottish Coon and were part of us within months.

Most of the other new arrivals did the same. We weren't quite the civilization some remembered, but those younger remembered only fear, cold, hunger, and being attacked. None of that existed here, and even if their elders would have contemplated leaving, none of the younger ones would have considered it.

We had books and musical instruments you could learn to play, loved pets, doctors and nurses so you didn't have to hurt for days or weeks. This was paradise and since most had little memory of any local culture, they took to ours with enthusiasm. Therefore, we moved on to our thirty-fourth year after the plague, and all of us as Cornish stood proud, strong, free, and that year, too, our wall was finally begun.

****

One attractive item that started about the same time as the first section of the wall went up was the Jamieson family's glassblowing. They'd spent the winter getting the house the way they wanted it and getting the glass-blowing equipment moved into a small barn separated from the house with insulated walls on either side of that.

It had been a twelve-year hobby Paul Jamieson said, right up to the start of the plague—when he'd been twenty-eight. Sharli had been his next-door neighbour, a year younger, and his best friend. She'd had a miserable marriage, returned home, and the next year, the plague hit.

Both families, long-time friends, had moved to an elderly uncle's home on a few acres down a dirt road—they'd removed the signpost, planted briers across the opening, and no one had found them. Sharli and Paul had married the year after, once they'd understood this problem wasn't leaving and would get worse over time. The uncle died the year after that. They'd had three children who were now twenty-nine, twenty-six, and Jay, the tail-ender at twenty-one.

It may have been a long time since Paul had practised his craft, but over the next months, he picked it up again. His children took it up in turn and proved to be good at it. His daughter, Caren, middle child of the three was also a reader, and while reading her way through a stack of old newspapers, came upon an article. She took that to her father, and the next thing we knew, the Jamiesons were incorporating the ashes of family members into beautiful glass sculptures people could display. It was versatile, cats, dogs even favourite larger animals all became urns in effect, and the Jamieson family had a paying profession while the wall lengthened.

Sadly, that was the year Di's doctor friend, Liz died. She went in her sleep, and we mourned. Di had seen it coming, bought a bronze urn, and now Liz/s ashes reposed in that, on a corner shelf in Di's library. Summer wound on and with two CBM's working—a programme of four hours on, two off, to let them cool, but both day and night—the wall was finished at the end of autumn. Two of—what many called the *Dinosaur Gates*— were installed, and the day after that we took Mic to see Thorne's wall. She smiled at it.

"Ninety-six, and I can still be surprised at the things people do. I guess I can go happy now, knowing you'll stay safe."
She made a face; we laughed, but I shall always wonder how
much she knew. Did she have a premonition? Like Liz, she went
silently during the day, napping in her armchair, we thought,
until she failed to wake for dinner. We mourned for weeks, as
did her cat, Iona. Then Thorne began the second wall, three hundred and fifty yards past the first — there would be cleared land
and booby traps between them, and if we were attacked, they'd
have a second wall to get past.

That wall, too, was completed and there was quiet in all
our lands, as we used the remaining materials, first for the
Manor, then village by village to expand protected lands or build
walls for new villages. Two years, three, five — and still the peace
held.

CHAPTER TWENTY-THREE

It broke in early spring of 2079. The year, Maureen and I were sixty-seven, and Doc Di was ten years older, but busy as ever. A year that marked the fortieth since the plague, since that day when our world changed, never to be the same again. The year we had refugees come knocking at the great wall Thorne gave us.

"S' bad out there, no food, you plant anything, some'un takes it. We lived St. Alban's aways out'a London. People we knew, they came here, we heard they got food, a house…"

"An' a *cat*," his wife broke in. "Had one when I was a kid, I loved Tibby, she went out one day an' never came home. Still miss her." *It couldn't have been that long ago*, I thought. She'd have been no more than mid-twenties, but she was gaunt, as were the children with her and her husband. One child was a toddler, the other a babe in her arms.

Her man nodded. "Figured to make it here before any others. Some been talking about it. Know we have to work." His gaze met mine. "Don't mind working hard, just hate working, then having it stolen."

We opened the gates. He'd told the truth; he didn't mind hard work. He took on for one of the Ruxtons; they got a house, his lady got a cat she adored, and two months later, the real rush started. He was given permission to spend time at the gates, and was able to identify many of those that came begging to be let in.

We never found him to be wrong or untruthful if he knew them. Thorne was often at the gate too; he was eighty-five now and had little strength for anything but talking, but he was as good a judge of people as ever. Towards the end of summer, when we'd taken in over three hundred people as new settlers, he sat talking to us, looking out towards the Manor gates one evening.

"I said once that I thought a time of darkness and flames would come. That was when we'd need a wall. Now we have two, and I hope with all my heart they'll hold back the night and the fire."

Maureen looked up from her crochet. "Not yet maybe, but it's coming. We should start sending scouts to watch beyond the walls." Thorne, Dray, and Lia, too, thought that a good idea, and so we began. Scouts went in hands, five men and an officer, and their only work was to prowl the land from the other side of our walls down to the old Cornish border. They did so, and the years turned peaceful again. Two, three, five, and it was 2084.

Thorne turned ninety. We celebrated, and the morning after that, a scout arrived on a lathered pony with a report, leaving us deeply grateful that years ago, we'd listened to Thorne. It was an army, the scout said. "Couldn't count them, hundreds for sure. On foot, on horses, in wagons. Got close to their leader one night; he was talking how we have the best land, drop seeds in and have more than you can eat in weeks. Animals are all fat; want meat, you just go out and throw a rock, hit a rabbit, a deer, and eat roast meat; fish too, all you want."

Dray snorted. "That's the silliest thing I've ever heard."

His father shook his head. "No, it's been forty years since the virus, son. Anyone younger than their late forties probably remembers nothing. Beyond the wall, they're dying of starvation, of diseases we were vaccinated against, of minor wounds we took a pill for, or wiped with disinfectant. They fight to the death for a single meal. And Doc Di says they may be dropping in numbers, one way or another. Too many women dying in childbirth. Long term starvation can render men less fertile. Beyond our walls, there's no civilization left, and what we have here is paradise to them."

"I see. Well, what do we do about this army?" Dray's eyes were a blazing amber while his face had shifted into a bitter scowl.

Thorne smiled and nodded to the scout. "Go back, tell Mel Merrison I want the scouts to do one thing, and do it ASAP. I want a count of the enemy as best as you can manage. I want it to the nearest twenty or thirty. Stay the night here, eat and sleep well, and ride at first light."

He did, and scout commander Mel Merrison came in his stead in three days, speaking officially. "Manor Lord, we have counted them. There are seven hundred in their army. They are in poor condition, most have eaten poorly for a long time, and had little food to bring with them, but their leader has convinced them all their privations are caused by us, deliberately. They swear to take our wall or die. They have sworn a blood oath to own all we have, and we shall be their slaves."

Thorne stared into the far distance where the wall stood. He gave his orders quietly then, and we obeyed. The enemy came trailing in scattered groups to our walls all of the next night and began their assault once it was light enough to shoot. We kept our own engagement with them light initially until Dray received the signal, and then twice, our numbers rose up on the second wall and shot.

We'd long saved the best rifles, the best ammunition for this, and we reaped a deadly harvest. We killed until the whole area between our walls ran red, until men slipped in the mud their blood had created, until their feet sank into the sodden ground. And, with over half their number dead, dying, or screaming underfoot—they broke.

It was then that those who had not known, realised that a wall had been only a third of Thorne's plans. Those of us on the council had known in general terms. We had never realised the effectiveness, or the brutality, but we saw them today. Once the army was distracted, once they were mad with battle fever, they ceased to watch behind them, and it was then Mel and some of his strongest scouts moved silently to shut the gates in the furthest wall. Between two walls now, the invading army were trapped.

As Thorne had told us years back when he proposed the

walls: "We build two walls, and between them shall be a killing ground for those who come against us."

It was. They tried to scale the inner wall to reach us, and we shot them down. They fought to climb the further wall to escape, and they died before they reached halfway up. And had they managed, we had reinforcements for the scouts waiting. Fresh, and well-armed. The last ones, their leader and those closest to him, screamed up at us then.

"Murderers!"

And with Dray's arm to help him, Thorne stepped up to stand waist-high to the wall top and answered, "No, we're defending our homes, our partners, and children. In other years, many came to us asking for a place, and they were given that. They or their descendants live here, our people, and they have houses, food, pets, and friends. They do not have to go hungry or die of small wounds. This," his hand swept out to indicate the dead and dying. "This was *your* choice. You could have come asking our help, sharing our knowledge. You chose to come armed in war. Die now by that choice."

He nodded to Dray, and the sound of guns came, dying slowly to single shots. And after the final shot, there was a long silence.

We took the bodies out to sea in a couple of the cargo ships. The sharks feasted — while the council considered and sent word around our lands, talking to those who come to us as refugees. As we'd guessed, out there, those who'd been old enough to be well educated by the time the plague struck, were dead now. Either that, or it was our fortune that those who'd specialized in types of knowledge had gone, leaving only those who had some vague ideas on the subject.

The brother of the leader was one, and they came a week later, presuming that as we'd won a great triumph, we'd have stood down our guards, and. be feasting, drinking, and congratulating ourselves. We'd feasted certainly, for a single night, and we'd kept the guards and scouts. Thus, when the big rafts drifted on the coast winds towards Polwithin, we were ready. Ships, armed warriors, and, in the village of Polwithin, three trebuchets that fired armour-piercing shells.

We smashed all but one of the rafts while they were out to sea, and before they swung towards the land. The trebuchet took out the last, and as those on the raft struggled ashore, far less in number than they had been since many could not swim — or not well — the villagers of Polwithin met them in the shallows — and again, the invaders died.

They had come against the walls in April, and by sea in May. At our final count, we had killed nine hundred. Some of our people had been injured at the wall, and there were two dead in Polwithin, but of all those that came against us, of all those that swore to take our lands or die — all died, and when winter came, those beyond the wall would know their effects of their loss.

The winter was quiet. This year would be known as the Year of the Great War, but it would be remembered for another reason too.

Thorne had begun fading after the sea battle. It was as if he had lived until he saw how well his plans had worked, and that his people, his lands, and the Manor would be safe. He'd seen, and he could leave us now in the hands of his own blood. He died on a soft-scented late-autumn day, with Dray and Lia, Maureen and I, and Doc Di, around him. At the last he reached out, clasped our hands in turn and smiled as Dray and Lia held him.

"I could never have had better friends, better kin. *Kernow bys vyken!*" And they were his last words, three slow dragging breaths and he was gone, lost to us now, but we would remember him.

Indeed, Dray and Lia made sure of that. They came to the council to ask, and they received. By now we had our artists, our craftspeople, and we raised a statue to stand by the gates of the Manor. A statue of Thorne in the days when the plague came and he stood firm, the days when Kernow started to become what it would be.

And once that was done, we voted Lia onto the senior council as well, and Cornwall, our land of warm summers, mild winters, where there are beavers, where the cats are three times the size of those beyond our walls, where the people live in harmony, sing the old songs, read books, and live long, Cornwall continues. *Kernow bys vyken!*

****

I was chosen by the council to write these notes. For your information, I am Jay of the Trelen line, of Lia Trelen, and in my early days, I knew some of those whose names I write now. Doc Di died at eighty-nine, Merr the year after her — of grief, I believe. Hugh and Maureen lived the longest of those who were founding members of the Manor and true adults when the plague came; they died together at ninety-seven in the year 2109.

In the Manor, there is a tribute room to those founders. In a section for each, it has their ashes, the diaries that Hugh, Maureen, and Mic wrote, the medical notes and ashes of Doctor Diane, of my grandfather, Thorne Trelen's diary and ashes, and the five are remembered, honoured, and we still sing the song of Kernow that Mic wrote.

****

I, Shari Ruxton Trelen, have been asked to write this now, but for the rest, I shall have eighteen months to complete it. That is to be a book, one that combines the founders' diaries of the time two hundred and fifty years ago, when death came calling and many answered, and I write, too, of the years following. My many-times great-grandfather had walls built to save and protect the people, and there were three others, kin to each other, bound by contact, so their diaries say, and the fifth, a doctor, whose courage and medical knowledge saved many lives.

The years after Thorne Trelen's death were quiet ones, Twice, armies had come against the people of Kernow, and twice they had died to a kin — I should note here that it was towards the end of Thorne Trelen's life that *kin* became a word through our lands that meant both male and female, explaining its use in

Mic's song, the first time it appears in our written words.

With peace in the year 2084, we did not stagnate; within a dozen years, trade groups were going out, both to trade and to salvage still, since that could still be found, although in truth, as often and near as effectively we were recreating our own necessities. Bandits became a rarity in the next century since where they appeared, many took Thorne's actions as a model, and bandits were killed without mercy

We walled in no more villages, but we kept Thorne's walls in good condition, and in time, we built new ships and fishing boats, replicated eco-electricity systems, from books and papers the five accumulated, and from those who had retained such knowledge when so many died, we learned dentistry, medicine, medical techniques, and sciences that gave us better lives.

Still, we have always been careful about such things. Doctor Diane wrote warnings in her dairies, saying that much of the reason the plague came, and that so many died, was because of science and that it pushed boundaries, ignoring safety and common sense for the sake of so-called knowledge that was often deadly. She also left warnings about the old ones' pollution of air, land, and water, and we remain wary there too.

Our borders have long since spread beyond Thorne's walls. One hundred and forty years after the plague, we planted our first settlement in what was known as Outer Kernow. It prospered, established a twice-yearly market, and those living in the lands beyond came for trade.

Last year, we began a new village; it is on the line that once marked where Kernow became — or so I think — a place named Daevion. That village flourishes, and already there is talk of starting to raise the walls for another, once the celebrations are finished.

****

A final note from Shari Ruxton Trelen: I named my book *Five Who Survived — Kernow after the Great Plague*. Fortunately, over and over, the machines that could print books, ways of making paper, producing ink, and other skills that allow this, were revived, improved, or recreated, continuing to our benefit and the benefit of all. My book came out a month before the two-hundred-fifty-year celebrations — it sold.

A census called by the Manor Lord has just been completed, and while not yet announced, I have seen the figures. In Kernow, we have just over forty-nine thousand people, and an estimate says that unofficial villages into DeVon, may now have some three thousand as well. In truth so many books did I sell, I think every family in the whole of our lands must have purchased one.

We believe a portion of the lands far north also survived and have become towns, with schools, doctors, and that they may have done nearly as well as we. Although, it's likely to be generations more before we ever know the truth of that. But this can be said: here in Kernow we survived, we thrived, and now we face the future in good heart.

Kernow bys vyken!

Shari Ruxton Trelen

<<<<<<<<<<<<<< (The book ends) >>>>>>>>>>>>>>>>

ABOUT THE AUTHOR

Lyn started writing professionally in 1989. By the end of that year, she had several credits which she has continued to acquire to this day. She has sold over 300 stories, plus a large number of articles and opinion pieces and won a number of awards from the (International) Cat Writer's Association and other organisations for them. She began to write books in 1991 and her first book — *Farming Daze* — published in 1993. Six awards from (New Zealand's) Sir Julius Vogal Awards followed for assorted books, and her fiftieth book appeared in 2023. *Forever Cornwall* is her 51st book and fifth in the post-apocalypse series.

www.ingramcontent.com/pod-product-compliance
Lightning Source LLC
Chambersburg PA
CBHW030104260626
47156CB00008B/2517